Content Warning

This book depicts events that some may find disturbing. Including some extensive sequences of gore and body horror.

You will find a list containing some of the subjects depicted on the very last page of this book.

Please read safely and know your own limits!

And don't worry, this book also contains some pleasant things.
Like hugs, wholesome friendships, and references to Matthew Lillard.

First published in 2024 by Little Grey Alien

Paperback ISBN 978-1-0686277-0-5
eBook ISBN 978-1-0686277-1-2

Cover Illustration by Luci Lemonseed
Additional Cover Assets & Design by B.C. Brown

Edited by Danny Lidstone and Muffin
(I owe them so much)

An emphatic thankyou to all of my friends and family.
I'd be surprised if a lot of you read this, and even more surprised if some of you
enjoyed it.

Thankyou Ben and Kat, for giving me a chair that made writing this book a much
more comfortable experience.
And thankyou to all the authors who write fun, pulpy horror, for helping to keep
me alive through multiple years of a terrible job that did its best to kill me.

The Prospect

by B.C. Brown

Chapter 1

The Vaughn drifted slowly through scattered chunks of what used to be a planet. Rocks as large as cities drifting amongst clouds of dust and debris.

Mining drones converged on the ship like bees bringing nectar to the hive. One other planet orbited within the same system, a cool blue star at the centre. A shimmering net of light surrounded the planet, emanating from a competitor ship. The other ship had arrived long before The Vaughn, staking claim to the planets, and the resources within. Now The Vaughn filtered through the remnants, scavenging for crumbs in the wake of another's feast. Waves of cobalt light illuminated the debris field, tinting the ship a cold, empty blue, despite the thrum of life within. The ship's body was circular, a thin Outer-Ring surrounding a domed interior. A bulbous lump protruded from the Outer-Ring, like the head of a turtle tentatively peeking from its shell. It was within the head, in a secluded office that a secretive meeting took place, away from prying eyes and far removed from the thousands of inhabitants living in the drifting city ship.

The Mayor's palms left streaks of sweat on the desk's wooden veneer as they fretted. The room had no windows, a single orange-hued bulb hummed overhead. Stark metal walls and a lack of ornamentation had him feeling ill at ease. He would have preferred to hold this meeting in his office, with its ornate comforts and broad windows. Instead they gathered in what, to him, seemed more suited as a storage cupboard than anything else.

Still, Octavia assured him it would keep the gathering discreet. He looked to a tablet on the table before him, its screen a near incomprehensible jumble of thin twisting lines and dots; it was a map of the galaxy, zoomed in to their surrounding cluster of stars, with reams of text scrolling past a few highlighted planetary systems.

"There's no other way about it, we *have* to go." He failed to hide the shake in his voice from his two accomplices. The chief Navigator's uncomfortable posture burst into a display of outright hostility, her arms uncrossing and flinging into rapid gesticulations as she yelled.

"Go *where*, Markus? You want us to just pick somewhere at random and hope we get lucky? You realise how insane that is, right? We use the charts for a reason!" The Mayor's pallid face flushed a bright red, brow knotting tightly above an angered glare.

"We use the charts so we don't get bloody *sued*! I'm not suggesting moving on somebody else's territory. We'd hardly be the first to mine outside of the charts." He could feel sweat pooling between his shoulder blades as he argued. His mayoral duties were a great source of stress, but things had never been this dire before. Navigator Duri chuffed a sound of indignation before rebutting.

"We don't just use the charts to avoid bureaucratic bullshit. They let us know what kind of planets we're going to find before we jump. We use them to know we'll find something worth mining. We use them, because we know we're in explored space, where it's safe!" The Navigator prodded her finger at the charts emphasising every word, exerting more force with each tap until she was tempted to ball her hand into a fist and punch the desk. Or the Mayor. When she realised how heated she was becoming, she threw herself back into her seat and tightly crossed her arms to keep them from doing anything regrettable. The Mayor scoffed petulantly and shook his head.

"Safe? Is *that* what you're worried about?" Previously his voice had betrayed his anger, but now he talked in a lilting and cocky tone, refusing to raise even an octave above casual conversation. He had studied the art of debate on the net for years, and he had read all about handling heated discussions like this. The trick was to avoid raising your voice. To let the other parties sound angry and emotional, where you appear cool and in control. It makes people take your side, even if your opponent raises good points. Nobody wants to side with emotional hysteria.

Navigator Duri faltered at the accusation of fear long enough for Markus to continue, free from any interjections. "I've met cartographer crews before. Even considered pursuing it as a career myself, before I was selected for leadership." This wasn't true, of course. Markus had been destined for politics from birth, taking after his father. But he'd read plenty of stories about the cartographers that mapped space beyond the sphere of human colonisation. They were a roguish sort, prone to fantastical tales and lofty embellishments. "Dull work by all accounts. Decades of your life jumping from rock to rock. Most never find a single thing of note in their entire careers! And here you are worried that we're going to be the lucky few that stumble on, what? Some

3

terrible creature from an old horror tale? What we find there will be exactly what we find everywhere else, barren planets and moons covered in rocks and dust. Only at least there we have a chance of finding one with some bloody materials worth mining, unlike any that these blasted charts have offered us in all the time you've had to scour through them." He put particular emphasis on the 'you' in the final sentence, pushing as much blame on the Navigator as one word could carry.

"And what if we don't find anything worth mining out there? If we waste our last jump and find nothing. We'd be better off collecting scraps from an old husk world than going back home with nothing," said Duri. She didn't like this at all. It was hardly her fault, she'd been given old used up charts to work with. This entire cluster of systems had been burned up long ago, every planet of note stripped clean by previous expeditions.

She'd spent the last few years guiding them to the few that hadn't been marked as visited, but the charts proved to be outdated. That, or previous crews were slacking and not reporting their work properly.

Each time they'd arrived to find planets hollowed out and devoid of value, or debris fields left behind after a planet crack. The first few times they'd simply moved on, but eventually decided scraping the few remains they could find together was necessary.

They had been burning through their fuel making so many jumps between systems and had barely anything to show for it. Usually expeditions in city ships like The Vaughn would last between five and ten years, on rare occasion as many as twenty. They would travel to systems and spend months, if not years, mining all the valuables to be found

4

there. Around half a million living within the intricate domed city that rested atop the ship, would all contribute in some way; thousands of miners ready to extract whatever materials they find, factory workers refining and condensing the materials, preparing them to be stored in the vast chambers that made up the majority of the ship's bulk. Often they would find materials to produce their own fuel and extend the expedition in the hopes of returning with their stores packed to the brim.

The Vaughn was just one of thousands of similar city-sized mining ships. Owned by Paxton Universal, one of a few leading companies focused on scouring the stars for their materials. All played a vital role in the life cycle of the ever-growing human empire. In years past, the city prospered, but their last expedition had seen their luck abate. Over the course of three years, only a tenth of their stocks were filled. They had wasted the majority of their fuel checking systems that had already been cleared, and only found two low-yield planets to mine. Markus had promised this time would be better, he would provide fresh charts, with more untapped systems. But now they found themselves in even more dire circumstances than before.

"Scraps won't do this time, Duri," Mayor Markus said, shaking his head emphatically. "We need something to bring in real money." A hard silence fell between the two that dragged over long seconds before Markus let out a long, exasperated sigh. He had hoped to find Duri more agreeable to the idea. They could keep the plan a secret from most of the crew, but there is no way one could reach uncharted space without the Head Navigator playing their role.

"Fine then. If we are so firmly at odds, we'll have to leave it to a vote. It's the only fair way to resolve this. We know where we both stand, Octavia can be the deciding factor," said Markus, turning to look at the third member of their party. Captain Octavia had remained silent during their entire exchange, listening absently while twisting a small metal token in her fingers. Her right leg rocked in a manner that would make most look nervous or agitated, but it was a constant for Octavia, who only ever seemed entirely comfortable and level-headed. Markus knew that Duri respected Octavia in a way she petulantly refused him. Whatever Octavia decided, Duri would accept. And Markus had known from the beginning precisely where Octavia's vote would go.

"I'm with Markus on this one, we should go," said Octavia in her husky, confident voice with a nod. Duri let her shock display fully in her expression and the sag of her shoulders. "I understand the risk we're taking, but we know the figures. Valuable systems appear more often than not. The chances of us jumping to a system with no planets or moons to crack is exceptionally low. If we see anything too dangerous, we can be ready to turn and start our way back home immediately and accept the consequences," Octavia said, placing the metal token in her pocket.

"That settles it then!" Proclaimed Markus with a self satisfied cheer that didn't entirely mask the ghost of anxiety that still lingered in his gut.

"Pick out a system and plot a course for us. We'll set off as soon as you're ready." Markus pushed himself out of his chair and set towards the door at a speedy pace. Duri reached for her tablet and swiped her hands over the screen in a few quick motions. When she'd found what she wanted she reached out a hand, blocking his path with the tablet displayed before him.

"This whole thing is your idea, *you* can pick the system. We only have one jump. I'll plot the course but if we end up leaving with nothing I'm not taking the blame." She made the statement with confidence, and a look in her eye that told Markus there was no point in arguing. What difference did it really make in the end, anyway? He took the tablet and looked at the star chart it displayed, a three dimensional representation of the countless systems reaching into the unexplored territory just beyond the cluster they currently rested in. Duri had highlighted the patch of space they could reach with a single jump, and it was vast. There would have been millions, maybe even billions of planets in the highlighted space alone.

A jump always used a set amount of fuel, but could take them as small a distance as the nearest star, which was currently a little over three light years away, or as far as a thousand light years. The energy usage was immense, however. It would take them a few jumps to reach inhabited space where they could refuel and begin the long process of selling their cargo, if they had any worth selling after all this.

They were already very close to the edge of charted space, a bright divide showed stars that had been previously visited. Pressing on one of these stars would bring up a list of graphs showing what planets and moons could be found there, along with all data collated on each expedition that had taken place, be it for mining, settlement or science. There were no settlements this far out, and only a small fraction of the systems discovered were claimed for scientific purposes. These days, the majority of the galaxy was claimed by corporations intent on wringing it dry of all worth.

Out beyond the edge, those explored spaces were scattered like the spray of drops around a puddle, thinning the farther from the edge you go. Markus now zoomed in on an area with no explored space whatsoever, with less chance of running into any cartographers or rogue explorers that were spreading out from one of those already noted areas. He kept zooming at random until he was faced with a cluster of around 100 stars. Here he paused, and slowly adjusted the position within the screen, observing and feeling for any kind of intuition or instinct to point him in a particular direction. He twisted the chart and stars rolled through the screen like frenzied fireflies, and a particular point of light stood out to him. It looked somehow more isolated than the rest, not held quite as tightly as the others in its local cluster. He zoomed in to look closer at this singular point of light hovering on the periphery of its peers. The intuition he'd been searching for began to tingle at the base of his neck. The system was entirely untouched, without a name or any information beyond a string of incomprehensible letters making up its stellar designation. Still, something about it called to him. He circled the star with his finger and passed the tablet back to Duri.

"There, that one will do as good as any other," he said, flippantly, as he turned to walk out of the room.

He wanted to maintain an aura of carelessness to his choice. After all, there was no way of knowing how it would turn out, and he didn't want any cockiness spat back in his face. But inside, he knew. He had an innate sense that he had made a fantastic choice.

Chapter 2

Drones zipped through the bay doors. Containers hung from their backs like swollen abdomens, filled with the minerals they had found floating amid the planetary debris outside. Less than a dozen people currently inhabited the huge equipment bay hall, and most were operating a console that aided the drones. The drone consoles themselves took up only one small corner of the bay, the rest acting as storage for colossal mining apparatus that lingered, silent and unmoving along the walls.

Aki found himself looking up at the mechanical goliaths with concern, a looming reminder of the dire situation they were in. He tapped a button on the side of an excavator, illuminating a small diagnostics screen embedded in the terminal's side. He lowered the brightness as the orange glow of the screen cast glares on his visor. He rhythmically popped his lips as he tapped through the information, checking over the status of the machine, before un-muting the microphone within his helmet.

"She's looking good, same as the rest. A bit of condensation after sitting so long, but nothing that won't clear up as soon as we get in-atmosphere. Assuming we *do* get in-atmosphere any time soon," he said, an electric blip sounded in his ear when he finished talking.

"Big assumption, given the way these last few jumps have gone. Alright, get yourself back in lad," replied Rob, his voice turned slightly electronic by the voice channel.

Aki turned off the screen and started back down the row of machines. Each step stuck his feet to the floor with a heavy clunk as the suit's magnetic systems counteracted the low gravity in the hangar. Aki left his voice call open, talking to Rob as he lurched his way through the bay.

"This is our last jump right? They're bound to make sure it's worth something."

"I dunno," Rob sighed. "Think we could be heading back with empty pockets this time. I'd put money down it's that bloody Mayor, useless prick he is. I bet—ah bollocks."

Rob sat in the control room high above the equipment bay, large glass windows stretching the length of the room allowed Aki to look up and see Rob sitting as his terminal. A flutter of high pitched beeps carried through the call as an alert appeared on one of Rob's monitors.

"What's up?" asked Aki, pausing his stride and watching Rob's figure in the distance.

"Problem with a drone. Few of them have been acting up lately. I'll have to send someone out for it."

Aki looked through the hangar doors into the empty space that lay beyond. "How far out is it? I can grab it, if it isn't too bad." Rob paused for a moment before replying.

"Not too far. About… eighty metres. Froze trying to line up with the doors. I can get one of the lot on intake to grab it, if it's a bit too far for you." Aki took a deep breath in, and slowly exhaled as he listened to Rob, stretching his fingers as best he could in his thick gloves. "No, it's alright. I'm already out here, might as well take advantage. Heading to the doors."

Large enough to easily fit the machinery held within, the bay doors towered above Aki. A faint shimmering film of blue stretched across the opening. Opaque webs of glistening light where photon-mesh barriers kept small debris from floating into the bay. The same technology was used to stop pieces of planet flying too far away when cracked open. It tingled ever so slightly as Aki walked through, stepping onto the ledge beyond.

Standing on the edge of the ship, Aki could look out and see what lay beyond, unobstructed. Drones buzzed past, hefting their loot, large rocks and fields of dust floating in the near distance. Beyond them, nebulae coloured the vista in vibrant greens and purples like static aurora. But mostly there was simply black, perforated by stars.

"Hook yourself up to one of the tethers, it'll be long enough," Rob said, breaking the silence that hung in the moments since passing through the door.

Aki looked back and located the tethers, a row of thick, coiled cables with clips on the end and a basic terminal to control them. His suit had a number of jets along his torso and limbs that would allow him to move freely in low gravity, but the tethers could make it much easier to return to the ship. That, and the extra security would help to steady his nerves.

"I'll keep the line open for you when you're out there. Let me know if you want me to send somebody else out, right?"

Aki fastened the tether to his belt as Rob talked, double and triple checking that it was secure before he replied. "Yeah, thanks Rob. I'll be alright."

Rob knew all about Aki's fear of spacewalks, and about the incident that had caused it. This had become something of

11

a routine between them, Aki taking opportunities to test his boundaries while Rob watched and offered words of support. Without another word, Aki straightened and reached for the handle mounted above the tethers. He took one last steadying breath, and disengaged the magnetic locks in his boots.

A shudder ran through his body as the sensation of weightlessness took over, his feet drifting from the floor. Still anchored to the ship by one hand, he focused on breathing until the shudders subsided. He opened his eyes and took a few moments. An icon floated on the inside of his visor, pointing in the direction of the drone. He followed the icon and saw the machine, floating still as the other drones flew past. It looked small at this distance, though the display told him it would be a trip of eighty-four metres. Less than he'd walked from the entrance of the hangar to the last of the machines he'd checked, but farther than he'd let himself drift in years.

"What difference does it make, ten, twenty or a hundred? The tether is there, and so are your jets," he thought, rallying himself. With that, he put his feet to the wall and pushed out in the direction of the drone. He tensed, fighting the desire to flail his arms. His mind told him he was falling, that he had tripped and needed to catch himself. Instead, he tried to reframe it as swimming, pushing himself through a pool of water like he had done in his youth so many years ago. His heart pounded in his chest, something Rob was no doubt aware of. He had probably pulled up Aki's suit diagnostics the moment he offered to retrieve the drone.

He let his imagination play in memories of youth. Drifting in the water, splashing friends from the orphanage. His mind wandered but his eyes remained focused on the outlined drone, and the numbers ticking down beside it. His heart slowed and settled. When the number reached sixty, the voice call illuminated in the top right of his visor, Rob's voice bringing him back to reality.

"You're doing good mate, really well. That's a good chunk done."

Heart settled, mind back in the present. Aki watched the numbers fall away. Fifty, forty-nine, forty-eight… The drone grew ever larger. Forty-five, forty-four, forty- three…

The tether trailed behind him, extending smoothly as he drifted away from the ship. Drones occasionally buzzed past, carrying their load back to the ship, or returning with bellies emptied and ready for more. He pressed the thumb and middle finger of his right hand together, and a menu appeared on his helmet's display. With small motions of his fingers, he tapped through the menu and activated the thrusters mounted across the suit.

Aki had been through EVA training a long time ago, and at one point had been quite comfortable in space. It came back to him naturally, despite his tensions and discomfort. He curled his fingers until the inner linings of his gloves stiffened, giving the impression of something held in each hand. Then, with small tilts of his wrists and rolls of each finger, the small jets mounted to his shoulders flared and aligned him with the drone.

At thirty metres he started tapping with his lower two fingers on either hand at invisible triggers. Pulses of jets caused him to slow, gradually, each metre ticking down over more and more seconds until the final few reached a near stop. The drone lingered before him, close to a metre wide on its own. Its metal legs and arms tucked tightly beneath its squat body, as well as the cargo container hanging behind it, gave the impression of an insect curled up and dead. Its body was coated in thick dust, including the protruding glass eye that hung from a stalk at its front.

"I see what the problem is," Aki's nerves were subsiding now that the drone occupied his attention. A thick layer of muddy dust clung to the glass. "The camera's blocked."

Rob mumbled and hummed for a moment, looking to one of the many screens before him. "Must be an issue with the cleaning spout, says here it still has half a tank of fluid. Drag it back in and we'll get it sorted."

Aki gently approached the machine with small taps of his thrusters, grabbing hold of its shell before lightly thumping into its side. He twisted the drone around in his hands and took a closer look at the dust-coated eye; a dark glass sphere with an array of lenses packed within. He used his hand to wipe away the grime, the glass reflecting the colours of the distant nebula. "Alright, let's get you back in and cleaned-"

With its eye mostly cleared, the drone buzzed faintly.

The eye stalk twitched to the right, pointed towards the hangar doors, and as soon as the drone could see its destination, it spun its body. The sudden movement rammed the heavy metal chassis firmly into Aki's torso, knocking the air from his lungs. The drone's jets flared heavily, projecting it towards the ship, and flinging Aki in the opposite direction.

Aki's vision blurred as he spun, stars twirling around him and the ship filling his vision in brief bursts as he tumbled. His heart thundered and panic shot sparks of electricity through every inch of his body, paralysing him. A heavy jostle hit him and tugged at his waist as the tether reached its limit and snapped him back roughly. The tether began to tangle in his limbs and wrap around his body, like a great snake eager to constrict and consume. Through the sounds of his own screams and the thundering of blood pumping in his ears, he heard his name.

"Aki! Aki you're alright lad, it's okay. I've stabilised you. Aki!" called Rob's voice, growing clearer as the chaos clouding his mind parted. Aki gasped in a deep breath and his screams subsided as he listened.

"You're okay. You're okay buddy. I'm here, you're alright." Rob continued, his voice urgent, turning soft and calming as Aki settled.

He opened his eyes, slowly, and saw The Vaughn still before him, obscured partly by the coils of tether drifting around him. Rob had taken control of the suit's jets and stopped his chaotic spin.

After a few more moments of heavy breaths and soothing words from Rob, Aki managed to reply.

"I'm alright. I'm okay," he said, a breathless whisper. "Thanks Rob." His heart still pounding and head spinning, the fear still rampant within him, Aki concentrated on breathing as he tried to soothe his frayed nerves.

"Good, good mate. Listen, I've got Joyce heading over to the doors. She's going to pull you back in with the tether. But you're gonna need to untangle yourself, or you'll just end up tumbling again. That alright?" Rob said, calm and confident, though his concern was still apparent.

"Yeah, I've got it," Aki said, looking down to see the tether tangled around him.

With care he pushed the tether away, freeing himself from its coils. Occasionally the jets of his suit would flare to keep him stable as he worked, the process helping to calm him even more. Once free, he again floated in a stable state, facing towards The Vaughn. In the distance, a figure in a grey suit identical to his own stood by the bay doors. She watched him, hand resting against the tether terminal, and raised a hand in a gentle wave when she noticed him looking. Aki waved back, and soon after felt the tether tug at his waist as Joyce started winding the long cable back into the ship.

Aki focused on his breathing, and let his eyes stay closed for long moments, doing all he could to stay calm. Eventually he opened his eyes and saw Joyce not far ahead, holding a hand towards him. He reached out his own and as they drifted together, Joyce clasped and pulled him back inside where his boots locked to the metal floor. The sensation of the magnets clicking into place was comforting, though not as much as actual gravity would be.

"Nice to see you Akachi. You doing alright?" Joyce's rough voice came through a local voice channel as she leaned in close and peered through his visor. Joyce was an older woman, strands of grey hair that matched her suit hung loose between her face and her own visor.

"Yeah, I'm alright. Thanks Joyce," he said, hunched and holding his knees as his legs shook. She gave him a moment, waiting patiently until he regained his composure enough to stand.

"If you need me to beat on Rob a bit, I'll do it. Always looking for an excuse with these management types, even the nicer ones," Joyce said as they began walking.

"Not this time," Aki chuckled, looking to her at his side.

"I volunteered to go out, pushing my limits a bit. It was my fault."

"Shame, I could have taken him when we were younger, he'd be *especially* easy now," Joyce said with a grunted laugh and a wink. They reached the airlock doorway at the entrance of the equipment bay, lights flashing as the doors prepared to open.

"He's one of the good ones, save the beatings for the

managers that really need it," Aki said, turning to look at Joyce directly as they waited for the doors to open.

"That he is, but I've known him a lot longer than you. That man got up to his fair share of mischief at your age. Not like you, you're a good lad. You sure you're alright?" Joyce said, patting him on the back.

"I'm good Joyce, really. Thank you," Aki replied as the airlock doors slid open. Joyce nodded and turned, heading back towards the drone terminals. Aki stepped into the airlock, the magnetic locks in his boots deactivating as he crossed the threshold and the ship's artificial gravity took over. He could usually make the transition smoothly, but his legs were still unstable and he nearly lost his balance.

The thick metal door slid closed behind him, and vents opened in the corners of the room, jets of atmosphere shooting out with a hiss as the room filled. A blue light illuminated the corner of the room, and Aki reached to his helmet, twisting the buckles that fastened it to the neck of his suit, and pulled it free.

Aki had a narrow face, slim and soft. Sweat beaded on his dark skin and trickled down narrow cheeks. He reached up and ran a hand through his short hair and felt moisture built in the tight curls.

He clipped the helmet to a latch on the suit's belt, breathing deep as the doors of the chamber slid open. Rob stood on the other side, leaning on a matte metal walking stick, a concerned smile crossing his face when he saw Aki.

"Sorry about that lad, I should have turned off the drone. Bloody foolish of me to leave it on like that." The depths of sorrow and guilt apparent with every word.

"Don't be stupid. I should have just dragged the thing back in like you said. Honestly it's fine Rob, I'm all good. It shook me up a bit, but that's exactly what I need to get used to again, isn't it? If I ever want to be back to my old self," Aki said, putting a reassuring hand on Rob's broad shoulders.

"You sure you're alright? I'm happy to help you do these little tests whenever you want, but you know we don't expect it of you, right? You're still plenty useful, even when you're not suited up." Rob patted Aki's hand through the thick suited gloves.

"I'm fine, and I know. You'd all be lost without me," Aki said, smiling. Rob grinned as Aki stepped away and started to remove the suit, a bulk of heavy fabric, rubber and metal plating.

"Don't get too cocky! A couple of years behind the desk, but I'm still the best!" Rob said, dropping to sit on a bench facing a row of lockers, each holding a grey EVA suit.

"With your knees? Unlikely. Besides, Joyce tells me you were a bit of a miscreant at my age," Aki said, hanging the suit in an empty locker and pushing the door closed.

"Joyce got into *plenty* of her own trouble. It was easier back then," Rob said in an almost wistful tone.

Rob was short and broad, still muscular, despite the weight he'd gained in his older years. His salt and pepper beard frequently framed a near-cherubic smile. In a few years he'd make a fantastic Santa Claus.

Aki collected a few possessions from lockers on the other side of the room as Rob returned to fretting over him. Aki reassured him another five times before he was allowed to leave, but with a final wave, Rob stood to return to his seat in the control room, and Aki stepped through the door into the wide corridors beyond the equipment bay.

18

Chapter 3

Aki emerged from the depths and headed into the Transport Hub. In stark contrast to the corridors behind, the Transport Hub was wide and open-air, and formed part of the dome that covered the Inner-City of the ship. He entered the hub just behind the great elevator platform that currently lay dormant, waiting for an opportunity to stretch out, should the ship find itself in orbit above a planet.

To either side, platforms of elevated trams continually traversed the city and the smaller districts of the Outer-Ring. Between them was a large paved pavilion that currently hosted a market of simple wood and cloth stalls. Beyond that was a wide road, lined with offices and shops that led to The Column, a towering building that marked the centre of the city.

The city was divided into districts, split like terribly uneven slices of pizza around the central structure. To either side of the Transport Hub were the Business District and Shopping Districts. In the far distance, barely visible behind The Column, Hydroponics helped keep the city sustainable, and that connected directly to the Industrial sector, which was by far the largest district, with its towering factory spires and deep silos reaching far below into the depths of the ship.

Aki climbed the stairs to a tram that would carry him to the Residential District, where he and the majority of residents aboard the ship lived.

The tram drifted smoothly, first passing through the Outer-Ring of the ship, a long stretch of suburban recreation. Lush green parks dotted between comfortable homes that were built to replicate the feel of life on Earth in centuries past. The tram coasted by a station nestled between scenic cafés and bakeries without stopping.

Very few who worked in the ship could afford to live in the Outer-Ring, and so the tram rumbled on. In time they reached the divide between the Outer-Ring and the dome of the Inner-City. The tram eased into a network of reinforced airlock systems, designed to allow the outer and inner sections of the ship to operate as separate entities. The process took a few minutes of slowly inching forwards and then waiting between each gate.

Aki leaned his head back against the window and closed his eyes, listening to the heavy clunks and whirs as they progressed. Hearing the rhythmic pattern of sounds multiple times nearly every day had fostered a comforting nature in them. With a final metallic click, the tram emerged into the narrow streets of the Inner-City Residential District, and settled to a stop.

Half an hour later, Aki worked his way through tight alleyways cramped between towering metal patchwork buildings. Neon lights buzzed above bars, restaurants and shops, all packed within tiny buildings stacked besides and on top of one another like cargo containers. The Inner-City was home to the majority of residents living within The Vaughn, and though the city was large, much of its space was taken up by additional industrial facilities. The Residential District was a jumble of pre-fabricated buildings, referred to as habs, packed tightly together and then again on top of each other. The lower layers hosted a number of businesses, growing more frequent towards the centre; small shops for basic necessities, occasional bars or fast food joints, all things that benefited from being closer than the Shopping District that lay on the other side of the city.

Aki was lucky enough to call an entire hab his own. He'd gotten a fantastic deal on a small hab when he first transferred to The Vaughn. They'd been desperate to find a new technician for some outdated equipment, and he was one of the few around who had recently found himself looking for a new ship to call home. He was fairly young at the time, barely halfway through his twenties, and under any other circumstance, would have found himself in a much worse job, likely sharing a hab with four or five others, as most people do.

He'd stopped off at home quickly to get changed, the thick layers he wore for work were far from necessary in the tightly packed, steam-filled corridors of city life. A thin tank-top was all he needed now, so he'd grabbed a mostly-clean one from the side and set straight back out, headed towards one of the many small pubs that peppered this part of the city.

The Copper Goose was their usual spot of choice. A city guard dressed in black armoured padding stood idly at the corner, watching people wander past. The armoured uniform featured a white circle within a dark ring printed along the chest and shoulders, the symbol of the city guards. Those guarding the Outer-Ring wore similar armour, though their symbols featured a white Outer-Ring with a dark centre. Another guard appeared, cups of coffee in either hand, and received a warm welcome from their bored colleague. Aki pushed his way through a chatting crowd that congealed in one of the tight spaces before a café and turned into a quiet alley off the main pathways. Jets of warm steam brushed his bare arms as he stepped into the opening of The Copper Goose.

Adie and Robin were already there, sitting at a corner table and laughing over well-diminished drinks. They exchanged waves and grins as Aki entered, it was good to see his friends after what had become a more stressful day than he had anticipated. The bartender greeted him with a smile of her own as he approached.

"G'day Aki, you good mate?" she said, reaching for a glass.

"Doing fine Tulie, ready for a drink. You alright?" he replied, pulling a card from his pocket and tapping it on the terminal to pay.

"First drinks covered bud, you can put the ident away. I was ready for you," she said, placing the filled glass on the counter. Aki shot a puzzled look to his friends in the corner who continued their conversation, paying no heed to Aki's accusing eyes. "From Rob. He blipped me half an hour ago, said he'd pay for your first drink whenever you got here," Tula said, winking one of her mismatched eyes. Her natural eye, pale green like ocean water. The other was a shimmering, semi-translucent purple that showed the circuitry and wires inside. "You must have done good work today! Or that Rob is as big a softie as I suspected."

"Soft as a teddy bear, I can attest to that," Aki said with a smile. He removed his hand from the pay screen and picked up the drink. He then slipped into the third seat at the corner table. Adie and Robin had cleared a space and continued their conversation as he took his first sip.

"Maybe you have lower standards, but personally, I like to be in peak shape before I hit town. I can't go out peacocking when I'm not presenting my best! Bad hair day. Bad back day. God forbid a bad dick day. Any one of them could throw me off," said Adie, leaning back into his chair.

Robin squinted and struggled to form words for a moment before bending forwards over the table. "What, exactly, is a bad dick day?" His face sported a bemused concern. Adie looked nonplussed at the question.

"A bad dick day my dude. You know, some days you just wake up and it's looking better than others."

"No, Adie, I don't know. I've never once heard anybody mention having a bad dick day," Robin replied.

"It's a thing! Sometimes you have a day where you look down there and you're rocking full length. Looking happy, looking healthy. Some days you look, and it's just not up to it. Maybe not everybody gets them, but it's definitely a thing. Aki, bad dick days, right?" Adie said, turning towards Aki with an energetic optimism to his question.

"I exercise my right to remain silent on the bad dick day debate," said Aki, raising his glass for another sip.

"That just means the poor dude's always having a bad dick day," said Adie, turning back to Robin. "Still love him, I have a lot of respect for people stuck with bad dick."

"I don't mind a small dick. I kinda prefer 'em a lot o' the time," said Robin, before he turned a cheekily sympathetic look to Aki. "Don't worry Aki, I know a lot of other people that prefer 'em small too."

"No, no you're getting it wrong dude. It's not small dick day, it's bad dick day. You can have a good day with a small dick," Adie said, entirely straight-faced and apparently devoid of humour.

"Well what the hell are you talking about? You said full length on a good day!" Robin gesticulated wildly at the absurdity of the conversation.

"It's just bad dude, I don't know what to tell you. Size is a part of it but, there's more to it than that. There's a *nuance* to it. Next time you're hooking up with a guy, ask him if he's having a bad day or a good day, take a good gander," Adie twiddled his fingers towards his crotch.

"Excuse me my dude, can I gander at your wang? I want to see if it's good today," Robin said, putting as much hippy twang in the 'dude' as he could, mimicking Adie.

"Exactly, you get it!" Adie shot finger guns at Robin who shook his head.

"You odd, gangly, Stu Macher-looking man."

"Who's that?" Adie said, cocking an eyebrow, beer paused just before his lips.

"Mm," Robin mumbled, having just taken a sip of his own. "Guy from an old horror movie. You're like, *spittin'* image of him. Well, if you chopped your locks. Surprised I haven't made you watch that one… We should watch it!" Robin said, face growing eager at the thought.

"We watched one of your weird old films last week my spooky dude! I need a bigger break than that. Aki too, I'm sure," Adie said, eyes darting to Aki for support.

"Yeah, I can't stomach films that old back to back. Add it to the list though, I'd like to see Adie with short hair," Aki said, putting his glass on the table. Adie and Robin sipped at their drinks in unison as Aki took the opportunity to shift the subject.

"You two heard that we're jumping again? I was just working in the dock, prepping the drills."

Robin hummed an agreeing tone and swallowed his

drink. "Thought I'd heard that, wasn't sure though. Last one right? Then we're out'a juice and gotta head back?"

"That's it, one last shot at making some money," said Aki with a nod.

Adie let out an exaggerated groan. "This entire trip's been a bust, so I can't say I'm feeling super jazzy about it," he said, draping his arms over the back of his chair. Aki nodded in agreement as Robin watched the bubbles of froth pop in his glass and let a beat pass before raising his head to speak.

"I'm pretty worried t'be honest. If we don't find somethin' this time the pay'll be rock bottom. No bonuses or anythin'."

Aki and Adie both looked to Robin with shared concern and understanding. "You got enough set aside to last? If we don't find anything this jump?" asked Aki.

"Nah, last run wiped me out. I had enough saved to renew my contracts once, but two bad runs in a row'll be rough. Never been the best at saving, and the refinery don't exactly pay top rate without a bonus to top it up."

Adie leaned forwards. "What are you going to do? You got a backup, right?"

Robin nodded and sipped his beer. "Yeah, I'll be alright. I'll have to buy a ticket back to Canis though. My family'll let me stay with 'em 'til I can find a job." He shrugged defeatedly, smiling sadly as he looked at his two friends. Adie cursed and slumped back in his chair, his sorrowful expression downcast towards the table. Aki felt the way Adie looked, a heavy pit expanded in his gut as the words took root. Adie and Robin had been his best friends for over a decade now, they had met when Aki was new to The Vaughn. The idea of losing one of his closest friends added stakes to this final jump that he had, until now, been spared. The lack of a bonus would hurt, but Aki's base pay was good enough to cover most of his living

25

fees, and he knew how lucky that made him. Technicians were paid a good bit more than many of the other workers on the ship, and he was luckier than most in his living conditions.

"Could you manage your licences if you had a cheaper place to live?" Aki asked, looking towards Robin.

"Maybe just about, but I'm already in a four-person hab. Don't think I could really manage anything smaller," Robin replied dismissively.

"You could move in with me," said Aki.

Adie's eyebrows shot up and he excitedly raised from his slump. "That's a great idea! You get to stay on with us, and Aki will finally have some company in his cave of solitude!" said Adie eagerly. Aki's living situation had long been a friendly joke amongst the group. It was well known that he had got lucky in his contract, and that he cherished his opportunity to live on his own.

"Hang on," Robin said, holding his hand up to Adie's energetic response. "I appreciate it Aki, but... I mean, honestly I couldn't afford to cover even half the cost o' your place. And I wouldn't want t' get in your way like that."

"I didn't say anything about paying half, I just said you could move in," Aki said. "I can cover the costs of the hab comfortably enough. We can get it converted for two people during the layover, give you a place to stay until you've got back on your feet. And, yeah I enjoy living on my own. But I don't mind giving that up, you're one of my best friends. You've stayed with me before, I enjoyed having you around."

Getting the hab converted to suit two people was easy enough, each container was pre-fabricated and had a number of modules that could be easily slotted in. All he had to do was request a change when the ship next parked up at a station. He'd be paying residence tax for two people, but that wouldn't be much more than he already paid.

Robin sported a look of deep consternation as he considered the offer. Aki knew him well enough to tell that he was heavily conflicted about the prospect. He wasn't one to easily rely on others when he thought he could manage something on his own, but surely the option to stay on The Vaughn would win over his last resort.

Adie looked between the two as the question hung in the air unanswered, before breaking the silence with enthusiastic encouragement. "Come on Robin, that's a great deal! It'd give you a chance to put some proper money away, even if the run after this is another bust. You two would be plenty happy living together, and I get another few years of hanging with my most delightful of dudes!"

Robin nodded solemnly. "I know, I just—"

"You don't need to decide right now," Aki cut in. "Think it over a bit. For all we know, this next jump could pay off. Get you a descent bonus. But if it doesn't, the offer is there. We can talk about it more later when you've had time to think, alright?"

"Yeah, yeah alright." Robin said with a slight smile. "Thanks Aki, I don't know but I'll think about it."

Aki reached over and squeezed Robin's hand affectionately, smiling in return. Adie bounced up from his seat, near bumping his head on the tall ceiling, and threw his arms around both friends, pulling them into an awkward hug.

"I for one think you would both have a splendid time!" he sang, smiling at his friends.

"It wouldn't be so bad living with me eh? Think about it, you could have been stuck living with Adie!" Aki said, patting Adie's shoulder. Robin laughed and Adie knotted his brow in mock annoyance, though he grinned and squeezed the two harder for a moment before releasing them.

"I'd like to contest that, but he's not wrong. You'd hate living with me," Adie said, falling back into his seat. "I'm an absolute nightmare."

Chapter 4

Everybody in the navigation chamber could tell that Duri was in a bad mood. She had been tapping her foot incessantly, slamming doors, and generally making noise all day. Nobody knew what the cause was, but many assumed the pressure of the final jump was weighing heavy on her shoulders.

She'd spent the morning preparing for their imminent jump to the unknown system. All of the work had to be done by her, of course. If she'd involved anybody else, they'd know at a glance that the ship was blinking into unknown space. It took near five hours to flesh out the system's information, just so that it wouldn't look suspicious if somebody decided to pull up the charts once they had arrived. A date of discovery, the name of the scout ship and its crew, some mundane observations, things that could be said of any system. Enough to make it look like the crew had only stopped briefly before moving on. As long as there was nothing especially unusual about the system it would do fine. If there was something unusual, well, she'd just have to edit the files again and hope nobody bothered to read them before she had the chance.

This entire situation was ridiculous, and left a deeply unpleasant sourness in her stomach. It wasn't just that she was technically breaking the law by fabricating this information, nor that she was doing it under the orders of one of the most insufferable men in the galaxy. Something about the star system unnerved her. A dreadful intuition had crept upon her, like a gigantic spider had crawled up her legs and perched on her back. The white dot hung on her screen, oddly isolated away from the rest of the stars in its cluster, like it had been shunned. Or maybe like it shouldn't have been there in the first place, an alien star that had appeared one day, hovering on the edge of a crowd and trying to blend in where it didn't belong. All of this was ridiculous of course. What information they could get from long range scans showed nothing of note. A small system with three planets, five moons shared between them. They would be balls of rock, or gas, like every other planet they came across. But still the spider clung to her, warning her that some ill omen lay ahead.

"My kin wait for you there, resting in the unknown. They're eager to meet you. They're hungry," it whispered in the shadows of her mind.

A shudder ran through her spine and she closed the tablet, tired of the thankless work. Pushing herself up from the desk, she shrugged the creature free from her back and started walking towards Octavia's office. The spider skittered behind her.

Captain Octavia sat at her broad desk, polished to a pristine shine. A single cleanly framed photograph of her long-deceased spouse as its singular decoration. She sat facing the large window that framed the desk, silently watching clouds of dust floating beyond the glass. Her leg bumped up and down rhythmically, one of many stims she had adopted as a child. She had trained herself to overcome the others, but this one she allowed to remain. It was the least invasive, but helped her focus her mind when she needed to, or became almost meditative when she wanted precisely the opposite.

She had sat like this for some time now, lost in the debris outside. This was her favourite thing about the job, views that let her forget herself, though she would never be lost for too long. Eventually she would snap back to herself, for better or worse. Suddenly aware again, of her surroundings, and her cravings. She took in a breath, long and slow, leg still twitching, and breathed out as she turned her chair to face the desk.

Reaching out a hand she clicked in one of the many compartments on her desk and produced a small plastic container. She held it for a moment, looking at the numerous pills within, each no bigger than a grain of rice. The cap she popped open with a thumb, when an electronic chirp sounded, informing her somebody was approaching. With a sigh, she closed the cap and placed it back within its compartment. She reached into her pocket and retrieved a small metal token, similar to a coin, and began slowly twisting it through her fingers. A rapid few knocks sounded at the door.

"Come in, Duri," Octavia said. The token rolled, and her leg jostled. Navigator Duri pushed her way into the office, clearly still holding on to her anger from the previous day's meeting. Octavia gestured to the chair across from her.

Duri started talking the moment the door sealed closed behind her. "I've done all the prep work, we can launch whenever we're ready. But Octavia, I'm still not happy about any of this," she said, firing the words like bullets.

"I know you're not happy, Duri," Octavia said. "I'm not thrilled myself. But you know how bad things will be if we don't find anything on this last jump. You also know that the risk is minute. Once we arrive, we can perform some routine scans and, if we find anything untoward, accept our loss and leave."

Duri held a stern gaze towards Octavia as she listened, then sighed and looked away as the room fell silent for a time. She looked at the debris floating behind Octavia, chunks of misshapen rock twisting lazily like leaves falling from a tree.

"Nearly four hundred. *Thousand*. People live on this ship. That means that any risk we take, however small, is a risk we are taking on behalf of near-half a million people. That, is why we use the charts. So we aren't putting ourselves, and those who live here with us, at any risk. At all," said Duri.

"You're right. We are putting those people at risk. We are putting each and every one of those people at great financial risk. Not everybody is as comfortable as we are, Duri. The majority of people that live on this ship earn a minimum wage. They rely on their bonus at the end of a trip to make ends meet. We've already failed to deliver that once. I have the data, here, on my terminal, that shows just how many were heavily affected by that loss. Hundreds of families had to leave The Vaughn, or were forced into smaller accommodations to survive another journey.

"A second run with no additional pay would be the end for many. Some will have friends or family on-ground or on other ships they could seek out for help. They are the lucky ones. Many will have no choice but to sign up to colony work. Some, those who trusted us with all they have, would find themselves living as transients. We will be destroying the lives of countless individuals. If given the choice, I'm certain most would agree that a small risk such as this is a better option than the certainty of that outcome." Octavia kept her voice even the entire time she talked. She had clearly known that this conversation was coming and considered her stance. Duri leaned forwards, trying to temper her irritation. She respected Octavia, and they had never been at odds like this before.

"You assume they would. *If* given the choice." Duri emphasised the 'if' with a particular ferocity. "We aren't giving them a choice. We're putting these people at risk and withholding that information from them. That doesn't sit right with me. I don't see how you're comfortable with this either, Octavia. It's unlike you."

Octavia let the last words hang in the air for a moment, looking away, nodding slightly as she considered the statement. "You're right," she said, eventually. "It is an uncommon choice for me to withhold information such as this. But, on this occasion, I do believe it is the correct thing to do. I have a responsibility to these people. Not only in the short term, but to their futures as well. The decision has been made. I am sorry you have to be a part of this, Duri. I know I'm asking a lot of you."

Duri pushed herself to her feet. She hadn't come here expecting to change anything, only in service of a moral obligation. But she still found herself disappointed in Octavia.

"I'll prepare my team for the jump. Choose a time and make the announcement. We'll be ready. You'll need to pick out somebody to run some scans for us when we arrive," she said, with a sorrowful acceptance, turned emotionless.

Octavia stood. "We'll make the jump in the afternoon. Give people time to rest tonight and prepare in the morning. As for the scans, once we arrive tell Rivka to meet us in operations. I'll be waiting for you."

Duri nodded, then turned and left the room without another word. Octavia remained standing for a time, looking at the closed door. She considered Duri a good friend, but she could feel herself losing grasp on that relationship. She had known this would come eventually. Ever since she signed her contract with Paxton Galactic, hand-delivered by Markus as though it was a gift. She opened her terminal and checked the time, not long after six in the evening. She tapped a button to connect to the ship-wide announcement system.

She paused for a moment, and looked at the metal token in her hand. She had stopped twisting it through her fingers when talking to Duri, but it had remained in her palm. She ran her finger along its smooth surface. It had once displayed an image, a picture of a rocket. She had been given the token as a child during a trip to the aeronautics museum in Kano. Only the faintest remnants of any pattern remained, but the token still brought fond memories of visiting her grandparents, and learning all about the early days of extrasolar exploration from her grandfather.

Pressing a button, a short tune played through speakers gaining the attention of passengers throughout the ship. The giant screens mounted to The Column in the centre of the city, and those spread throughout its narrow streets, paused their adverts and displayed the Paxton logo.

"Good evening all, this is Captain Moore speaking. A course has been set for our next stop, and I'm here to inform you all for the jump that will take place tomorrow, at one PM. Everybody please make any necessary preparations, and rest well. Your station heads will provide instructions following the jump. Enjoy the rest of your night."

With that, she turned off the speaker and leaned back into her chair. The token began its journey twisting through her fingers once more, but stopped as another chime sounded through the speakers.

"Greetings all! This is your Mayor speaking. I'd just like

to chime in on Captain Moore's announcement, to say that I'm, personally, *very* optimistic about our prospects on this new venture! I hope you will all share this optimism with me, and prepare yourself, to bring your very best work to your stations. We are all in this together, and I for one, will be doing my very best for all of you! I believe I will treat myself tonight by cooking up some fine food, and maybe even partaking in a little drink to prepare myself for the hard work ahead! Bless you all, and good night!"

Octavia could picture him gesturing his pointed fist with each unnatural pause in his speech, carefully practised in mimicry of his favourite politicians. She felt the shimmer of anger rippling through her veins thinking of the man. Leaning forward, she tapped her terminal and locked the office door. She opened the compartment on her desk and retrieved the pill bottle once more, popping the lid open and dropping two grains into her palm. She swallowed the pills and leaned back into her chair, waiting for them to take hold. Her eyes met with those of her late husband, his photograph sitting across the desk, watching as her pupils swelled. He would have hated to see her like this. But then, if he was still here, she never would have found herself lost enough to take them. She turned away from him, back towards the wide glass window, and drifted into the stars.

Far below, in a broad and lavish house surrounded by the lush gardens of the Outer-Ring, Marcus settled into a plush and comfortable chair. He felt particularly pleased with himself, certain his impromptu announcement had gone quite well. He sipped a half empty glass of brandy, and reached for his tablet. He connected the voice channels and called his personal assistant, who answered within the second.

"Jim! I'm growing rather peckish. Order me a steak and

kidney pie. And a creme brûlée."

Chapter 5

From within the ship, the only discernible way to tell that a jump had happened was the lightest of shudders. Across the city, small, light objects would topple from precarious perches. A minor annoyance, if any at all. From outside however, the jump was marked by an intense flash of white light. The glass dome surrounding the city would tint pitch dark in response, blocking the light. All windows to the exterior of the ship could do the same. Without the protection, the light would likely blind anybody watching.

Viewing busy space ports from a distance gave the impression of countless stars blinking in and out of existence. On this occasion, their arrival went unnoticed as the light dissipated into the vacuum unseen, the new star system welcoming the arrival of the ship only with silence.

Octavia and Markus stood either side of a terminal in a room filled with similar devices, screens blinking between images of celestial bodies and maps of the stars around them, an electronic hum filling the air. Eight wireframe spheres rotated on the screen, serving as simplistic representations of each of the bodies within the system.

"That's eight," said Markus, leaning into the monitor.

"Eight chances for us to not fuck this up. Who knows, maybe this is going to be a goldmine for us. Anything could be out there."

Octavia hummed in vague acknowledgement. "It's unlikely to find a system with this many bodies and nothing worth mining. But you know how slim the chances of anything exceptional are. We'll fill the silos and head home with something to sell, let's be thankful enough with that."

Markus gave Octavia a sour look before turning back to the screen and idly tapping at the panels around each planet. "Have some faith in our capacity for luck. We've had more than enough bad karma to have earned a little. You may enjoy floating around in space for years on end, but I'm ready to settle down somewhere with an atmosphere. We find a planet with enough pure copper, maybe one brimming with platinum? That would be early retirement money!"

"That, if we're lucky, would be enough to pay off all of our debts and give all the workers their hard earned bonus," Octavia said, with the intonation of a calm teacher correcting a petulant child.

"Oh bugger the workers, we've done more than enough for them," Markus snapped, clearly with more to say, but cut off by the sound of the door sliding open. Navigator Duri stepped into the room, followed closely by Rivka, a member of the Planetary Geology team. They primarily acted as quality assurance for the materials gathered during a trip.

Duri continued smoothly towards Markus and Octavia, but Rivka paused briefly before crossing the room. The sight of the Mayor and Captain before her brought a lump of panic to her gut. Her mind wanted to race with possibilities, but instead turned blank with anxiety-induced stupor. She had only frozen for a moment, but already Mayor Markus had closed the gap between them substantially, sporting a welcoming cheshire grin.

"Rivka, hello! I have it on good authority you are one of our finest surveyors. I'm Markus, an absolute pleasure to meet you!" he said, voice full of faux charm, hand extended towards her. Rivka stiffly shook the hand and nodded as Markus guided her across the room.

"Yes, uh—I... know your name, Mayor Bailey. I'm sorry I just... didn't realise you or the Captain would be here," she said, glancing towards Duri with panicked eyes. Duri offered a faintly apologetic half smile before Octavia stepped forward.

"Yes, we're sorry for the inconvenience. This is somewhat short notice. Can I offer you a drink before we begin? My assistant Jim here will happily bring you a coffee, or tea?" Markus said, gesturing to the corner of the room. Rivka turned and saw a small man in a dishevelled suit. He sat on a chair like a child in time out. At the mention of his name he jumped from the seat, brushing his crumpled suit in a fruitless attempt to remove its multiple creases. She hadn't noticed the man at all, despite walking within a foot of him when she entered the room.

"Uh, I'm fine, thank you. Can I ask what this is about?" she said, looking back to the Mayor cautiously.

"Well, you see, we've run into some issues with the charts. I'm hoping, you can help us fill some gaps," Markus said, with the unusually staggered speech pattern he adopted any time he was talking in public.

"Oh, well, yeah that shouldn't be an issue," Rivka said, lowering herself into the seat before the terminal.

"It seems those that mapped the place, did a bit of a sloppy job. Marked the system but didn't note down any details before they left. It wouldn't be the first time, somewhat common, in my personal experience," said Markus, leaning down to look at the screen. Rivka started tapping through menus. With a few motions the scanning array on the exterior of the ship whirred to life.

"They didn't do any of it? That's not great. I mean, it's inconvenient at least. But it's nothing we can't deal with I guess," said Rivka. Data began scrolling across the screen beneath each planet and moon. She would watch one for a moment before tapping on the planet and typing numbers and code, altering settings and adjusting dials. "The moons are all fairly standard, a few minerals and metals. One of them is mostly made of ice so we could test the purity, get a good amount of water. One of the planets, this one, is a gas giant. Pretty similar to Saturn back in Sol, mostly hydrogen. It has a metal core, but it's pretty small."

She swiped away from the vibrant gas giant and its two moons and then towards the second planet, a cool blue with patches of pure white with three moons of its own. "This one has some ice caps, and a few decent metal deposits. The core here is bigger but I don't know if we'll want to crack the whole thing to get at it. I dunno, maybe if we're desperate enough?"

She swiped again and centred the screen on the final planet, its surface a near uniform yellow-grey colour. The planet was ringed. A wide, thin band of pastel colours hovering above the equator.

"This is a weird one. Rings usually have a lot of metal, they're basically a naturally cracked moon, but this one looks like it's pure mineral dust, nothing worth mining. The surface too, the whole thing's empty. But, then you take a look inside—" she tapped a button on the screen and the coloured rendering of the planet turned to a green wireframe diagram, slowly rotating and displaying what the scanners had detected within. A doughnut-shaped ring of dark green circled the inside of the planet. "There's this mass, just above the mantle. It seems to be a pretty dense liquid. Most likely a metal, but I can't say what. Whatever it is, there's a lot of it."

The mass was near-perfectly uniform throughout, though upon closer inspection, a webbing of intricate roots stretched out from the centre. It created a thin net that evenly covered the entire planet. Markus reached forwards and zoomed in to observe the pattern. The webbing reminded him of the marbled fat you found in wagyu steak, a favourite of his father's.

"Remarkable. Dense is good, yes? Valuable?" Markus said, looking towards Rivka, whose nervous disposition flared again at his proximity.

"Uh, well… usually, yes. It's hard to say without a sample though. My team can get a probe ready, send it down to gather some. It'd be back in a few hours and I can tell you more then," Rivka said. She noticed a shift in Markus's demeanour, though it was brief enough that she couldn't say what it had been. He stood straight and looked towards Octavia, who stepped forward and placed a hand on Rivka's shoulder.

"About that, Rivka. I'd like to ask a favour of you. I would appreciate it if you can keep this exchange between us." Rivka furrowed her brow in confusion, her mouth dropping slightly before Octavia continued, cutting off any questions that were about to seep forth. "I know it's unconventional, and I apologise to put you in this uncomfortable position. See, the charts we are using were provided by a friend of mine. An old veteran who works as a cartographer. I realise I am asking a lot of you. But should this become an official matter, we would be forced to report the error. We would put not only his career in peril, but that of his crew as well. After the last journey, we had some issues procuring a new set of charts. Seeing our concerns, he offered to help. I would hate to see him punished for that." Octavia maintained a steady eye contact with Rivka, not to intimidate, but to properly express the weight of her words.

Rivka's expression softened slightly, but she still felt uncertainty, and discomfort, at the situation. She liked the Captain. Octavia had never been anything but good to the crew and had always been warm in her interactions in the past. She would have believed what she said without question, had it not been for Mayor Markus. The shift in his expression, and the way he looked towards Octavia as he stood.

"We won't be able to know what's down there before we have a crew set up," Rivka said after a moment of contemplative silence.

"Not a cause for concern my dear, we have some of the most experienced and talented crew in the universe! They are more than capable of handling what we find," said Markus with a cheery optimism.

"We still have access to topographical data," said Octavia. "We don't need to know the specific material to safely extract it, only its location and consistency. I assure you we will give the department heads all necessary information to keep their workers safe."

Rivka looked towards Duri, who had remained silent during the exchange and now looked pointedly away. Tapping on the screen a few times to finish the process, Rivka raised out of the seat and turned to face Octavia directly. "I'll leave the rest to you then. Duri can update the charts, I best be getting back to my duties."

"Thank you," Octavia said with a simple nod, her

expression held firm. Rivka began walking back across the room, quickly pursued by Markus who reached out and clasped her hand in an enthusiastic double-handed shake by the door.

"I really must express how much we appreciate your cooperation! If you ever find yourself in need of aid, please, feel free to ask me, whatever you need." He held a hand out to the silent man still sitting in the corner by the door. Jim started, and quickly reached into a pocket, retrieving an antiquated business card. Markus took the card and pressed into Rivka's hand. "These are Jim's details, feel free to contact him any time!"

Rivka looked at the strange object in her hand quizzically for a moment, before thanking Markus and turning to walk down the corridor.

Markus watched until she turned the corner, closed the door and rushed back to the terminal. Duri had taken the seat, already transferring the new data to the charts that would soon be distributed throughout the ship.

Markus leaned in and swiped across the terminal monitor a few times, bringing it back to the third planet, and swapping to the wireframe view.

The light lines that depicted the ring orbiting the planet contrasted the darker lines of the deposit within. Where the ring in orbit followed the equator of the planet, the interior ring was tilted a near perfect ninety degrees. As the image rotated and the two rings twisted, they intersected and formed a cross that neatly divided the planet into four even quadrants.

"Start moving us there now. If we have a crew work late, we can get samples ready to test by the end of the night," Markus said, tapping his finger on the screen where the two rings converged.

"We'll find our treasure. X marks the spot."

Chapter 6

Aki and Robin sat in a café a few floors up in The Column. The food wasn't great, but it was cheap, and anywhere in The Column had the benefit of a great view. Broad windows pointed out over the twisting streets leading towards hydroponics. Glass towers filled with greenery poked above the buildings like a test tube jungle. The city's lights shone a light blue, mimicking the early evening of a sunny day.

Aki scribbled at the screen on his tablet, a half finished halloumi wrap pushed aside. He added notes to a very rough but vaguely accurate diagram of his hab. He was busy defining the layout he envisioned for their hypothetical cohabitation.

Robin took a bite of a bacon sandwich, watching the scribbled blueprint take shape. "No, no," he said, muffled through a mouth still full. "If you're paying more you need the bigger room. We don't need an even split."

"If I'm paying more, I get to make the decisions, and my decision is we're going to share the place evenly. I'm not sticking you in a closet!" Aki said, pointing accusingly at Robin with his pen.

"The room I have now ain't much bigger than a closet, I'll

be fine!" said Robin dismissively.

"I don't care what you want. You're going to live comfortably whether you like it or not," Aki said, writing "Robin's Room" on one section of the diagram and underlining it for emphasis.

"Gimme that, I'll show you," Robin said, leaning across the table and reaching for the pen.

Aki shot his hand away, holding the pen out of reach. "Not a chance! I'm not letting you ruin my careful planning!"

Robin offered a weary glare that was undermined by the smile pushing at his cheeks. "I'll just bribe the guys when they show up. Tell 'em to make it how I want," said Robin, taking another bite.

"I can bribe them more, you have no money," said Aki, adding additional detailing to the clumsily drawn rooms. "Does this look right? It's a bed," he said, pointing at a rectangle tucked into the corner of one room.

"Low blow. And, no, s'too skinny. 'Less you got a custom bed, made to fit your waifish form." Robin indicated Aki's slim physique with his free hand.

"I have a perfectly normal bed for my waifish form, thanks," Aki said, tapping the pen on the screen. "Do you think Adie has a custom bed? Or does he just sleep with his feet dangling off the end?" he said after a moment of contemplation.

Robin shrugged and sipped from a can, washing down the final bite of his sandwich, before he pulled his own tablet from a bag and tapped the power on. "Y'know, there's a good chance we won't have to do this. You looked at the charts yet?" he said, pulling up the display of the new system they had arrived in.

"Yeah, took a quick peek. Looks like we're the first ones

here," Aki said, turning off his tablet and setting it aside. An icon showed the progress of The Vaughn towards its new destination, a ringed planet in a fairly sickly looking yellow-grey tone. They would arrive in two hours, at which point the ship would split in two. The Inner-City would descend to the planet, an elevator and a tangle of pipes and wires forming a tether leading all the way back to the Outer-Ring that remained in orbit above.

"Looks like we'll finally make a bit o' money!" said Robin, tapping the planet to see the meagre information the charts offered. "If there's anything good there anyway. Jus' looks like a big rock t'me."

"There's something in there. Had a meeting with Rob about an hour ago," Aki said, twisting the tablet so he could make out the data listed beside the planet.

"Any word on what it is?" Robin asked.

"They didn't say. But they're sending us in pretty fast so it must be good," Aki said.

Robin nodded. "Or they're desperate."

Aki twirled his finger in a circle above the screen. "Nah, there's this ring of something around the whole planet. Even if it's just a load of slag, there's enough that we could clean it up and fill a few silos. If it's good quality stuff we could even get multiple trips out of it."

"That'd be nice. A few easy trips'd make up for the last couple years," Robin said, looking at the planet for a moment before leaning back in his chair.

"Hang on. If you're so certain we're gonna get paid, why've we been sat here talking emergency plans for half an hour?"

"Oh!" Aki said with genuine surprise. "You're right, sorry. I guess I'd just got a bit caught up in the idea of you moving

47

in. I forgot why we started planning it in the first place."

Robin grinned. "I'm already such a fantastic hab-mate that you're sad to see me go before I've moved in!"

Aki laughed. "You're not wrong. It's been a long time since I lived with somebody, even longer since they were fun to be around."

"Yeah, I think it woulda been fun too. Maybe another time," said Robin, twisting the remnants of liquid around the bottom of his can.

Aki looked at his friend for a moment. "We can still do it, if you're up for it? Even if we do get a bonus, I mean," Aki said.

Robin looked back and thought for a moment. "I dunno… It's one thing when I don't have another choice. I don't want to take up your space if I don't have to."

Aki shook his head. "Stop thinking you're going to be invading my space. I have more than enough room, and I enjoyed having you stay with me a couple years back. Plus it would stop all the hermit jokes from you and Adie!" This comment won a smile from them both.

A few years prior, Aki persuaded Robin to stay while he recovered from surgery. A bilateral mastectomy that left him largely unable to use his arms for two months, or move much at all for the first few weeks. Without the money to recover in hospital, and with his small and overpopulated hab, Robin had agreed to stay with Aki, hoping to recover faster.

He'd spent the majority of his two month stay laid in a sofa bed, sleeping through the haze of pain medication or re-watching centuries-old horror movies.

Aki had gone out of his way to keep Robin comfortable, helping to keep him fed and medicated, and chastising any time his restless nature won over. It had been a surprisingly

48

good experience, better than you'd expect recovering from a major surgery to be.

Aki picked up his tablet and turned the screen back on, presenting it to Robin. "Besides, we just spent half an hour planning this out! Are you going to waste all that?"

Robin pushed his seat back, rocking on its hind legs. He scrutinised the drawing, and Aki's expectant face. "I'll consider it, okay?" he said, dropping the chair back to the floor. "But! If this dig pays off and we get paid, we're re-negotiating the money. I'll pay half rent."

"I can agree with that. Only if we do get a proper payday though. And I don't know about half," said Aki, reaching across the table to shake Robin's hand.

"If the rooms are even, the rent is too, Aki!" Robin said, batting his hand away. A chirp sounded from Robin's tablet and he glanced down to a notification appearing on the screen. "Ah, I'm gonna have to head off, they need me to help prep the drop," he said, reading the message.

"Yeah, that's alright. I should probably get down to the dock and see if they need my help with anything. I'll check in with you tomorrow when my shift is done," Aki said.

Robin finished off his drink and departed with a quick goodbye. Aki looked at his roughly drawn blueprints again as he finished his forgotten food. Once he was done he packed up his things and set off to the trams.

The trip to the Transport Hub took a little under an hour, delayed by heavy traffic as people moved in waves through the ship. Once it arrived, the Inner-City would be detaching from the Outer-Ring of The Vaughn and descending to the planet below, so it was important everybody arrived where they needed to be before the airlocks sealed and blocked passage between the two sections of the ship.

The Transport Hub was an overwhelming jumble, crowds pouring in and out of each tram. The market that had been operating in the pavilion below was being disassembled, the stalls and wares stored and toted away. Aki passed the platform where a crew prepared the elevator that would soon stretch between the two halves of the ship. A huge metal capsule sat in the centre, waiting to ferry people between the orbiting Outer-Ring and the city on the ground below.

Passing through the Transport Hub and the hallways behind, Aki walked into the control deck around an hour before the ship would be settled in orbit. Rob sat at his terminal, flipping through images on the monitor and checking items from a list. He waved Aki in with a smile before continuing his conversation with whoever was on the other side of his headset.

A few others were in the control room already, working at different terminals. Once the ship had arrived, an outpost would be constructed on the surface, and the administrative staff would be split. Half working from the control room above, and half working from the outpost below. Aki was a head engineer for the mining department, and had to spend a good chunk of time in the outposts or control room. But his job gave him plenty of opportunities to work manually too, helping the crew at the dig sites directly. Truthfully, he preferred that side of the job. Riley, one of Aki's fellow engineers, sat on a sofa tapping at their tablet. When they noticed him, they called a greeting and beckoned him to join them on the sofa.

"Hey Riley, how things looking?" Aki said as he lowered onto the sofa, peaking at the tablet in Riley's lap.

"We were expecting a few more hands in the bay, but a fair chunk of crew got trapped in the city. It's been so long since we actually touched a planet that everybody's out of practice. We're managing though," Riley said, swiping the tablet screen as they talked. "Rob says you checked the printers already so we've got a crew setting them up. You got something to be doing?"

"No, nothing specific," Aki said, shaking his head. "I just prefer taking the elevator down. Figured I'd see if I can be helpful here."

"Yeah? I always preferred riding the city down. Adie is down there if you want to give him a hand," said Riley.

"Sounds good, I'll grab a suit and see what I can do," Aki said, pushing away from the plush sofa. Five minutes later he had pulled on a grey EVA suit, and waited for the airlock cycle to complete. Despite his discomfort with space walks, he actually liked the feel of the suit. He'd always thought they looked cool, especially the more colourful ones they wore on the surface. As a child, his favourite book had been about a crew of space explorers who wore similar suits. The book had been commissioned by a subsidiary called Tau-Visser Inc, the company that owned Paxton Galactic, and by extension, The Vaughn. They also happened to own a lot of the companies that produced the suits.

Illustrated children books donated on mass to orphanages, schools and libraries across the system. Looking back, he was uncomfortable at the idea of corporations advertising directly to children, directly influencing them from such a young age to idolise the industry. Even so, he couldn't help feel a nostalgic joy any time the suits reminded him of the characters in those old books.

An electric tone played over the ship's speaker system as Aki exited the air lock, his boots magnetically clamping to the floor as he left the ship's gravity behind.

51

A notification appeared in the corner of his heads up display, along with a similar tone playing from the speaker in his helmet. It was the signal alerting all crew that the Inner-City was now detached and departing from The Vaughn.

Prospecting ships often shared the ringed design, allowing the centre portion to descend to planets, whilst the Outer-Ring remained in orbit. A long, broad cylinder of cables, tubes and panels followed behind the Inner-City as it descended, keeping the two halves of the ship tethered together and acting as transport for materials and people alike. The process effectively allowed the ship to replicate the space elevators that had played a large part in humanity's early days of space faring. The entire process would take roughly fifteen minutes. Once settled, a number of docks would extend around the perimeter of the city, offering transport between the sealed city dome and the surface of the planet.

Aki walked towards the shielded doorway to the bay.

The horizon of the planet below crested into view and quickly grew in scale as he approached. From this distance you could observe the layers of atmosphere, the curve of the planet, and pick out details of the terrain far below.

Even on a relatively nondescript planet like this, the sheer scale would always maintain a degree of wonder, for Aki at least. The planet's ring stretched past them, curving into the distance and vanishing behind the horizon. From here he could see just how unusual the ring was, its texture was unlike any he'd seen before. Planetary rings were traditionally made up of dust and trillions of rocks and asteroids varying in size, debris left over from what had formerly been a moon, or from some large solar object that was ripped apart when colliding with the planet. This ring looked smoother, almost uniform.

Whatever it had been before must have been particularly fragile to disintegrate into such fine debris.

The planet itself looked quite unusual. It was a large solid mass of flat yellow-grey, the colour of years-old tobacco smoke staining the walls of an ancient home. The surface only ever varied in slight, gentle inclines. No mountain ranges or plunging valleys. It was almost ugly somehow, distinctive in its lack of defining features.

"Fuckin' weird dude," came a voice from beside Aki. He turned and could just barely make out Adie's face through the side of his visor.

"Looks like somebody polished it up, nice and smooth," Adie said, glancing to Aki, then back to the planet.

"It is bizarre. I wonder if they'll want to study it? Could have formed in a weird way. Or maybe the crust is made out of a rare material?" Aki mused, nodding imperceptibly within his bulky suit.

"I remember a few years back, Robin made me watch one of his ancient films. You might have been with us," said Adie, leaning forwards to glance down over the ledge of the ship as he talked. "The crew of a spaceship are flying over some planet. See some weird alien shit going on down there. Then this one dude says something like, god doesn't build in straight lines," he stepped back and turned to look at Aki. "It stuck with me, because I remember thinking, that's fuckin' dumb! Straight lines are all over the place my dude. Crystals and minerals and all kinds of stuff grow in straight lines, right? Plop a snowflake under a microscope and it's all straight lines and angles." He turned and looked back towards the planet. "This shit though, this is fucking weird. That ain't natural."

The group started to stray from the opening and return

to work. Aki and Adie joined the effort, preparing machines for departure from the ship. The machinery ran along tracks in the ceiling leading to the bay doors, where they extended outward, hanging above the planet before silently dropping from view. One at a time they fell, large propulsion ports on each side adjusting their descent.

The jets would slow the machines, and soon, with a heavy thump, they would land on the surface not far from the Inner-City. Much of the machinery used in mining was designed to be dropped from orbit, and had the capacity to launch itself back into space where drones would retrieve them. Not every ship had the capacity to split itself like The Vaughn, and not every planet was safe to land on; uneven terrain, unstable crust or any number of possible complications.

The first machines dropped were large scale 3D printers. As soon as they landed, they would set to work. Sucking in regolith, dust, dirt and debris from the surrounding area to use in construction. By the time the work crews arrived there would be a series of what effectively amounted to high-tech mud huts. But they were strong, quickly erected, and most of all, very cheap to maintain.

After a few finishing touches by the crew, the buildings would be the foundation of an outpost for the crew in their time away from the city.

When the last of the printers started its descent, the crew took a short break. There was plenty more to be deployed, but not until the crew on the surface were ready for it.

"You headin' down now?" Adie asked, stretching one arm across his body and groaning as the tender muscles pulled.

"Yeah, figure I'll see if I can be useful at the outpost," Aki said as the two started walking towards the airlock doors. Adie struggled to find more comfortable positions to stretch out his muscles with the limited movement of the suits.

"Man, I'm out of practice with all this. We've barely started and I'm already feeling stiff." The doors opened and they huddled their way into the chamber, other crew shuffling in besides them. Adie started unscrewing the latches on his gloves and helmet in anticipation of the air cycle, and the moment that the safety light turned green, he sprang them from his body and shook his scruffy hair loose.

Aki started to unfasten his own suit. "Some day you're going to lose an eye or something if you're not careful."

Adie waved a hand dismissively. "I wait for the light, it's fine. Rob good?"

Aki pulled his helmet loose, his hair too short to shake free like Adie. "Yeah, we're good to get a move on. The elevator's dropping in ten minutes, we should be able to catch it if we're quick." They stored the grey suits and set out through the corridors towards the elevator chamber a few floors above.

Far below, the city settled and prepared to work. And even further below, deep beneath the city newly nestled upon the jaundiced crust, ripples quaked throughout the substance that webbed its way around the planet.

Chapter 7

The elevator rumbled down from the orbiting ship. Aki and Adie sat amongst a few dozen others who didn't quite fill the wide seat rows. Half of the space was dedicated to storing crates of material or equipment, all strapped tightly into place with thick black tethers. Gravity fell away as the shuttle departed The Vaughn, harnesses holding the passengers in the brief period before the planet's gravity eased into place.

The trip to the surface of the planet took near half an hour for the Inner-City. A slow descent to land safely with as little disruption to the city and its inhabitants as possible. The ship was designed to absorb the tumult of atmospheric re-entry, with turbulence dampeners leaving most of the effects entirely indiscernible to those within. But there would be a consistent vibration, the sensation of pins and needles creeping up through the floor and into your feet.

The elevator was a much rougher ride by comparison.

No turbulence dampeners and a much faster descent made the metal container feel like a submarine rocked by towering tsunami waves. Though Aki preferred the turbulence to the dampened vibration of the city's descent. The tingle would climb up through his legs and seep into his stomach.

A growing, tumbling ball of unease that left him feeling light headed and sickly. It brought back memories of his previous placement on a small ship called The Shining Prospect.

Unlike the massive Vaughn, The Shining Prospect had been home to barely a hundred people. They had been a pickup crew, a team that filtered through the materials left in the wake of larger ships. Occasional transport jobs eventually landed them a contract with a scientific colony, in a system near the edge of the galaxy. The scientists were established on a comfortable moon in the system's Goldilocks zone. They would ferry samples of minerals and microfauna across the system, and got paid a comfortable wage to do it. The Shining Prospect had been small enough to fly down into the atmosphere entirely, no need for an orbital platform or space elevator like those on The Vaughn.

Aki thought about his time on The Shining Prospect often, and most were happy memories to relive. But those vibrations of dampened atmospheric turbulence, they only reminded him of the very worst, the memories of his greatest trauma. A panic would grip him, squeeze him tight. Until they had landed he would find the air reluctant to enter his lungs. His heart would pound so loud no other sounds could permeate the deafening thrums of blood gushing through his ears. He was getting better at space walks, but those vibrations would only feel like an omen to tragedy. No, the elevator was definitely the better option.

Adie bumped his head against Aki's just as his thoughts were wandering to his last day on The Shining Prospect again. "What are you gonna do if we get a big bonus this time?" Adie said. "Sounds like they're pretty optimistic about the place."

Adie knew exactly what Aki would do with the money. He'd do what he did with all of his money. Most people couldn't seem to tell when Aki was falling into one of his low moods, but Adie just had a talent for distracting him when he needed it. Aki had struggled with it ever since the event on The Shining Prospect. Memories of bad times led to a spiral of involuntary negative thought that inevitably wiped him out for a few days if they went unchecked.

"The usual, plop most of it into savings," Aki said after a thoughtful moment. "I think I'll spend a bit on the hab though. Fix up a few things so it's all set for Robin if he ends up moving in."

"Yeah? You two sticking to the plan even if we get a big payout then?" Adie said with a curious tilt of his brow.

"I think so. We've talked and he knows I'd be fine with it either way. He's being a little stubborn about it, but I think he likes the idea of moving in," Aki said, head clearing already.

Adie smiled. "Robin being stubborn? Never," he said sarcastically. "I knew this'd happen. I think it'll be good for both of you. Two best buds chilling every day."

Aki nodded. The more he considered it, the more he agreed. He'd spent a long time living alone, out of habit more than anything else at this point. Ahead of them, mounted above the doors to the elevator, a screen displayed the progress of their descent. They were close. The gravity was still not quite as strong as The Vaughn's own artificial gravity, but it was close enough to feel comfortable. Aki looked back to Adie. "You good to head straight out, or do you need to stop off anywhere in the city first?" he asked.

"Nah, I'm good. I'm pretty eager to stretch my legs, check out the new neighbourhood," Adie said with a smile. The elevator travelled through the airlock system into the glass dome of the Inner-City and came to a rest on the platform below. Stepping through the doors, Aki and Adie paused for a moment. The elevator platform offered a fantastic view of the city, unobstructed all the way down the wide road from the Transport Hub to The Column at its heart. The shutters had receded away from the glass dome's thick panels. The city lights were still bright, replicating the early evening of Earth, but beyond the windows a dark night sky loomed above, the planet's ring creating a pastel slash arching into the distance.

Robotic arms whirred and began to unpack the heavy storage crates from the shuttle behind them. The Transport Hub was much calmer now. A few guards, outfitted in black plastic armour with the white ring emblem emblazoned on their chests, idled beside the platform looking bored as they watched the few commuters moving between tram stations.

Aki and Adie descended from the shuttle platform and crossed the now empty stone pavilion towards one of the tram stations. With the city now nestled on the planet's surface, what used to be airlocks between the two halves of the ship were now converted into docks where workers and vehicles could transfer to the planet's surface. The only one currently assembled was in the Industrial sector. A few familiar faces appeared as they boarded the shuttle, mostly mining crew on their way to the outpost. The tram skimmed along elevated platforms through the city, first passing through the Shopping District, neon signs and advertising screens scattering multicoloured light through windows as they passed. Small crowds gathered before cafés and bars, gatherings for celebrations at the final jump being a success.

Soon the bright lights of the Shopping District vanished and the towering brutalist structures of the Industrial District took over. Iron towers wrapped in pipes and wire. Steam pouring into the streets from low vents, chimney stacks high above that would spew smoke plumes once the refineries were at work. The district was near empty now, but tomorrow it would become one of the busiest sections of the ship.

The tram smoothly slid to a halt and its passengers alighted towards the docks, a large archway leading to a section of ship protruding out from the glass dome. Aki and Adie scanned their ident's at the row of terminals in its centre and split up to retrieve new EVA suits. Unlike the grey suits in the equipment bay above, the suits used on planets came in a number of varieties suited to the atmosphere and terrain the crew found themselves in. They also came colour coded, a means of easily identifying crew at a glance.

Aki pulled his suit on. Tough synthetic fibres with light metal plating. A thick tool belt clipped to the waist with a number of pouches and hoops at his side. His suit was mostly white, with a line of vibrant orange crossing the chest, and shoulders. He tapped at a small screen on the wrist of the suit and watched it connect to the sub-dermal ident chip below it. When his name appeared, he slipped his tablet in one of the belt pouches and picked up a matching white and orange striped helmet.

He tucked the helmet under his arm and found Adie waiting beside the surface elevator. Adie's suit was identical, though mostly dark red in colour. He leaned against the wall and peered through a window, arms crossed, his helmet hanging from a hoop on the back of his belt. Aki nudged his shoulder.

"Come on, get your helmet on," Aki said, tilting his head towards the elevator doors.

Adie reached into one of the pouches on his belt and pulled out a pack of gum, throwing a piece into his mouth as Aki pressed the elevator call button. "Want a chew dude?" Adie said, holding the pack out to Aki.

"You're getting high for work?" Aki asked, scrunching his brow.

"No! I mean, it wouldn't be the first time, but not on important jobs. It's just minty gum," Adie said laughing, showing the packaging as proof. The elevator doors slid open and one person in a dark slate suit stepped out,unfastening their helmet.

"No thanks. We might not get these helmets off for a couple of hours," Aki said, stepping into the elevator. Adie followed behind, happily chewing his gum as they both pulled their helmets over their heads and fastened them in place.

The elevator started a leisurely descent, metal walls illuminated by a soft white ring around the roof. Aki leaned against the handrail and watched a timer tick down on the screen above the door. After a few minutes, Adie nudged his arm. "Watch this," Adie said, tilting his head forwards. He used his tongue to press a shiny glob of white gum to the inside of his visor, then looked directly up and held his mouth wide open. The gum hung for a moment, then dropped loose and fell back into his mouth. Adie grinned wide, looking pleased with himself. Aki watched with mild amusement.

"Little bit of entertainment when work goes slow," Adie said. Adie stuck the gum to the visor again and lifted his head. This time the gum fell past Adie's open mouth and tumbled out of sight. "Ah shit, it fell into my suit..." Adie said, trying to tilt his head to look down the neck of his suit.

Aki laughed hard. "You're an idiot," Aki said fondly between chuckles. "My eyes are watering and I can't get at them," his hands reflexively reached to wipe tears from his eyes. Adie smiled, giving him a light jostle with an elbow.

A chime sounded and a small image of Rob appeared within Aki's helmet. He accepted the call. "Hey Rob, everything going on alright up there?" he said, the laugh still lingering in his smile.

"Hey Aki. Sorry, I'm gonna need you to head to the outpost soon as you can. I'm just setting off on my way down too. It's a bit of a shitshow up here and it's going to be one down there too if we're not lucky," Rob replied. He sounded out of breath, and the microphone occasionally picked up a clink of his walking stick tapping at the floor.

"I'm already on my way down with Adie, going to help set up the outpost. You alright?" Aki said, growing concerned.

Rob stayed silent for a moment, then with a beep, Adie was added to the call.

"I'm glad you're both on your way down. Adie, I was going to call you next but, two birds one stone. I've just got out of a call with some of the boffs up in the operations centre. They want us to start drilling tonight, Captain's orders apparently," Rob said, huffing slightly between sentences.

Adie visibly recoiled before responding. "They want us to start drilling, like, right now? We've literally only just got here!" he said.

"I know. I've been arguing with them since you finished up in the bay. But they insist." Rob said, letting out a heavy sigh.

"They want to get some samples by tonight. But listen, I managed to talk 'em down a bit. We're just doing a single line. One drill, one crew. I want you two on it, I'll get a few of our best and we make sure this is done as safely as possible, alright?"

As Rob talked the elevator reached the planet's surface and the doors opened. Aki and Adie stepped out onto the dry, fine soil for the first time.

"Why are they in such a rush? This sounds weird, Rob,"

said Aki.

The clicking of Rob's cane stopped and he let out a heavy breath.

"I know Ak, I just... I think it's that joke of a Mayor. Too eager to know he's getting paid after all this. Listen, I'm about to get on the elevator down to the surface. I'll get back in touch soon, you two just head to the outpost and start getting what you need."

With that, the call disconnected. Aki and Adie looked to each other, standing for the first time in near-three years on natural ground, wind pushing grains of yellow dust around their feet and sun glinting on the metal of their suits. Adie shook his head and gave Aki a gentle slap on the shoulder.

"Come on dude, let's get started on this bullshit I guess."

Aki turned and looked up at the high metal walls of the city's underside, where the pipes, storage silos and electronic systems of the ship were stored. He saw the glass dome of the city above, and then the thick cable of the elevator trailing far up into the sky. The cable and the pipes that stretched up with it always looked like an impossibility, stretching out of the planet's atmosphere where they connected with the Outer-Ring of The Vaughn. The ship was tiny at this distance. Occasionally a burst of bright light would mark its location, as heavy thrusters pulsed to keep it stable and worked to find the best position to suit the new planet's orbit. Aki saw the burst of light now, then took a few long steps to catch up with Adie.

The outpost was a ten minute walk from the city. Once fully operational, vehicles would shuttle workers back and forth between the two, but for now they were occupied with industrial cargo. Towering metal pipes extended out of the city, three storeys high, mounted on heavy struts that held it high enough for workers and vehicles to pass beneath. The pipe stretched far beyond the outpost, with a thick band every quarter mile that would maintain the internal flow back towards the city.

The majority of the outpost had been constructed by the printers they had helped deploy earlier, causing each building to take on a similar yellow hue to the surrounding landscape. Workers were fixing heavy metal doors to the shells and adding oxygen pumps to the perfectly fitted ports that the printers had left in place. To the side of the chaos surrounding the outpost, a small group congregated beneath a gazebo made of unfolding metal pipes and coarse white cloth. A cargo truck parked beside it, half-prepared with equipment for a single drill site.

Near-twenty crew members gathered around a table in the centre. Most wore varying shades of red and orange.

When Aki and Adie approached they were welcomed by a sequence of familiar voices, many of the crew known for their particular talent or work ethic. Riley stood at the head, wearing a white suit with a charcoal grey stripe. A small projector displayed a topographical map of the area on the table, with markings indicating each location drill sites would eventually be prepared.

"This will be our last two I think, head engineer and drill operator makes for a full set," Riley said, nodding towards Aki and Adie respectively. "I've got the equipment you'll need on its way down. Rob's given everybody an idea of what's going on, and just forwarded this onto us. You'll be headed here."

Riley pressed a fingertip to the table and slid along the surface, leaving a circle in the projected image. Aki looked to the map, then up in the direction they would be heading, the same direction the pipe was heading. Eventually the pipe would be split, stretching out in multiple directions, but for now it seemed that everybody was purely focused on getting this singular drill site operational.

"The planet is already fairly small, and this site seems to be where the crust is thinnest, only around sixty kilometres. The substance isn't too far below that, and it's especially high right here too. So, it should be a quick job for the drill. Get the pipe down there and you can all be back in a few hours."

One of the crew spoke up. It was Joyce, the older woman who had helped Aki after his space walk the day before.

"We know what it is we're drilling for down there yet? Or they still acting like we don't need to know," she said, a surly rasp ringing in her voice.

A rumble of agreement circled the table. Joyce had been on The Vaughn since long before Aki arrived, and was a well-liked, and very outspoken, member of the crew. Riley's head shook.

"Not specifically. But we know it's metallic. Very dense, viscous and heavy. That's enough for us to work with, you know what precautions to take."

"They think they've found something special down there. Something worth a lot, I reckon," Joyce said, crossing her arms.

"And they either don't trust us to know, or they want to hide it from us. Just going to tell us that it's slag, pay us as low as they can manage and keep the rest for themselves."

"If that was their intention, which I highly doubt, they wouldn't get away with it long. We all get the chance to see what we're drilling for. If one of us doesn't know what it is, we have plenty of friends in processing that would let us know," Riley said.

They tapped the projector and the map vanished from the table, a circle left behind in the yellow dust that had built on

65

its surface.

"It is unorthodox, I will give you that. And I am just as uncomfortable with it as you, and I'm sure everybody else here is. But, they've told us the information we need to do the job safely, and that is what we are here to do. Now pack up the last bits you'll need, you set off in ten."

With that, Riley walked away from the table. Most joined and set to work immediately, a small few lingering behind to share in uneasy looks. Aki helped Adie attach one of the printers to the back of the truck. The machinery was much more cumbersome now that they had gravity to contend with.

The larger portions of the drilling equipment would be dropped from orbit like the printers. All of it would be waiting for them at the site by the time they got there. Aki returned to the table and pulled his tablet from its pouch, laying it on the dust-covered table. Checking the manifest, he confirmed that all the equipment they needed was accounted for, and those that would be dropping from above were being processed. All they had to do was hop on the truck and put together the pieces when they arrived. Turning off the tablet and placing it back in the pouch on his belt, Aki noticed fresh marks in the dust on the table's surface.

Somebody had drawn a grid around the circle Riley had left, and played a game of noughts and crosses in the yellowed dust. The crosses had won.

Chapter 8

A small convoy rolled easily along the smooth surface of the planet. The truck loaded with equipment rattled ahead, towing the printer, as a second truck transporting crew followed closely behind. The outpost shrank into the distance behind them, but the colossal pipe continued alongside the trucks, stretching far from the city.

A bright light burned towards the planet's surface some distance ahead as the jets of a pipe segment were ready to be assembled by the crew waiting beneath. The pipe, as with many of the technologies used in prospecting, were modular, each section telescopic and interchangeable. It would arrive on the surface compacted, attach to the previous segment, and stretch out over a vast distance under the directions of the workers assigned to it.

Another large item began its descent through the atmosphere. The final components for the drill site.

Aki watched as the blazing object descended to the distant ground. Joyce appeared beside him, leaning her arms on the top of the cabin at the front of the transport.

"What you think of all this, Akachi? All this.. secrecy," she said, squinting in the bright sunlight despite her tinted visor.

"I'm not sure, to be honest," Aki said, still watching the trail carved into the air by the falling equipment. "I have no idea what reason they could have for it. To avoid telling us what we're digging for. We're going to find out as soon as it gets back to the city," he said, as he looked down to meet her eyes. "You've been on the job a lot longer than me, has this happened before?"

Joyce shook her head. A lock of grey hair hung loose on the inside of her visor, swinging free along with the motion. "Not in my time, that's why it's giving me the jeebs. Nobody hides things for good reasons. Not management types, at least."

"As long as they've given us the right info, we can make sure the dig goes safely. That's my main concern right now. I have a friend that works in processing, if I hear anything from him I'll make sure you know as soon as I do, alright?" Aki said.

Joyce nodded and patted his back fondly. "You're a good'un," she said, and returned to her seat with a grunt of discomfort. The convoy eventually overtook the tunnel with friendly waves between crews, and arrived at the dig site soon after. The site looked identical to the rest of the planet, a flat and featureless expanse of yellow dust, only signified by the drilling equipment that waited for them there. It had taken half an hour to reach the location, and as soon as they did, everybody departed the vehicles and set to work.

With a crew of their best it took three hours to assemble the drilling site. A large construction of metal bars held the drilling platform aloft, a small control room where Adie would operate the mechanism, overlooking the drill from high above. The equipment dropped from orbit included a sequence of tube-shaped grinding drill heads, each as big as a house when assembled. Heavy jagged claws stuck out of each cylinder, designed to crush their way through soil and rock as they spun. Each head mounted to an arm and spread out across the drill site with the ability to expand or contract like the iris of a camera.

Fully extended, the machine was capable of drilling a hole as wide as four hundred metres across, though now was only set to half that. The entire contraption gave the impression of an old ferris wheel laying on its side, with each carriage replaced by a spinning wheel of metallic, hungry teeth.

The printer had constructed two small buildings on the site, a rec room with a few bunks, and an office where Aki would monitor the drill.

Aki sat at a worn chrome table inside the office, watching a simple render of the drill as it worked its way through the planet. The monitor marked the drill as thirty-four kilometres deep, progressing slowly but inexorably downward. The large claw-like protrusions on the drill heads funnelled all of the rock and dirt through pipes embedded in the arm of the drill. The system then deposited the debris onto an ever-growing mound above.

Had the crew not been wearing their helmets, the sound of the drill would be overwhelming; a constant metallic grinding singing in the air above the crunch of the planet's matter being dislodged. The process was slow, but the layers of crust and mantle that lay beneath them proved every bit as featureless as the surface. The small planet only had a thin crust, near sixty kilometres thick on average. The substance they sought only slightly farther below that.

Still, it would take a while longer for the drill to reach that depth. As it churned, the dirt filled the air with particulates, giving the impression of a sand storm surrounding the drill site. Despite the diminished visibility, a crew assembled the final segment of pipe network beside the crater. Some of the crew had departed back to the outpost, while most rested within the barracks, waiting for the next stage in the process to begin.

Aki finished typing a report and submitted it to The Vaughn, then connected to a voice channel with Adie who sat high above operating the drill. As soon as the channel connected the heavily muffled whirring of the drill burrowed through the call. The helmets did a good job of dulling the sound, but the thick walls of the printed office did much better than Adie's cabin atop the towering machinery.

"How are you holding up Adie, you going to need a break any time soon?" Aki asked, checking the time.

"Nah, I'm good! Been listening to some tunes and vibing. It's kinda nice to be back up here," Adie replied. He'd been operating the drill for two hours now, and spent a few more helping to construct the machine beforehand.

"I know what you mean," Aki said, leaning back in his chair and smiling. "It's nice to touch dirt again, you know? It's odd to think we've been floating for so long."

"I've been running drones for, what is it, two years now? That's fine and all but, big chunky machines. That's the good shit," Adie said, affectionately patting the metal console before him.

The monitor before Aki chirped a light tone as the depth indicator continued ticking up. Forty-six kilometres, well over half way to the deposit. The heavy grinding drone of the drill had eased away, filtered out like the ring of tinnitus temporarily forgotten. Another chirp from the console, and then a new sound puncturing the mundane. A high metallic whine, a heavy crunch.

The grinding sound of the ground below was replaced by the pained motors fighting to turn the drill head, and failing. The control cabin high above rocked heavily, and Adie clutched the arms of his seat tightly. "Woah! The fuck was that?" he said, eyes darting to the monitors around him in search of an explanation.

Aki leaned forwards and tapped at the monitors before him. "I don't know, the charts don't show anything!"

"Well there's something down there. Something tough if it's—" Adie was cut off when another heavy churn whined out of the hole like a siren calling for aid. Aki tapped at the console and pulled up a video feed of the crater. At first he couldn't see anything, just the top of the drill, stationary. Another heavy groan. Adie rocked within his cabin, and then on the feed Aki noticed the growing pools of dark material around the sides of the drill.

"We've hit the deposit," Aki said, swiping through files on his tablet, looking for confirmation.

"What? We shouldn't be anywhere near it yet!" Adie said, flipping at the controls before him.

"Shutting off the drill, we need to get it out of there." The constant high whine of the drill mechanisms faded and a silence descended on the site. Outside, a small congregation of workers appeared from the rec room, trying to see what was happening through the dust filled air. "Every chart says the same thing, they must have got something wrong, or… Or there was some geological shift, maybe?" Aki said.

"Ak, I'm gonna try pulling the drill back out. Whatever that shit is could be doing all kinds of damage to it," Adie said, already starting the process. Aki agreed, nodding lightly as his eyes continued to scan the documents he found. He looked back towards the camera feed of the drill and saw

71

that somehow the drill had sunk even farther down into the viscous substance.

He opened his mouth to speak when a new screeching sound filled the air, the sound of metal slowly straining. Adie let out a yelp of surprise as his cabin began to rock again. This time, the screeching continued, followed by the heavy ping of a metal beam snapping somewhere along the structure outside. Aki's eyes shot wide, the monitor showed the drill growing evermore subsumed within the dark mass.

"Adie you're not pulling the drill out, you're just pulling the whole structure down! Turn it off!" he yelled, pushing up from his chair and peering out the window towards the drill site.

Through the settling dust that filled the air, the silhouette of the structure was visible, a mountain of crossed metal bars. It looked wrong, ever so slightly tilted or malformed.

"I didn't get a chance to turn it on yet. That ain't me," Adie said, his voice carrying a chill that rode through Aki's spine. The groan continued, another ping of metal snapped, followed by a chorus of cracks and high ringing chimes as the entire structure of the tower began to buckle.

"Adie get the fuck out of there!" Aki shouted as he sprinted from his console towards the exit, rushing to fasten his helmet as the airlock doors opened. The doors to the airlock closed behind him and the process began. Decompression and disinfectant spray dragging through long seconds, the sounds of Adie racing to free himself from the drill control cabin carrying through the voice channel. "I'm on my way out, I'll meet you at the base and we'll get some distance, alright? You just have to get down that tower," Aki said.

Adie unfastened his harness, struggling through

panicked, fumbling hands, then pushed himself out of the low chair. Another heavy lurch sent him tumbling, catching on the console with a heavy grunt. In the short time it had taken to free himself from the harness, the tower had already taken a distinct tilt, the windows of the control room leaning to peer into the gaping maw it helped to create.

Adie stumbled his way to the cabin door, and as he turned the handle it fell open with ease, gravity pulling it down to smack against the outside wall. He ran across the platform as best he could, fighting against the uphill tilt. Aki continued talking, but the words were drowned out by metallic groans and the pounding of his own heart. He reached the stairs to the floor below and held the railings tight, struggling to descend safely. The entrance to the tower elevator sat in the middle of the lower floor, directly before Adie as he reached the bottom of the stairs. Another lurch threw him to the floor where he rolled and slid, hitting hard against the folding metal doors of the elevator. The groan of pain that shot out of him cut off Aki mid-sentence.

"Are you okay?? What was that?" he asked, urgency and concern swelling to new heights in his voice. Adie rolled to his side and peered down the gaps between the door. The elevator was at the bottom of the tower, and the elevator shaft was twisted and crumpled along with the rest of the structure. He grunted as he pushed to his feet, using the wall for support.

"The elevator is shot, I'm going to need to climb down," Adie said, pulling open the manual access hatch behind the elevator. He leaned over, looking to the ladder struts embedded into the side of the tower. After years of operating the drill, he was comfortable with heights. But looking down the hatch, seeing the pit below, it made his stomach lurch. He pulled a tether from his belt and clipped it to the top of the ladder, and started lowering himself through the hatch.

As soon as the airlock opened, Aki raced out, skidding to a halt when he saw the tower again. The entire structure was curling in, like a withered beckoning finger. He couldn't comprehend how quickly it had decayed. He could hear Adie's exertion as he struggled to make his way down the twisted wreck. A worker ran past from the rec room in the direction of the tower and Aki followed behind. A group congregated not far from the base of the tower, watching in horror at the events unfolding before them. Aki arrived amongst them, bending and breathing heavily after his sprint. One of the crew raised a hand, pointing up towards the structure, where Aki saw that high on the tower, small with distance, Adie clung to the metal structure. The red metal panels of his suit glinting as they caught the sun.

When he first started climbing, the ladder had been heavily angled, and had only gotten worse with each cry of metal. He used a safety tether that extended from his suit, clipping it to the rungs of the ladder as he climbed. Every few steps he needed to unhook and reattach it. Four steps down, hand over hand, and then he would reach up, unhook the tether, and connect it to the lowest rung he could reach. A further two steps and another heavy groan rocked the tower, the shaking so intense it caused him to lose his grip. Gasps came from the crew below as Adie fell momentarily, then slammed hard into the metal beams of the tower, saved by the tether that left him swinging loose in the aftermath of the quake. Adie heard a yell of horror through the communication channel.

"Fucking hell!" Adie screamed.

"You're alright Adie, you're doing fantastic! You just need

to get back on and keep using the tether," Aki said, recovering quickly from his momentary despair.

"I cracked my fuckin' arm mate," Adie said between heavy breaths. "Not broken but, fuck me that was not good." Adie swung from the tower, dangling precariously above the vast opening the drill had made.

"Shit! Shit... Alright, I'm going to climb up. I'll meet you part way and we can get back down together." Aki said, starting towards the base of the tower.

"Don't you fucking dare Aki!" Adie yelled, as one of the crowd grabbed Aki by the arm and pulled him back. Aki couldn't hear the person who'd grabbed him, but he could read their lips clearly enough.

"Too dangerous!" they yelled.

Adie pulled himself back to the ladder, using the metal beams of the tower for purchase. Pausing for just a moment to catch his breath once he held firmly to the ladder's rungs again. He continued down. His left arm seared with pain, but he needed it if he had any hopes of getting off the tower.

A few more steps down and Adie paused, the pain in his arm growing exponentially with each step. Maybe it was broken after all. He looked down and saw the gaping maw of the drill site below. He still had a long way to go before he would reach the bottom of the ladder, but the edge of the hole was getting closer. "Ok, Aki, dude. Here's what's going to happen," he said, breathing heavily as he transferred the tether hook to a lower rung. "I'm gonna climb 'til I'm above solid ground, get away from the hole. And then I'm going to drop, alright?"

Aki remained silent as he absorbed what Adie was saying. "That's gotta be, what, fifty foot?" Adie said. "The gravity's a little weaker than Earth. The suit'll take some of the blow, if

I'm lucky," he was panting between each sentence, struggling to climb as fast as he could. "You just, get ready to drag my ass outta here before it falls on me, alright?"

Aki looked at the tower. From here the drop looked much more than fifty feet, maybe as much as double that. But the tower was crumbling fast, it looked like it could collapse at any moment. "Yeah, yeah okay. You're probably going to get hurt pretty bad, Adie. But we need to get you out of there, quick as possible," Aki said.

"I don't doubt it," Adie said with a weary smile. "This is gonna suck. But listen, I love you dude. I trust you to get me back safe."

Aki turned to the man who had grabbed his arm and tapped into a voice channel with him. He'd try to soften Adie's landing as much as he could, and then they needed to get as much distance as possible. Somebody ran off to fetch the truck as Adie, high above, continued his painstaking process down the tower. His muscles burned white hot as they supported his weight in the bulky suit, legs burning and shaking between each step. Sweat drenched his back and his visor began to fog. Despite it all he persevered, a mantra forming in his mind, narrating each step like a good luck charm. He just had to repeat the process enough times, and then he could let go, just a momentary fall and then others would take charge.

Down four steps, holding firm with one hand. Unhook the tether, reach down and attach it to the lower rung. Down four steps. Unhook the tether. Attach it to the lower rung. Another heavy metallic groan shook the tower, intense like a beast trying to shake him free. As the tower shook, his hand missed the lower rung, the hook didn't latch, and then the tower was gone. His hands empty and the world a sudden blur. The screeching groan from the vast dark hole filled his mind, drowning out any thoughts he could have as he saw the tower fall away. The sky became an ever shrinking circle of light above him.

For a moment, through the cacophony, he heard Aki's voice, shouting his name, as he fell out of the world.

Chapter 9

Captain Octavia sat at her desk, fingers knotted tight in her hair. She stared ahead, eyes fixed on the grain of her wooden desk. News of the incident had arrived a few minutes before. People died in this line of work. Inevitably machines would fail, planets would prove unpredictable. Any number of factors beyond their control could lead to a situation where life was lost. She felt a great sorrow at those losses when they did occur. But deaths due to pure human negligence, they weighed heavy on her in a way nothing else could.

It wasn't clear yet exactly what had caused the incident, but her intuition told her that whatever they found, it would inevitably lead back to her. Markus had pushed for this, for them to rush the mining crew, to get the drilling started the moment they had landed. Markus had insisted they start drilling without testing the site first, without acknowledging their incomplete data. Markus caused this, but she had been complicit. The Captain was supposed to be the highest authority on the ship, her decisions would have overruled his demands. But she owed him a debt, one that lurked in every interaction they had, hiding between words and in knowing looks. Markus loved nothing more than to make suggestions, giving the illusion of choice, knowing that in reality they were commands.

The terminal on her desk chirped, or had been chirping for a time before she acknowledged it. A box centred on the screen with block capital letters. MARKUS BAILEY. She had been anticipating this call.

"It's about fucking time Octavia! I've been calling you for nearly ten minutes!" came his voice, bursting out over the speakers the instant she tapped to answer the call. "I assume you've heard the news. We give those ingrates a simple job, and we are burdened with their incompetence. You realise how this will look, right? This is going to raise questions we do not want to answer, Octavia!"

Octavia sat firm in her chair, allowing the words to tumble from him without response.

"I need you to keep this quiet, if it isn't already too fucking late. We need to control the narrative. I need to make a plan, figure something out… The mining crews are probably already talking to each other, it's only a matter of time until it spreads to the rest of the ship!" The dialogue rolled out of Markus as a stream of consciousness, his mind racing faster than his words could keep up with. He stumbled over words, and Octavia took the opportunity to interject.

"All crew from the site are being held in closed offices, and have been instructed not to contact anybody until they have been discharged. It was a small outfit, twenty-four in total. No doubt there is a degree of rumour, whispers that an incident occurred. But I was quick to contain it."

Silence for a few seconds, and a quick relieved breath from Markus. "Good… Good! You did the right thing, we have time," he said, pacing the length of his lounge.

"But, we can not hold them for long. And expecting

them to follow any false narrative is off the table. These are individuals who witnessed the event with their own eyes. They lost one of their own. If you say anything to contradict what they witnessed, they will challenge you," Octavia said, picking up her metal token.

"All we need to do is stop anybody asking questions about the charts we're using. We need to give them a distraction. I can do that," Markus said, his pacing coming to an end.

He dropped into his seat and flipped open a notebook. "How long will the crew be held?"

Octavia looked at the time. The incident had taken place late in the day. By the time the crew arrived back at the outpost, most workers had returned to the city. It was now coming up on eight in the evening.

"Not long, but we will ask them to maintain discretion until an official statement has been made tomorrow morning. We will also request that they remain at the outpost tonight, in the instance more is needed from them," Octavia said, the token twisting between her fingers.

Markus nodded. "Ok... Yes, I should be able to manage that. I can head down tonight. I'll give a talk in the morning, assuage any fears and suspicions. Maybe I'll work from my office in the city for a time so I'm able to monitor the situation up close." His pen scratched along the notebook, roughing out his speech for the morning as he talked.

Far below the orbiting ship, Aki sat in a cold, sterile room within the main outpost building. Crew from the site perched on stiff metal chairs, mostly in silence. Bare yellow walls with no ornamentation reflected orange-tinted light from the fixtures above, visible wires stapled across the ceiling.

Every member of the team had been interviewed, Aki twice. They'd asked him to recount the events in as much detail as possible, and he had done so with ease. He could pull every second to his mind with crystal clarity. In reality it had seemed to pass so quickly, but now replaying each moment in his head it seemed excruciatingly slow. The image of Adie falling seeming to play at half-speed.

In Aki's mind, Adie's head turned to look towards the crowd that bore witness to his demise, and his eyes met with Aki's. There was no anger or judgement in them, only sorrow. It isn't what happened, it couldn't have. Adie was so far away when he fell, and it was so fast. But still in his mind, the image was there as clear as the rest of it. Adie's eyes, filled with fear, dropping beyond the edge of the great pit they had built together.

He wanted to talk to Robin. He deserved to know what had happened, that their best friend had died. When he'd first sat in the nondescript room he considered calling him, or sending a message. But how would he word it? Can you just send somebody a message out of the blue with news like that? If he called, what would he say? Maybe it was better to wait until they could talk in person. At least then they could cry together. He hadn't cried yet, which was strange, wasn't it?

Shortly after the crew had settled in the waiting room, a woman with a white suit and a badge denoting some level of management had asked them all to avoid communications until they had been released. Maybe that was for the best, he decided that talking in person was more appropriate.

It had been some time after six when they arrived at the outpost, and was close to ten by the time they were finally allowed to leave the sterile offices. The woman in white had asked them all to stay in the bunkhouse for tonight, in case they had any more questions in the morning. It was still light outside, but the sun was getting low in the sky as Aki trudged across the outpost. The Vaughn ran on a set twenty-four hour cycle, simulating a day on earth, which didn't line up at all with the daylight hours of the yellowed planet. A few more hours of dwindling daylight would pass before the still yellow landscape would be plunged into darkness. It felt strange going to bed with the sun still hanging in the air, but the day left Aki exhausted. Many of the other crew headed straight to their cots, where others solemnly sat in the rec room within the same building, eating or chatting amongst themselves in mournful tones.

When Aki fell back into the cot, he could swear it compressed more than usual, like the weight of his sorrow had manifested and lay atop him. Despite his terrible weariness, he struggled to sleep. He lay in the cot, heart aching in his chest. But still, he didn't cry, and that bothered him. Almost as if his body simply wasn't ready to accept what had happened yet. Maybe he was in shock. Still, he tried.

In time the few remaining crew joined him in the surrounding bunks, the low murmurs from the recreation room diminished to nothing. Aki lay in the stillness for what felt like hours, long enough for the sun to set. By the time the clocks ticked over to four AM, Aki finally lay asleep, muscles tensing and face twitching at the discomforting images his dreams brought.

Far away, across near eight miles of unshifting yellow dust, the dig site lay still. The site had continued to deteriorate for a time after the crew had fled. The tower had continued to deform until eventually the structure had torn free and plummeted into the pit, leaving only jagged metal debris behind. The edges of the pit had crumbled and cracked, spreading out into a funnel. One of the outpost buildings had partially crumbled and fallen into the pit, like an ancient seaside home succumbing to the sea. The ground had buckled beneath part of the pipe network and the last segment collapsed and unfurled into the hole, and then everything had become still.

Two drones from The Vaughn hovered above, watching the process, arriving shortly after news of the incident had reached the orbiting ship. They scouted the site and made note of the damage, before settling still in the air as their operators finished for the night. In the morning, the operations crew would arrive to find alerts from the drones signifying movement had occurred during the night. Clips of ground giving way and crumbling into the pit. Of dust devils twirling across the debris. One clip would go unnoticed until much later, capturing the movement of an obscure shape.

Through the distance, the darkness of the night, and the haze of yellow dust that still lingered in the air, it was hard to make out precisely what the shape was. An indefinable silhouette emerging from the crater, pausing at its edge for a time, and then lurching its way out of the drone's view.

Chapter 10

Robin rolled out of bed, eyes blurry and back stiff. His tablet was somewhere in the room playing his wake up playlist, but it wasn't on the side table. He must have fallen asleep watching videos or reading again. He dropped to the floor and reached around under his bed, pulled the tablet out and tapped to turn the alarm off.

A few notifications waited for him on the screen; a reminder to renew his prescriptions, a charged subscription he was reluctant to cancel despite his lack of funds, and one alert that mentioned a public meeting, some talk by the Mayor being held in the city centre this morning. He could catch it on the way to work.

No messages. Barely past six AM, Aki and Adie were probably still asleep at this time. He tossed the tablet back onto his bed and stretched as best he could in the tiny room. He pulled on some sweat pants and shuffled out.

As soon as the door opened, an upbeat tune sang out, and the sound of tinkering came from the kitchen. One of Robin's hab-mates, Kimi, was a morning person. She was still wearing her exercise gear and was preparing some kind of elaborate breakfast. Robin slipped out of his room and into the bathroom without drawing her attention. He needed to wake up a little bit before he could interact with other people. He washed up, brushed his teeth and then spent a moment studying himself in the mirror.

Robin had a rectangular but soft face, a defined chin and angular jawline, all features he liked. The lines under his eyes made him look like he needed a few more hours in bed, but he could live with that. He ran his hands through his hair, straight, limp strands that flopped to the side like the teen star of a movie made in the late 20th century. He wouldn't admit it, but that was precisely the look he was going for; a touch of Billy Loomis. He really would have to make Aki and Adie watch Scream soon… He had a stocky build, muscular, though not without some fat to cushion it and add bulk. His skin a pale tan shade, the light brown contrasted with the much paler scars curved beneath his chest, another thing he liked to see. He felt good about himself today.

He left the bathroom feeling more alert and ready to tackle the day. The door opened and Kurt stood directly outside, looking like a prop from a zombie movie. "Okay Kimi I'm using the bathroom now," he said, pushing his way past Robin and eagerly closing the door behind him.

Kurt was very much not a morning person. Kimi stood at the end of the hall with a cheerful smile, a smoothie in one hand and a spatula upright in the other. "Morning Robin! You're looking well today! You want anything for breakfast? I can make you a smoothie if you want!" she said, twirling the spatula and returning to the kitchen.

Robin smiled. "Thanks Kimi, I'll skip it today though. You got a shift this mornin'?" He walked to the kitchen and grabbed a cereal bar.

"Not on the morning shift, Kurt is," she said, gesturing to

the bathroom door with her spatula. "I'll walk into town with you two though, I have a few chores to do."

The three of them all worked at the processing plant and often walked there together. Their fourth hab-mate, Elliott, worked the night shift at a restaurant and was rarely seen. Robin returned to his room and changed into some proper clothing for the work day, ate his cereal bar, and tucked a pill between his lip and gums. He took the pill twice a day, and liked to spend the ten minutes it took to dissolve laying on his bed and checking news and social media.

The news was more of the same. Updates on an ongoing scandal with a megacorporation called Hinkley Industrial that had been found running unlicensed and unethical studies on their staff. Progress reports on the rebuilding of Earth. He flipped to a local news channel for Canis Minor. Most of his family lived in stations and colonies in the Procyon star system, back where he was born. Finally, he checked updates from within The Vaughn. Issues reported with the first drill site, something had caused a delay setting up the pipeline, but details were scarce. Mayor Bailey was expected to give more information at his gathering today. Robin finished reading the article before flipping to the schedules for the processing plant. No changes made.

He pushed up from bed and tucked the tablet in his bag. He leaned over the small desk built into the hab wall and tapped a button, the desk's surface illuminating and displaying a partially filled jigsaw. He studied for a moment, then tapped a piece and swiped it into a gap at the centre. The piece completed a green glowing syringe in the hand of a still-not-quite-completed Herbert West. A character from one of his favourite ancient horror movies, one he had an inexplicable crush on that even Robin couldn't quite justify.

He tapped to turn the screen off again, picked up his bag and left the room.

Robin, Kimi, and Kurt left the hab and started their trek through the city. The narrow walkways and stairs leading down between layers of habitation chambers bustled, flowing out of the Residential District. Their hab was only a short walk from the city centre, where the repeating dull grey of the hab chambers eased into the colourful neon lit grid of shops, bars and restaurants. No light shone through the glass dome above, so lights within the city provided artificial daylight in its stead.

"What do they expect us to do if the pipe isn't set up?" Kurt said, eyes still tarnished with the deep desire for more sleep.

"I'm not sure. We already finished up all the prep yesterday. You know Harris though, he'll find somethin' to keep us busy," Robin said. Kurt grumbled in acknowledgement and took a heavy gulp of coffee from the thermos he carried every morning. The Column came into view, the many screens mounted to its towering walls displaying advertisements and news in bite-sized strings of text. The flow of foot traffic began to converge ahead as they approached the plaza, the sole public park within the Inner-City. A broad patch of neatly trimmed grass intersected by a web of footpaths. A stage was permanently erected at one end of the plaza, prepared for public announcements, concerts or plays. A screen atop the stage displayed a countdown until the Mayor would give his morning address.

Some people simply passed through, eager to start their day, or uninterested in whatever the Mayor had to say. But a few hundred gathered at the base of the elevated stage. Kimi waved goodbye and walked around the crowd towards the

Shopping District on the other side, while Robin and Kurt found themselves a space to settle within the crowd. A small few guards stood at either side of the stage, as they often did when Mayor Markus made a public appearance. None of them looked particularly alert.

Mayor Markus stood in a small cabin connected to the stage, holding a sheet of paper with scrawled notes and pre-prepared sentences. He read them aloud as Jim styled his hair. Tidy and proper, but not perfect. He had spent many years refining his image. Not one of a rich politician or the son of a wealthy CEO, but a Mayor who could relate to the everyman. A bloke you could meet at the pub, though he admittedly despised his occasional appearances at the local taverns. Octavia had been true to her word, and news of the incident had remained scarce and limited in scope through the night. This was his opportunity to control the narrative. Waving Jim aside, Markus straightened his jacket and climbed the steps onto the stage.

A sparse scattering of claps and some sarcastic jeers sounded as he walked to the podium, waving with one hand and displaying his well-practised smile. The screen above the stage flicked to a live feed of the Mayor, as did screens around both the Inner-City and the Outer-Ring of The Vaughn in orbit.

"Good morning all, and good day! I hope you're all, settling in well, to our new, temporary, abode," he began, adopting his unusually staggered speech pattern. He paused for a moment, as though expecting a response that never came. "Now, I'm afraid that I arranged a meeting this morning, as the bearer, of unfortunate news. Many of you, have an intimate knowledge, of the processes, used by our, fantastic mining crew. But for those of you who do not, it usually takes a day, or, a number of days, for our crews, to ready dig sites, and begin extracting the materials, we are here to gather." He paused again here, looking over the crowd as though checking they understood, a teacher ensuring his students follow the lofty concepts he was conveying.

"Yesterday, a small number of the mining staff, volunteered to head an early expedition. A prospect, you might say, to set up a single pipeline. Their hope, was to have the quality of the materials tested, so that we could reassure all of you fine folks, that our so far unlucky journey, was about, to pay, dividends!" He gesticulated with a soft fist, thumb protruding unnaturally as he emphasised each unnatural pause in his speech. "Well, unfortunately, though they did work effectively, and safely, I am assured. An incident, occurred. A malfunction, in a piece of mining apparatus, lead to the loss, of a great deal of company property, as well, as the possible loss, of a human, life." Markus made sure to present the last statement with as much sorrow and gravitas as he could muster. He lowered his head and solemnly closed his eyes, a display of sorrow that also afforded a moment for the ripples of whispered chatter that spread through the crowd.

"Now," he continued. "We don't yet, have a firm explanation, of the cause, of this, incident. An investigation is underway, and I assure you, we will provide, more details, as soon as we have them. The crew were all very talented, and proficient, in their jobs. And though we cannot rule out, that human error, is at play, I urge you all, not to speculate, or place blame, on those poor individuals, suffering, with the loss, of a colleague, and, friend." He shook a finger along with this statement, as though chastising the hypothetical abusers he addressed. "The machinery will be checked for faults, but

I assure you, that all of the equipment we use, is the best, that money, can buy! Business, will continue, as normal today. I will be staying, at my office, here in the city, for a time being. So that I can keep my eye on the situation, as it evolves." He gestured up, towards The Column, towering in the centre of the city behind them. "Now, I believe, I have held you all long enough. If anybody has questions, please, don't hesitate, to contact my office!"

The Mayor left the stage as the crowd turned inward, discussing with one another, or taking to their tablets to message friends and family. Robin's gut clenched at the thought of something bad happening to any of his friends, and reached to pull his own tablet from his bag.

"Shit. Well, that seems like a bad omen," said Kurt, rubbing the back of his head idly. "Some of your friends are on the drill crew right?"

"Yeah, Aki and Adie…" Robin replied, flipping the tablet open and checking his messages for any sign from his friends. "You too, right?"

"Ah, nah, nobody on the drills I don't think. My brother and a few buds work out there but, I think they're all like, transport or somethin'," Kurt said, rubbing the back of his neck. People pushed past as the crowd dispersed, back to starting their day as Robin tapped away at the tablet. He pulled up a group chat between himself, Adie and Aki.

The last message sent had been sent at nearly two AM the day before. Adie posted a picture of an overstuffed burrito.

'We not been to Chizi Grill in an age. I CRAVE BURITOES! Should go soon, get some bud grub with my dudes' Two small thumbs-up icons in the corner meant that Robin and Aki saw the message when they had awoken a few hours later. Robin typed a new message.

'You two okay?? Mayor just gave a talk, said something went wrong, somebody got hurt??' The message popped into the chat and Robin stood waiting for a reply to appear. The message sat at the bottom of the screen undisturbed. After a minute passed Kurt cleared his throat.

"Hey, I'd try not to worry too much. I mean, I know you'll worry but. There's what, hundreds of people that work on the dig sites? Thousands maybe. Chances of it being your boys, or, one of your boys I guess, are pretty slim. You'll hear back soon."

Robin nodded and flipped the tablet closed, but kept it in his hand as they walked through the Shopping District, and into the Industrial sector. By the time they were at the processing plant, the group chat remained undisturbed, his message sitting heavy, eager for acknowledgement.

Robin sat on a bench in the locker room wearing thick overalls and rubber boots, gloves pinned under one arm. Harris, the floor manager, leaned into the room, counting heads. Before he turned to leave Robin noticed and jumped to his feet. "Harris! Hang on a sec. Is it alright if I keep my tablet on me today? I just want to—" he started before being cut off.

"No tablets Robin, in your locker like always," Harris said, sounding annoyed already.

"I just wanna keep an eye on it, I've got friends on the drill crew that might have been in the accident this morning," Robin said, trying to maintain a calm tone.

"No exceptions, Robin. It wouldn't be fair to the rest of the team if I let you break the rules that everybody else is expected to follow. If any news comes through I'll see it on my tablet and let you know," Harris said, then swiftly exited the room.

Robin looked at the tablet one more time before throwing

it in the locker and slamming the door shut with a muttered expletive.

Chapter 11

Red lights flashed and an artificial voice churned through the speakers as Aki ran, panting down the metal corridor of The Shining Prospect. Heavy metallic whines sounded through the ship as the hull struggled to maintain its integrity. The grated metal floor felt sticky, clinging to his feet as he ran, like the steel was melting and the soles of his shoes were sinking in with each step. The words sounding through the speakers were garbled and made no sense, but they were loud and threaded fear through his veins. The entire ship vibrated, the turbulence dampeners still active and trying to diminish the evidence of the ship's degradation.

He reached the door at the end of the corridor and pulled it open, stepping into a small room with EVA suits lining one of the walls and a heavy airlock bulkhead across from the entrance. He was surprised to see the room empty, not a single other member of the crew rushing to escape ahead of him.

He grabbed a suit and pulled it on, sweat running down his face, his hands clumsy. He pulled on the gloves and fastened the seals quickly before picking up the helmet and straightening. His hands froze as they lifted the helmet, when he turned and saw Adie, standing in the open doorway. Adie's eyes were wide with panic, his mouth hanging open slightly and his chest rapidly expanding and shrinking with heavy, strained breaths.

Aki let the helmet drop to the floor, reaching forwards, ready to step towards Adie when a bright flash of flames illuminated the corridor behind him. The ship tore apart around them as the cabin flung itself away from the body of the ship. Aki rolled with the explosion, falling backwards, and then was outside, tumbling in space, the wreckage of The Shining Prospect visible in the distance as he drifted ever farther away.

He slowly twisted, the ship and the planet it had just left shrinking with each rotation. On the other side, only vast empty space. And then, with another turn, Adie was there, floating in the space before him. With every rotation the ship and the planet grew farther away but Adie remained the same. His eyes and mouth open in a frozen scream, arms reaching for a ladder that wasn't there, legs writhing in a slow motion mockery of his final moments. For just a moment, their eyes would meet, and it would feel like a jolt of electricity rocking Aki's body.

With each rotation the emptiness grew, the planet vanishing faster than it had any right to, and Adie's eyes still jolting his body for that brief moment they met. He tried to close his eyes, but the darkness behind his eyelids rotated too, revealing stars, and the ever shrinking planet, and Adie's eyes. The shock. A current of electricity like a splash of acid.

He awoke with a jolt, the image of those eyes fading in his vision as he shot upright in his bunk. He took heavy breaths and felt his heart pounding in his chest. The room was dim, all of the other bunks empty. The clock mounted on the wall

94

said it was getting close to eight in the morning.

Aki rubbed his face and climbed out of the bunk, staggering to the door to the common room. He squinted in the light when the door opened, the radio inside playing at a low volume. The room was near-empty, but Rob sat in an armchair flicking through a book. He looked up as Aki entered the room, quickly reached for his cane and began to push himself up from the chair. Aki waved him down and fell into the chair beside him.

"Morning Ak, you manage to get much sleep?" Rob asked, leaning over the arm of the chair to get a better look at Aki.

Aki shook his head slowly. "Not much, but, I got some. Where is everyone?" he said, looking around the room.

"They're out, doing odd jobs or loitering about. I told them to let you stay in. I was hoping you'd manage a few more hours to be honest but, we'll take what we can get, eh? You should grab something to eat."

Aki looked towards the cabinets and appliances on one side of the room. Boxes of cereal and fruit were stacked on the counter. The prospect of eating seemed unappealing, though he knew he should. "I'll grab an apple or something in a bit. What you reading?" he said, nodding to the book in Rob's hands.

Rob tilted the book to display the cover, a collage of birds. "Just looking at the pictures really. Don't know much about birds, but, they remind me of my dad. Old bugger spent half his time stood at the window, binoculars and all," Rob said with a smile.

Aki reached over to the book and flicked through the pages. "Janet, my mum, she had this real big thing for penguins. She had a shelf stacked with teddies and figurines," Aki said. He found a page of penguins and the image brought a small smile to his face. "I didn't call her mum very often. Not because I didn't think of her that way, you know. But it took a few years after she'd adopted me to feel brave enough to do it. I remember, it was mothers day. I got her this penguin toy, you know those ones with the yellow crown? The toy was nothing special, she had so many. But I handed it over to her, and I said, 'happy birthday mum!'" Aki's smile had grown as he talked, the memory crystal clear in his mind.

"I remember, she looked so happy when I was giving her the thing, and as soon as the word left my mouth, I thought I'd upset her. Her face just, shifted so suddenly. And then she scooped me up, gave me the biggest hug. I'd called her by her name for years and never really got out of the habit, even after that. But I'd slip out a mum here and there, and every time I'd catch this little smile jump up on her face. She tried to hide it, but she could never hold it back. Not completely." He sat silent for a moment, looking at the pictures in the book and remembering that smile. "I wish I'd said it more, to be honest."

A faint smile lingered on his lips as he flipped the book closed, letting the image of his mother linger in his mind as long as he could. He took a heavy breath and handed the book back to Rob, who was looking at him with an expression Aki couldn't quite place. Rob looked away for a moment before returning his gaze to Aki, sorrowful and heavy.

"Look, Aki. Can you talk to me about yesterday? I've read the reports, and talked to some of the others. But, you were in the control room. What the bloody hell happened?" he said.

Aki nodded his head silently for a time, thinking about everything that had happened. Thinking of Adie.

"The deposit, it wasn't as deep as we thought. I was watching the depth chart and, we were barely even halfway down before we hit it. The scans must have been wrong somehow, or maybe some geological anomaly, a tectonic shift or… or something. Whatever it was, that stuff down there, it was way higher up than we expected," Aki said, thinking back, trying to recall every detail, looking for explanations.

"And, that's it? Aki there has to be more than that," Rob said, his voice remaining soft and filled with concern.

"It's not just that," Aki said, looking to Rob, still considering the sequence of events in his mind, replaying the images again and again. "Adie dropped the drill, as soon as we noticed anything was wrong. He didn't try to retract it, or push it further or anything. But, something…" he paused for a moment, considering his words.

"Somehow, it got pulled further in. I don't know if the substance down there is just so dense, or if there's some kind of magnetic field or, whatever else could possibly explain it. But once the drill reached the deposit and stopped moving, some force started to pull it further in. Not gradually but, in these heavy waves. Like somebody was tugging on it.

"The support system held, but the tower started to buckle. Before we had a chance to really even figure out what was happening it was already starting to bend. I just told him to get out of there. I ran out, and by the time I was through the airlock he was already on his way down. The whole tower, in just a few minutes it was bending forwards over the hole, the rear struts snapped completely. It was completely sideways, I'm amazed he could even climb on it like that. And then he…" Aki took a breath, Rob listened patiently.

"There was another shockwave or, whatever they were, and he fell. The tower kept pulling and a few more beams snapped and the whole thing started coming down not long after. Somebody, I think it might have been Janice? They started pulling me away. A few of the struts pinning the tower down were being dragged forwards. The edges of the hole cracked and started falling in. We got away as quick as we could, didn't hang around to see just how bad it was going to get."

Rob sat listening, brow furrowed as he tried to make sense of the situation. He sat back in his chair and took a long, deep breath. His hand rested on the cane beside his chair, fingers tapping on the handle. Eventually he shifted and looked back towards Aki. "We'll figure it out lad, whatever happened. You did good, right? You did all you could. We'll make sure that this doesn't happen again." Aki nodded in reply before Rob continued.

"I'm gonna send you back on up to the city. I'll check in on you, and let you know what's goin' on. But you need to take some time off. I'll make a call to refinement and request a leave for Robin too, so you're not just sitting in that empty can all day, eh? You can take as much time as you need. If anybody at the plant gives Robin any bother I'll sort them out. You need anything, or anybody else contacted, just let me know, okay?"

Aki could see the dedication in Rob's eyes, his compassion. "No, no that's enough Rob. I mean, thank you. But, I'm doing okay. I'm alright," he said, trying to smile to reassure Rob that he was alright.

"Don't be a bloody idiot, you're clearly not okay! I know you well lad, and I have done for years. You're far from okay and I won't have you hanging around making it any worse. You know how irresponsible that'd be, if nothing else," Rob said, sounding sharp but not cruel in his reply. Aki knew he was right, and knew even better that trying to dispute him would be fruitless, and so he agreed. Rob seemed satisfied and softened quickly, leaning back in his chair again.

With Rob settled, Aki reached for his tablet. The mention of Robin had brought Aki back to reality somewhat, and suddenly he found himself worried about what, if anything, Robin had heard. Did people in the city know what happened? His notification tab was flooded, messages and alerts from both friends and acquaintances, and one from Robin. He knew something had happened, that was clear. But he didn't know what. He didn't know about Adie. Aki sat, hunched over his tablet staring at the message, wondering what to do. He started typing.

'Hey Robin, I'm okay.'

And then, he stopped. How did he continue? Would he just tell him what happened?

'But, Adie...'

He erased the message and started again.

'Hi Robin, I'm safe. There was an incident last night and I'm okay, but we need to talk about Adie.'

He looked at the message, and at the send button, but erased the message again and tried a third time before slumping back into the sofa. It didn't feel right, sending this over a text message. It was such a heavy weight, the burden of such news. He needed to handle it right.

Eventually he sat up straight and looked at his tablet again, flipping to his contacts and pulling up Robin's profile. He was looking at the button to start a voice call, when the door of the room slammed open and somebody ran inside.

"Rob! Somebody—" they said in a fast, panicked, cracking voice. It was Chuck, a kid who had only recently joined the crew. He froze and looked to Aki for a moment, then back to Rob. His eyes wide and hands splayed.

"There's—there's somebody walking to the outpost. From the drill site. Riley told me to get you," he said, stumbling over

99

his words.

A crowd gathered outside, standing at the edge of the outpost and looking into the distance. A figure, silhouetted in the low light, was staggering its way towards them. Aki ran to the side of the crowd and skidded to a stop, still tightening the seal on his helmet. Rob struggled to keep up, his cane tapping through the yellow dust. Chuck raced to the crowd and found Riley, pointing to Rob, easily identifiable in a white and yellow EVA suit.

The figure was distant, and difficult to make out, but moonlight glinted on the metallic surface of a red EVA suit.

"It's Adie," Aki said, low and disbelieving, before yelling and starting to run towards the figure. "It's Adie! Get help, it's him!"

Aki's feet slipped on the dust and sand, the suit and the adrenaline coursing through his system making him clumsy and uncoordinated. Others started to run behind him. The figure continued to approach, reaching the perimeter of the outpost and stepping into the floodlights that surrounded the workspace. Aki and the running crowd came within a few feet of the figure. The running crowd paused, and Riley, catching up, grabbed Aki and pulled him back. The figure took a few more steps forward, and then paused, facing the crowd. The visor of the helmet was entirely obscured from within, a shimmering opaque black substance coating the inside of the glass. The figure wavered slightly, its stance twisted, before its knees buckled and it fell flat to the floor before them.

Aki yelled Adie's name and tried to run to the figure, but Riley held firm, another running to help hold Adie back.

"Aki! We can't, we don't know what that stuff in the suit is. It could be toxic. And we don't know how he's hurt, moving him could make things worse," Riley said.

Rob huffed as he reached their side. "Jesus," he said, looking to the figure collapsed and unmoving on the floor before them. "Aki, calm down lad. We can't do anything that'd help. We have doctors coming." Even as he spoke, two medics carrying a stretcher ran past and dropped to the side of the figure. One used a small torch to inspect the suit, calling out to the person trapped within to no response. The other laid out the stretcher behind the prone body and looked to the crowd before waving his hands.

"Move aside! Transport's coming, we need room," they yelled to the crowd before turning to look at their partner. The crowd split and moved to either side, Aki still held back by Riley, though he had stopped fighting and instead stood, tense, watching the medics work. A small truck with medical symbols emblazoned on either side pulled up, and the medics rolled the body onto the stretcher.

Aki watched as they carried the figure, Adie, to the truck. Laying on its back, motionless, except for a slow turn of its head to either side, watching the crowd left behind. The helmet turned to look in Aki's direction, and Aki watched to see his friend, but saw only black within the helmet.

One of the medics climbed into the truck, where the other stepped back and closed the doors, watching as the truck sped away. It drove towards the city elevator and quickly vanished. Aki fell to the floor, overwhelmed and uncertain. Riley let him fall, but kept a supporting hand on one shoulder. Rob stood beside them, watching the elevator ascend towards the city.

The crowd dispersed as the medic returned to the spot where the figure had fallen. They blocked off the area with thin metal poles and tape, retrieved a canister from their back, and used it to spray foam over the ground. When done,

101

they turned and scanned the area, landing on Rob.

"Make sure everybody keeps their distance. There could be traces of dangerous chemicals. Until we know for certain, best to play it safe." They turned away and started speedily walking back in the direction of the city.

"Wait!" Aki yelled, pushing himself back to his feet. The medic paused and turned to look. "I'm going with you. He's my friend, I want to keep an eye on him!" Aki said, running to catch up with the medic.

"That won't be possible, they're going straight into quarantine. A lot of tests will need to be done before we know if it's safe, but you'll be able to request more information by calling the medical wing. Just give it a couple of hours."

With that, they turned again and ran in the direction of the city, leaving Aki standing there feeling weak and afraid. Rob and Riley approached, Rob then placing a hand on Aki's back.

"Come on lad, let's get back inside. I'm not sure there's much good we can do out here," he said, still looking towards the city. Aki turned to look back in the direction the figure had come from, towards the drill site. Then he looked to Rob.

"We should go back, take a look. There's no way he could have survived that fall, he must have... He must have landed on something, or, I don't know. But we left him there. He found a way to get out and we had just driven off. We didn't even check. I want to see how he did it, I need to know what he went through."

Rob looked in the direction of the drill site, then back to Aki. "Yeah, alright lad. We can do that. Give me ten minutes, I'll set a few things in order, then me and you can get in a truck and we'll go together. That okay with you, Riley?" Rob said, turning to look at Riley, who nodded.

"Fine with me, I can keep an eye on the crew while you're out. I'll go set up a truck for you," they said, then turned and walked towards the vehicle bay.

Aki looked out towards the drill site. Nothing felt real, not since the accident. He needed to make sense of it all, to know that it was real, and that Adie had a chance.

Chapter 12

Dr Brennan pushed through the doors and into the hermetically sealed surgery room. The doors sealed behind her with the sound of a muffled gasp. The room was pristine white, counters and tables of chrome sterile steel. A glass wall bisected the room, on the other side a body lay on a gurney, unmoving within its red EVA suit. Dr Merlow was already in the room, stood at a monitoring station. He turned towards Brennan and nodded in acknowledgement of her before turning back to the monitor. Beyond the glass, a robotic arm whirred up and down the body, a camera mounted on the end studying it with an array of glass eyes.

"What's the status?" Brennan asked, stepping up to Merlow and peering at the screen over his shoulder.

"Deceased. The suit's internal systems don't seem to be working, but the stethoscope couldn't detect any signs of a pulse. There's a constant static sound being picked up. Presumably interference from broken components in the suit. Medics reported movement initially, so he must have passed some time during transport. No signs of elevated radiation or vapours from the substance."

Brennan looked through the glass to the body lying on

the table. "Can we identify if death is from the substance, or trauma from the fall? Broken bones, signs of internal haemorrhaging?"

"I can't tell," said Merlow, turning to look at Brennan. "The material is coating the entire interior of the suit, and it's completely blocking x-rays and anything else I try. Whatever it is, it's dense. Suit tells us the body is Adrian Clines. Last recorded weight at around sixty-four kilograms, that was two weeks ago. The table is picking up an extra forty-three kilograms. That's adjusted to account for the suit too."

Brennan tapped a thick pen on the table. "If he has any broken bones or internal bleeding, he managed to walk for what must have been, four, five hours? While carrying all that extra weight." Brennan crossed her arms as best she could in the thick protective suit. "If the substance is what killed him, then it took as many hours to do the job. And it's coating him head to toe, how is that possible?"

Merlow leaned forward in his chair.

"You haven't noticed the weird bit yet," he said, his tone suggesting he had been waiting for this moment in particular.

Brennan's brow scrunched in annoyance. "The entire situation is weird, Pete. If you found something then just tell me," she said, impatient.

"Look at it again, the body," Merlow said, gesturing towards the glass with a tilt of the head. "The suit is filled with this, oil or metal whatever-it-is. But the suit is pristine. Not a drop on the outside. How did it all get in there?"

Brennan turned to look at the body. Merlow was right, the suit didn't have a drop of the stuff anywhere on the exterior.

"If he fell in, and it got inside the suit... How is he not covered in the stuff? Rain washed it off, vaporised during the walk back to the outpost maybe?" Brennan said.

"No rain, I checked. And whatever that stuff is, I think it's too substantial to evaporate in this atmosphere. Even if it had run off, there'd be some caught in the panels and creases of the suit, right?" Merlow replied, tapping the pen on the counter top again.

"We've speculated plenty, I want to get a look at the stuff," Brennan said, then walked promptly to the entrance of the glass chamber. Merlow pressed a button to open the door and began the quick air cycle when Brennan stepped inside. The camera retracted into the ceiling as Brennan entered.

She approached the table, studying the body. The visor remained entirely obstructed by the black substance. She paced around the table and studied the suit in detail, though nothing else seemed amiss. Merlow was correct, not the slightest remnant of the substance was anywhere to be seen. She pulled the trolley of equipment from the corner of the room and retrieved a set of thick tongs.

"I'm going to begin opening the suit, I want to start by getting a sample of the material so we can identify what it is. After that we can determine cause of death," she said. An acknowledgement came through her earpiece as she gripped the helmet clamps firmly with the tongs.

Careful movements twisted each clamp free with a click. She swapped the tongs for a thin chrome pry bar. Levering the bar down, the helmet popped up, eagerly releasing and leaving an opening a few inches wide. A viscous black material spilled out of the suit like innards from a gutted fish. Brennan studied the surface of the material as it pooled on the table. The surface caught the sterile white light above in small shimmering glints, like sun catching on a field of dark snow.

"It seems to feature some particulate, or fine solid

material. It's not quite granular flow, possibly some non-newtonian properties," Brennan said as she watched the last of the ooze trickle free. A glint caught her eye, something revealed on the rim of the helmet. Rows of small, multicoloured crystalline structures uniformly deposited along the inside of the metal.

"There's… some kind of mineral deposit forming on the suit interior. It's almost iridescent, similar to bismuth." She reached out toward the top of the helmet and carefully pushed, lifting the helmet up and revealing the head beneath.

"Fuck me…" came Merlow's voice over the speakers. The camera apparatus ahead buzzed as it zoomed in on the head. Even through the layer of thick ooze, it was clear much of the soft tissue had been worn away. There was no definable raise to the surface where the nose should be, and the liquid dipped over the eye sockets lower than would be possible had anything remained within them. The material didn't coat the head entirely, but in strange clumps leaving areas of exposed flesh and bone. And strikingly, large deposits of jagged, crystal-like structures protruded from portions of the head and face like haphazardly scattered horns.

"What the fuck is this stuff?" Merlow continued as the camera whirred and shifted. "Why are only parts of it dissolved? It's eaten completely through in some spots and left others totally untouched. Look, by the right temple. It's eaten away at the bone." As he talked, Brennan took a new implement from the cart. She carefully scooped part of the substance from the table, transferring it to a wide panel of glass. She turned and cautiously walked to a table of instruments on the far wall of the room, where the glass panel slotted neatly into a large microscope. She tapped on the screen on the side of the device.

Blurred black shapes, gently undulating, appeared on the screen. Merlow quickly linked his screen to the microscope to watch. Brennan reached for the dial on the side, and as she twisted it, the blurred shapes came into focus. The screen displayed a number of dark, smooth objects. Near perfectly spherical, aside from one flattened plane. Thin lines ran along the surface like an intricate maze. Slowly, the lines shifted along the surface, flowing organically like the ridges of sand dunes rippling across a desert of metallic black sand. A membrane of cloudy dark liquid surrounded each sphere, undulating and twitching in a rhythm that seemed in tune to the maze-like ripples.

"What the fuck is that thing," came Merlow's voice. Brennan watched in silence for a few more moments before responding.

"I'm… not certain. It's.. a single celled organism, maybe. A complex nucleus, around forty microns in diameter, surrounded by cytoplasm and a membrane making for a total of near seventy microns. The central structure, the nucleus, look closely. It's iridescent, possibly made from the same material as the deposits on the corpse, or something very similar. I think—" she was cut off when she and Merlow both gasped in unison.

The central structure of the cell twitched, and wisps of the clouded liquid rippled and converged into strands. Thin trails connected to the central system on one end, tapering to a fine point at the other, like a child's drawing of a sun turning to worms from an apple as each strand began to writhe and undulate in snapping, rapid motions. The tendrils began forming small angular pieces of a clear material and feeding them to the inner structure, which hungrily consumed each piece.

"What is that? What are they doing?" Merlow whispered, overcome with wonder at the sight. Brennan leaned back from the screen and looked down to the glass panel within the microscope. Minute multicoloured deposits had appeared along the edge of the black substance, which undulated ever so slightly as the microscopic structures worked.

"It's deconstructing the glass," Brennan said, breathy with awe. "It's taking it apart and… the nucleus is reconfiguring it at a molecular level. Pete, look at the flattened side of the nucleus. The entire thing is unlike any naturally occurring cell we've ever seen, there are seams around the perimeter of that edge. This isn't natural at all, this is constructed. Intentionally designed. Pete, we—" Brennan was cut off when a scream pierced her ears painfully. Merlow shot up from his chair, sending it clattering to the floor, pointing as he screamed.

"Behind you! Nicola!" he yelled. Brennan spun around, and saw a looming figure, dressed in a red EVA suit. Its helmet completely gone, the semi-skeletal face looked down towards her. The black substance had shifted, revealing more of the face. Brennan quickly noticed that one eye remained, but had simply fallen inward. The substance had completely consumed one eye, but only the socket from around the other. The multicoloured crystal structures protruded from its skull at random. Her eyes continued to scan the face, unable to move as it lurched towards her.

The arms of the figure raised and, preposterously, reached around her, enveloping her chest and pinning her upper arms to her body in a gesture that almost seemed intimate. The creature lowered its head, and as it did, the black substance began to reach out in pointed peaks, eager to touch her. One arm took hold of the hood of her suit and pulled back, tearing the material loose and exposing her face to the cold air.

She began to scream the moment the black substance made contact with her flesh. The creature placed one hand on the back of her head, holding it firm, and pressed its concave cheek to her own. The ooze spread across her face, pushing its way beneath her left eyelid. Lumps of the substance fell from the creature and landed on her torso, immediately starting to eat its way through her suit. The horrific embrace lasted only moments before it released her and raised back to its full height. Brennan's screams became a wheezing drone and she dropped to her knees as the black liquid spread further along her face and body.

The creature stepped to the glass panel and paused for a fraction of time. Merlow, collapsed to the floor on the other side, found his arms and legs shaking too violently to pull himself from the floor. The creature raised its arms and placed its hands and forearms flat against the glass, and the fabric of the EVA suit quickly vanished, black liquid appearing in its stead and spreading across the glass. Metal panels of the suit diminished shortly after, taking slightly longer for the microscopic creatures to tear apart. Shimmering deposits of crystal began forming around the edges of the liquid and Merlow's eyes widened in understanding.

"Oh, no. Oh fuck no!" he yelled, pushing himself to his feet and running to the heavy door. The ooze worked its way through the glass until the creature's right arm crashed through the thinned pane. As soon as the panel shattered, a whooping alarm began, and the quarantine lights illuminated the room in red hues.

A heavy metallic chunk sounded from the door. Merlow grabbed the handle and tried desperately to force it open, pleading for the resistance to give and free him from this nightmare. Behind, the creature held the glass and black liquid slid down either side of the surface, thinning the material until it crumbled away. The thing pushed its legs through the glass and took a clumsy, lurching step into the next room.

Merlow spun and saw it approaching, his legs giving way at the sight. He pushed across the floor, backing as far away from the creature as he could, until trapped in the corner of the room. He looked up to the counter beside him and reached up, pulling a tray of glassware to him where it smashed across the hard floor. He picked up a shattered beaker and held it out, sharp edge of the glass pointing towards the creature that continued inexorably in his direction. The creature's head never tilted to look towards him, only ever facing forwards at the space directly ahead of it. As it grew close, one hand lifted and its torso hunched, reaching towards his face. The ooze-covered withered hand pressed against the stiff plastic of his suit's visor and pushed against his mouth. The pressure forced his head back painfully into the corner. He stabbed fruitlessly at its arm with the jagged glass, shredding his own hand and flinging blood across the pristine room with the motion.

The black ooze quickly ate through the plastic visor, and the creature's hand jolted forwards, forcing its way into Merlowe's screaming mouth, where the fingers curled and gripped tight at the soft tissue of his throat. He gagged and wailed as the thick substance pushed its way down through the opening, and he felt the flesh it touched begin to crumble away.

He grabbed at the arm and tried to pull it away from his face, groaning in anguish as his fingers began to burn and shrivel. The creature pulled its hand free and turned away, leaving him in the corner. He stared at his hands as the ooze spread down each finger and across his palms. The liquid seemed to increase in quantity at a staggering pace, drops expanding and spreading as they consumed. In places, it burned away the surface layer of his skin, in others it burrowed below, eating at muscle and flesh and leaving the skin above, tinted dark. Two of his fingers fell limp as the bones within were consumed, the muscle and flesh left to hang loose. The pad of one thumb diminished to nothing, the bone beneath turned black and shrivelled and the thumb snapped free, falling to the floor.

The ooze roiled in his stomach. He grew close to fainting at the lack of oxygen before a portion of flesh fell from his throat, exposing the opening of his trachea, which twitched and convulsed. The ooze worked its way up his spinal cord, slowly exploring each vertebrae on the path towards his brain. His left eye began to blur as the fluid tendrils punctured its outer layer, a trail of clear jelly squeezed from within, trailing down his cheek like tears. The remaining eye watched as beyond the dissolving glass partition, Brennan slowly raised to her feet. She staggered forwards, obscured by the ooze and cracks spreading over the glass. When she reached the still-expanding hole the creature had left and stepped through, Merlow was dimly aware through the thick fog of pain-induced shock that only her jaw now remained. The entire top of her head was gone, either disintegrated, or left behind on the floor. The quarantine alarm continued to blare as the creature pressed itself against the sealed door, and the ooze began to eat through its surface.

Chapter 13

Much of the processing plant was a maze of gridded metal walkways and thick iron pipes. Silos of coolant ensured a near-constant dampness lingered in the air, making droplets of water form on the exterior of cold metal. Meanwhile, industrial furnaces and generators ran at intense heats that perforated their walls and raised the temperature around them. As a person moved through the structure, they would find themself exposed to intense cold, fierce heat, or trapped in a steam-filled, humid fog where the cold and the heat collided. Robin spent the first hour of his shift at the bottom of refinery C, as heavy gloves, full face mask and goggles protected him from the intense chill that lingered in the lower levels.

He'd been instructed by Harris to prepare all storage silos, which meant arduously uncoupling a series of thick pipes and adjusting them so that each silo would feed into one another, sharing their volume rather than acting as individual storage for disparate materials. Constant drops of liquid falling from above gave the impression of a light rain. Robin disliked the lower levels in particular. All the moisture had a tendency to absorb into one's overalls and make them feel that bit heavier.

And the chill that would sting at the face and fingers, despite the body feeling so hot from the many layers and hard work. He was glad then when his work was done and he could finally begin the climb back up.

Tall ladders lead him between metal walkways, where he squeezed past other processing crew that were trying their best to look busy. Two ladders up and he gratefully pulled off the thick gloves, face mask and thick outer jacket he wore, and placed each on the equipment rack. The goggles left a patch of pale skin around his eyes where the rest of his face was a vibrant red, and his hair a tousled mess. He pulled on a thinner pair of work gloves and continued his climb up into the steam-filled mid section of the tower. Heavy fans tried their best to clear the air of steam, but mostly served to fill it with noise. Kurt was ahead, looking at the pipe intake monitors. Robin yelled a greeting over the sound of the fans and Kurt turned and waved in response. "Hey Robin. Been in the freezer?" he said, glancing at the fading redness of Robin's face.

"Yu-huh, jus' finished up," Robin replied, wiping his dampening hair back from his face. "What's he got you doin'?"

"I've just been trying to look busy to be honest, managed to dodge the big man sticking me with anything. Come take a look at this, I was just checking the input and it says we have something on the way. Anything been mentioned to you?"

Robin squinted at the screen for a moment. The pipe network was active, the pumps working as they usually would, and according to the pressure readouts, something was on its way to the city. Robin shook his head to Kurt as he reached up and pulled a handheld transmitter from a unit on the wall.

"Hey uh, Harris, you there?" he said, holding the button on the side with his thumb. A moment passed before Harris' voice responded through the tinny speakers in the wall unit.

"Harris here, what's the problem?"

"It's Robin, I'm 'ere with Kurt at the input valve. We're seeing somethin' comin' in, is that right?" A few moments of silence passed.

"Hold there, I'll be out in a sec," came the metallic voice again. A few minutes later Harris stood looking over the monitor, seeing precisely what both Kurt and Robin had seen, yet still feeling the need to double and triple check.

"So what we gonna do?" Robin asked, once Harris looked content.

"What do you mean? We do our jobs and process the stuff," Harris said, giving a derisive look to Robin.

"They don't usually have any sites set up for another day o' two. I know they had that one group that went out earlier, but the Mayor said there was an issue settin' it up," Robin said, glancing at Kurt for support.

"He said there was an issue, not that they didn't get it done. Workplace incidents happen all the time Robin, people still get the job done," said Harris.

"Harris, we don't even know what it is they're drilling up. How are we supposed to process it if we don't know what it is?" Robin replied, not entirely tempering his aggravation.

Harris gave an exaggerated faux sigh. "How far out is it?" he asked.

Kurt turned and looked at the monitor, leaning in close. "It's moving pretty slow, but it should be here in like, ten minutes? Little less?"

"Alright then, we'll just check when it gets here. We have the sample chamber, we'll use it to sample," Harris said. A U-shaped section of pipe extended from the side of the input valve, with a small cylindrical chamber in the centre. Switches either side would let any materials flowing through the valve enter the chamber for observation through the thick, clear panel on the front, and a spout beneath could be used to extract liquid samples.

Harris left to retrieve some testing equipment. Robin and Kurt waited, watching the input display as it marked the progress of the material through the gigantic pipe network. The network was built to handle vastly higher quantities than they were currently seeing. Upwards of fifty drill sites could all be running at once, feeding in through the same pipe network, but even one site could deposit many thousands of litres an hour. The pipe network split the liquid evenly over a number of facilities, each containing a number of storage silos with a capacity of nearly half a billion litres of liquid each.

The input valve began to rumble lightly, building to a loud cacophony of metallic rumbles as the liquid arrived and began to pour its way through the pipe and deposit into the silos. The noise was particularly loud, more often the case when the liquid within was especially thick. Kurt reached to the switch on the right side of the U-shaped testing chamber and turned it, letting some of the liquid find its way into the chamber. Harris returned, a large glass container in one hand and a black rectangular device in the other.

"Step back, give me some room," Harris said, waving a hand. He set the glass container to one side and peered at the transparent panel on the front of the sample chamber. The panel only showed a featureless black within. "Looks like oil to me," said Harris, looking back at Kurt and Robin.

"I doubt it," said Kurt. "Oil isn't something that shows up on planets like this. Aside a few rare exceptions. Not the kind you're thinking of, anyway. Could be ethane."

Harris glowered at Kurt briefly and pulled on a face mask.

He removed a cap from the top of the small black device he had brought. It had a screen and a number of buttons in the front, and a thin metal probe protruding from the top made it look like an old-fashioned mobile phone. It was the kind that business men would use before inevitably wandering into the killer's trap, Robin thought.

Harris placed the device beneath the chamber and pushed the metal probe up into the spout that hung beneath with a click. He held it for a moment and watched the screen before a green light beeped on.

"Not radioactive so that's a good start. Keep back, I don't want to get into shit if you breathe anything toxic or get it on your skin," he said, pulling the device back down. The probe retained a small amount of the black material on the end. Harris held the device at a distance and used his other hand to move the glass container beneath the spout, turned the valve, and took a step back. They watched as the material began to trickle down into the glass vial.

It ran at varying speeds, slower and faster as though changing in consistency as it poured. There was a strange shimmer to its surface that reminded Robin of the frost that would often coat the metal exterior of the ship. The liquid that pooled in the glass rippled and shook, twisting around the glass unnaturally.

"What's... what's it doin'?" said Robin, noticing a thin layer of shimmering material beginning to build around the glass at the top of the liquid. Kurt squinted and leaned in, then stepped forward, trying to observe the growing halo of crystalline structures on the inside of the glass. Without warning, the bottom of the glass shattered, making Kurt and Robin both jump backwards at the shock. The liquid spilled across the counter and began trickling down to the floor.

The upper half of the glass remained intact, resting upon the thin pool of black ooze, and then slowly began to shrink, as though sinking into the liquid.

"What the—" Robin began, before being cut off by a high-pitched screech of pain to his side. Harris dropped the testing device, which was now coated in the black substance, its antenna and casing seemingly shrivelling away. Somehow, the minute amount of black liquid that had been on the device had now become enough to not only coat the device entirely, but to spread to Harris' hand, where it had quickly made its way through his thick rubber gloves. Harris continued yelling, looking at his hand as it curled and twitched. He started shaking the hand, the glove loosening and eventually flinging away from him, narrowly missing both Kurt and Robin as it arced through the gap between them and landed with a heavy thump.

Harris fell silent when he saw that part of his hand was gone. Presumably remaining inside the glove that he had launched away. His smallest finger along with the ring finger were gone, a mess of visible bone and muscle protruding from the hand below them. What remained of the hand was stained black or coated in more of the liquid which seemed now to seep from his skin and drip loosely to the floor. A wet snap rang through the air, somehow louder than the churning of the pipe before them, and the hand slid down and away from Harris, his entire forearm falling to the floor with it, raggedly separated at the elbow.

Harris made a horrible, breathless groan as he looked at the partial limb laying on the floor in a spreading pool of shimmering black. He looked up towards Robin and Kurt, who stared back. Robin blinked for the first time since the entire process began, glanced towards Kurt whose eyes were firmly locked on the arm, and then to the communication unit mounted on the wall.

He ran to the unit and started to reach for it when he saw small beads of black liquid beginning to appear on the bottom of the pipeline. The droplets were appearing exponentially, and just as Robin turned to run away, the bottom of the pipe gave way with a heavy groan. Viscous black liquid splashed out across the metal floor and began to gush down through the grating, vanishing into the depths of the silo chambers below. Kurt staggered backwards, snapped back to an alert state, and reached a hand out to Robin who stumbled and began to fall, catching him and pulling him back to his feet as they narrowly avoided the splash of liquid. They retreated a few more steps and looked on as Harris attempted to step forwards before limply collapsing into the growing pool. His head hit the metal beneath the liquid with a heavy thunk, half of his face immediately coated.

"Go hit the alarm!" Robin yelled to Kurt, before turning and running towards the walkways. The odd dark liquid continued gushing down, a midnight waterfall that would already be coating the floor of the lowest level. Other workers began to emerge, rushing to see what had happened. Robin saw the glint of metal in the hands of one and reached to grab the tool as he raced past. A crowbar in his hands, he reached the top of the walkways and began to bang it hard against the metal, the sound ringing out to the layer below.

"Climb up!" he yelled, cupping one hand around his mouth. He saw familiar faces looking up at him, all gathered together where they had been gawking at the falling liquid. "Tell the others, climb up!" he yelled, banging the metal again.

He watched as one of the workers below ran to the edge of the walkway and began to bang the metal with a heavy

119

wrench. They leaned over the side and he heard a woman's voice yelling, repeating his own message. The rest of the workers jogged to the ladders and started to climb their way up. A third voice faintly came from below as the message propagated down the layers of walkways, but new sounds began to mingle amongst them. Screams of pain and terror started to echo from the hollow silos and metal walls, soon after drowned out as a loud siren blared to life. An artificial voice spoke through the alarm call.

'An incident has occurred. All employees please evacuate the area. Please shut down your work stations and proceed in an orderly fashion to the nearest exit. An incident has occurred—' The call repeated.

When the first of the workers were approaching the top of the ladder, Robin turned and started back towards the entrance, and quickly jumped back, hitting his ribs painfully against the railings behind him. A figure, their overalls peeking through a blanket of dripping black viscous liquid, staggered towards him. One arm raised, fingers pointed towards him, eager to share their infection. The sleeve of the other arm hung loose. The left side of the head was black and skeletal, a pit growing as he watched in the top of the skull, and a strange multicoloured spike protruding from within and seemed to be growing rapidly. More of the spikes dotted the face and perforated the clothes and ooze. The creature took another step closer, and then another, its remaining arm coming close.

Robin swung the crowbar hard, arcing through the air and colliding with the arm at the wrist. A small spray of the liquid flung free and fell in heavy drops to the ground, as the arm snapped and spun free over the railing. The figure, Harris, seemed entirely unfazed. Robin looked to the crowbar and saw black ooze sticking to the surface, tendrils beginning to creep down towards his hand, and he quickly flung the bar over the side.

Harris took another lurching step towards him, and then froze, beginning to turn away from him when Kurt appeared. He held a metal chair by its back and jammed it into the creature that held its stubby arms up and tried to push back against him. The Harris-thing staggered backwards, catching against the railings as the chair legs pushed into its shoulders. Robin dashed away from the ledge to Kurt's side, put his hands on the seat of the chair and added his strength to the push. The creature struggled for a moment more, and then tumbled over the barriers, falling silently out of sight, the chair plummeting after it. Black ooze dripped from the dissolving metal bars to the floor, and started creeping its way slowly across the floor towards Kurt and Robin.

Robin noticed a growing crowd gathering at the top of the ladder, watching in bemused silence. "Don't touch the black shit," he said, panting, before he and Kurt turned and started their way towards the exit.

Chapter 14

In the faint light of the moon, the yellow sand and dust coating the planet's surface appeared a dark, sickly tar. The pastel streaks of the ring stretched high overhead, darkened as the planet cast a heavy shadow across the bands of orbiting dust. In the distance, a point of bright colour stood just beyond the horizon, where the sun's light reached the ring in advance of dawn.

Lights mounted to the side of the pipe network illuminated their path, as Aki and Rob drove towards the drill site. The site was enshrined in darkness, but twisted metal beams remaining from the tower were visible, silhouetted against the night sky. The truck travelled easily across the featureless terrain, but Aki still felt a growing unease, akin to motion sickness that grew as they approached the site. Rob had remained uncharacteristically quiet, clutching the wheel of the slow truck, conspicuously glancing at Aki regularly during their drive.

Aki spent much of the journey watching the lights on the side of the pipe passing. He was trying to figure out what could have happened. How Adie could have survived, not only falling such a distance but landing in whatever that substance is down there. He thought of the visor, coated in black, turning to look towards him as Adie lay on the stretcher. He pulled out his tablet and again looked at Robin's profile, pondering over the call button. He pressed it and watched as the call symbol spun in lazy circles waiting for a response, but minutes passed without any reply. Aki ended the call and leaned back into his seat.

"We're about there," said Rob, breaking the silence. "You managing alright?"

"Yeah, I'm doing alright," he said, leaning forwards and peering through the windscreen of the truck. The remaining metal bars of the tower stretched high, distorted. Some had cracked cleanly, where others had been twisted and pulled into pointed spikes that jutted up from the pile of debris. The drill site appeared within the bright beams of the truck's headlights.

Deep cracks ran along the ground,and up the walls of the printed yellow buildings. They parked beside the control room, where Aki had been when the incident began. The narrow cone illuminated by the vehicle's lights was filled with scattered debris from the tower, the smooth flat ground giving way to a shallow slope where dirt had crumbled into the pit.

Aki and Rob pulled torches from the storage bin behind their seats and climbed from the truck, Rob leaning heavily on the seat for support as he lowered slowly to the ground. Aki looked back to check on him, already a few steps ahead, then turned forwards and scanned the space with his torch. The beam of light was narrow, but intense enough to reach far around the circumference of the pit.

Where the tower had been, the ground was intensely deformed. The rivets used to pin the structure in place were gone, steep gouges like claw marks left behind. The top layer of dirt had fallen away, dragged into the pit along with the rivets. Many of the support beams that stretched around the perimeter of the site had been dragged in behind the tower, leaving similar scars scattered along the edge. A gateway to hell, scarred by the claws of some enormous beast trying to escape.

The rec room was partially destroyed, its walls crumbled, and furniture scattered along the slope below. The pipe that had been built to rest on the very edge of the pit was now vanishing into its depths. Aki drew closer to the ragged earth as he walked through the scene, looking towards the edge of the pit. "Not too close lad," Rob called, catching up to Aki. "Could still be unstable. All that dirt ground up, like a sinkhole."

The ragged ground put too much space between them and the pit to see beyond the edge. Aki traced the sides as best he could with his torch.

"The support struts got pulled in after the tower, but it looks like at some point the cables snapped. Look over there, some of them are still up. Could be safer," he said, shining his light across the gulf and noting the vague shape of a standing structure on the periphery of his torch's reach.

Together they set to walking past the half-destroyed building and approached the pipeline, careful to keep a good distance from the collapsed portion. They passed beneath the huge structure, between two support columns that remained intact. The metal of the pipes whined, and emitted a low rumble. On the other side, the hole continued to stretch out before them, the edges of the circle becoming smoother the further they got from the tower.

Aki jogged the last few feet once a clean edge to the pit was close. He slowed and placed a hand on the metal support structure, leaning to peer over the side. His torch shone town into the pit, seeing only shadows. The light drifted across the darkness until it met the wall of the pit, where the darkness began to stretch up in heavy fluid tendrils, like wax dripping from a candle in reverse. He struggled to understand what he was seeing, and moved the torch along the wall of the pit searching for an explanation. All along, the viscous, dark substance that had been down in the pit was clinging to the sides of the wall, creeping up the rock like vines of glistening charcoal ivy. Aki looked back over his shoulder towards Rob who was drawing near to the edge.

"This isn't right Rob. The stuff down there, it's too high. It was about half way down when we hit it with the drill, but this... It's a lot closer now."

Rob took hold of the metal support structure and warily leaned over to look into the dark pit. Aki moved his torch until it met the metal pipe that hung loose into the pit. The end of the pipe was resting against the wall a few metres below the highest peaks of the black substance. It seemed to congeal at its entrance, a concentrated, thickened mass. There was a strange shimmer to the liquid, almost as though waves rippled along its surface.

"It's moving," said Rob. Aki turned to look at him, then followed the trail of Rob's torch back into the pit. He pointed it at a nondescript section of wall, tendrils of dark ooze stretching up the rock. Nothing looked different to Aki at a glance. But Rob held the torch in place, the circle of light wavering only slightly in Rob's unstable hands. Together they watched, and then Aki saw it. The tendrils of black liquid weren't just clinging to the sides of the wall, they were climbing it. It was hard to judge the distance at a glance, and Aki had been too eager to move his torch, searching for ledges or platforms Adie could have landed on. Watching like this, holding in one place for a time, you could see how it inched its way upwards.

"What the hell is this stuff…" Aki asked.

"I've no bloody idea lad, but I think we should be getting ourselves back," Rob said, taking a few steps back from the edge. Aki looked once more down at the pit, then stepped back and nodded.

"We should get back quick if we can, I'll run ahead and get the truck, then come pick you up," he said. Rob agreed, and started walking as Aki sprinted ahead. He tried to find an explanation for what they'd seen as he ran. What could this substance be? And what had happened to Adie? His mind returned to that black visor. This stuff that was trying to climb free from its pit, it was inside Adie's suit. What could it have done to him? He hoped he was doing okay, and that the doctors would have some answers for them soon.

He passed under the pipe again, the low rumble tickling his scattered brain. The truck was in view, its headlights left on, a beacon in the dark. Between confusion at what he had seen, concern for Adie and the unusual nature of this inexplicable sequence of events, he felt like his mind couldn't keep up with itself. There were simply too many contesting thoughts fighting for his attention. He reached the truck and opened the door, when the itch became a realisation. He looked back in the direction he had come from, a panic catching his breath. He climbed into the truck and drove back, passing under the humming pipe and seeing Rob approaching, waving his torch in the air. Aki slammed the truck to a stop and jumped out of the door.

"Get us ready to head back, I need to check something!" he yelled to Rob, instantly running back towards the pipe.

The hum rang out in the air as he approached the closest support structure. A terminal embedded in the wall illuminated when he arrived and flipped the heavy switch by its side. The screen immediately confirmed what had concerned him. The pipe network was active, the pumps inside working to transport any substances it detected back towards the city. He thought of the way the dark liquid seemed to grow thicker around the entrance of the pipe. The truck approached behind and Rob parked close, the idling engine mixing with the hum of the pumps working overhead. Aki flipped through menus and found the shutdown sequence for the pumps. He hit the button and watched as each section of the network turned dark on the screen. The hum from the pipe above faded.

He ran back to the truck, and as he did, deep bass groans screeched out from the metal of the pipes. He climbed in and slammed the door shut. "Go as fast as you can, the pipes were on," he said, breathing heavily.

"You mean that crap's already at the city?" Rob asked, eyes widening.

"I don't know, but I hope not," Aki replied. The truck wheels spun for a moment in the thick yellow dust, before catching and lurching towards the city. The vehicles were designed to operate in any conditions, on any planet, but they were not designed for speed.

Even so, Rob pushed it as hard as he could. The metallic groaning continued to ring out from the pipes, even as they crossed the distance between the pit and the outpost. The sound shifted, changing in tone until suddenly, with the silhouettes of the drill site growing small behind them, the pipeline ruptured. The bottom of the metal structure burst, and heavy, viscous liquid plummeted out and spilled across the ground beneath it. Rob swerved to gain more distance between themselves and the pipe as the substance spread, fast at first, then slowing as it thinned.

They paused for a moment and watched as the segments of pipeline in view each buckled and spilled their strange innards out onto the floor. They began to drive again, but continued to watch in horror. The black substance began climbing slowly up the support columns and coating the exterior of the pipes. Holes appeared seemingly at random in the dense metal, entire sections collapsed to the ground as their support dissolved away. Aki watched the destruction of the colossal structure, and he despaired as the image of that black visor came to his mind. And what could have been happening within it.

Chapter 15

Markus sat in his office, rocking back on his chair as he clicked through a list of films on his wall monitor. Nothing that suited his mood was showing up, which was typical. Thousands of choices and not one worth watching. He reached the bottom of the list, frowned, and jumped back to the top, ready to start scrolling again, standards suitably lowered. Glancing to his right, a light flashed on his phone, and a number of notifications displayed on his desk terminal. He stretched to reach towards the desk, careful not to tumble from his chair, and grabbed a box of chocolates, popping one eagerly in his mouth.

The phone had been flashing for hours now, pretty much since he got back from his rousing speech this morning. He thought it better to leave them for Jim, that's what he was paid for, after all. In a few hours Jim would have filtered out the time-wasters and Markus could deal with the ones that were worthy of his attention, if there were any at all.

He kept scrolling through the list. A movie about a secretive order of knights fighting, what appeared to be, gigantic slugs. A film about some kind of solar apocalypse piqued his interest, but the synopsis put him off when the word 'polycule' appeared in the very first sentence. Liberal tripe.

A rapid knocking rattled his office door. He looked towards it with a heavy dismaying harrumph, turned off the wall monitor and checked himself for crumbs before rising from his seat. The knocking didn't stop as he crossed the room, a cacophony of rushed raps, like a horse galloping across a marble floor. He struggled to maintain his composure in the short walk, feeling the urge to yell swelling as he reached for the handle. As soon as the door opened, his mouth opening in turn, Jim pushed his way inside and spilled a rapid array of panicked words.

"Where the fuck have you been Markus! I've been calling and messaging and I'm sure other people have been blowing up your inbox and have you not even looked outside?" he rattled the words with barely a pause, crossing the room to the desk.

Markus remained by the door, stunned by the uncharacteristic entrance. The irritation was festering into a rage, his face growing pink and hot. Jim leaned over the desk and clicked a notification, flicking the scroll wheel twice.

"Fucking hell Markus. Something is going very wrong out there. The pipes are collapsing, there's this black stuff spreading on the dome and there are riots by the hospital!" Jim said, pushing from the desk and pulling the blinds open, revealing the city behind.

The mayoral office was high up in The Column, the vast central skyscraper in the direct centre of the city. Markus didn't spend much time at all in the Inner-City, but when he did, he appreciated the view it afforded over the plaza below, and the distance from the general populace. Nothing unusual appeared through the window, and Markus struggled to piece together Jim's words with anger clogging his ears. Jim pressed his face against the window, trying to look around the corner of the building, then pulled away, leaving an oily impression on the glass. Markus shook his head and let a fraction of the anger ease away.

"What the devil are you on about, riots? Why in heavens would anybody be rioting all of a sudden?" he said, approaching the window.

As he grew closer, his view of the exterior widened as the plaza and streets below came into view. Still, nothing too strange was apparent, but the crowds did seem a touch hectic. From one side of the plaza, a hurried flow rushed out, away from the Municipal District. He didn't see why that would be the case. The district was mostly office buildings, a few small businesses, and the hospital on the far side. Away from the hurried flow of the populace, large crowds gathered, seemingly gazing into the distance towards the Industrial sector. Jim finally pried the window open and leaned precariously out, peering to the side before swinging back inward. As soon as the window opened, a wave of hectic noise flooded into the office; the chatter of dense crowds, and something else less definable.

"Go on, take a look!" Jim said, gesturing to the open window.

Markus looked at him, the dregs of his anger dissipating as a rigid confusion settled heavily in its place. Cautiously, he stepped forward, placed his hands on the ledge, peeked his head out of the window and looked to the side. From this height, he could see a large portion of the city quite clearly, and the grass plaza below, bustling with its chaotic crowd. The Municipal District's buildings, where much of the chaos seemed to originate, nestled between the Residential

131

District and the Transport Hub. He could just make out the stone pavilion of the Transport Hub in the distance, it too, looking unusually hectic for this time of day. He looked to the Municipal District one more time, trying to ascertain what could be causing this erratic behaviour. Trying to catch a glimpse of any riotous activity, but tall office buildings blocked too much of the view.

He still didn't understand what was happening, but clearly there was some unrest within his city, and he had to quell this behaviour before it got out of hand. He pushed back from the window and reached for his suit jacket.

"This is ridiculous. What is this even about?" he said, pushing through the office door.

"I don't know!" said Jim, following behind. "I told you, there's something growing on the dome, and people are rioting in the hospital. There are reports of incidents at the factories too, they're coming in too fast for me to follow!" Markus shot a disgruntled look at Jim over his shoulder as they approached the end of the corridor. He pressed a button to call the elevator, then walked to a window beside it, looking out over the side of the city he couldn't see from the office. He studied the ugly metal block buildings and towering chimneys of the Industrial District. Again, crowds were rushing through the streets, but he saw no discernible source for the chaos that seemed to be infecting his city. The glass dome that surrounded the city offered a view of the night sky beyond, just beginning to tint towards a cobalt blue as the sun approached the horizon, the planet's ring growing increasingly vibrant in the distance. Then he noticed a dark gap within that cobalt blue sky. It was easy to miss at first, but there between the buildings, and just beginning to reach above them, the sky was obstructed by a black mass.

Something ragged and indistinct coated a portion of the dome.

Tapered lines reached out from the central mass, tendrils of pitch dark reaching up to scale the glass dome. Markus stared at the mass silently, eyes focused hard to define the shape against the dark sky. Then he noticed the mass was moving, the tendrils squirming and stretching.

The elevator chimed and its doors slid open. Markus spun, a frenzied look dawning in his eye. "Why didn't you come get me sooner, you bloody idiot!" he spat to Jim as he rushed into the elevator. "Call Octavia!"

When the doors opened on the ground floor, Markus flew out of the building and across the street toward the plaza. The noise swelled as they approached, the crowd expanding every moment. Markus impatiently buffeted his way through the shifting mob, Jim followed in step behind, holding himself as small as he could. Jim held his earpiece, worried that the jostling crowd would knock it loose, as he tried to call any of the guards assigned to the city.

He'd been unable to reach Octavia, or anybody else so far. The ship's communication system had been overburdened with the huge number of users at once. "Turn on the speakers. And keep trying to get through to the guard station," Markus said as they reached the stage at the back of the plaza.

The scrolling banner above the stage illuminated, and a few musical tones played from the speakers ahead as Markus climbed the stairs and crossed the polished wooden boards. A light static hum began as Jim turned on the microphone. The clamouring noise from the crowd continued, though a scant few faces turned up towards the stage.

"Good fellow citizens! Please, calm yourselves!" Markus called, gesturing in sweeping motions like he was attempting to fan a light breeze over the crowd. He continued waving and calling for attention for a time, succeeding with only a small section of the crowd closest to the stage. Noise still filled the plaza.

"Please, we must remain calm! I understand your concerns and confusion, but I assure you, there is no need for this degree of uncivil behaviour! We have the very best enforcement team, working to gain control over the situation. The local guards will no doubt find themselves—" Markus was cut off as an item flew from the crowd and arched past his shoulder.

He flinched away. Thick pink liquid spilled out of a cardboard cup across the wooden boards behind him. "The guards are fucking dead!" came a loud voice from the crowd.

Markus straightened, looking angrily into the throng of faces below, trying to discern who had launched the projectile. More voices rose up, many shouting about the guards and the hospital and other words that got lost in the churn.

"Hush, quiet now, quiet!" Markus said, growing louder with each demand. "I assure you all the guards are most certainly not dead! A ridiculous claim. My assistant is in contact with the guards right now," Markus said, turning and looking towards the door at the back of the stage.

Jim stood in the shadow of the door like a meerkat watching for lions. Something in his face caused Markus to pause for a moment, near-stumbling over his words. Jim was shaking his head and twisting his hand in a strange motion that Markus couldn't decipher. Markus placed a hand on the microphone and leaned in Jim's direction.

"What are you doing?" Markus said, projecting the words through gritted teeth, firing them across the stage like bullets.

"I told you to get in touch with the bloody guards!"

Jim mouthed something in reply, or said something that couldn't be heard over the noise of the crowd below. Markus gestured for him to come closer. Jim timidly stepped from the shadows, paused momentarily looking towards the crowd, and then scurried towards Markus, careful to avoid stepping in the milkshake between them. "I couldn't get through to any of them," he said, trying to speak loud enough to be heard while maintaining the rasp of a whisper. "I got through to command but, they say all of the guards in the city, or most of them, they've just stopped responding. Any that were in the area got called to the hospital and, well, their suits have just cut out. They said there was… Some kind of altercation."

Markus glared at Jim, hand still held on the top of the microphone. The crowd had been growing increasingly restless, the volume of the scene inching up, with more angered shouts projected towards him, there was an electric air of discomfort radiating across the stage. He knew this situation could turn very messy. He turned back towards the crowd and felt a hot sweat form on his back and in his armpits. He waved his hands, trying to quell the crowd again.

"Please, all of you, please! I understand your distress. But I assure you, we will see to it that this situation, whatever it may be, will be dealt with! Me and my assistant here will personally investigate, and open up communications again with the guards. Please, all of you return to your homes or places of work, and I—we, will keep you all updated over the communication systems in due time!"

Markus turned from the crowd to Jim, whose face had somehow grown even more gaunt. He stammered out words in a staccato tremble. "W-we? We will investigate?" he croaked. Markus spun on his heel and stepped close to Jim, their noses a hair away from touching.

"Yes, Jim. We are going to go and find out why these useless buffoons are struggling to do their job," Markus said, in a low, breathy growl. He stepped to the side, then walked quickly to the back of the stage. Jim looked across the city, towards the strange black mark defacing the dome. Whatever it was left him feeling immensely discomforted. The door at the back of the stage slammed heavily and startled him. He turned and ran to catch up with Markus, who was now storming his way towards the Municipal District.

The streets were still bustling with panic-stricken civilians fleeing towards the centre, many of whom seemed to be sporting untreated injuries. A few dressed in medical scrubs ran among them. Jim noticed that one man wearing an open-backed patient's gown was limping heavily, swinging his arms in an attempt to move farther with each heavy jolt of movement. Two men brawled in the middle of the street, grappling at one another. One had a heavily bleeding nose that had left both of their clothes stained in streaks of red. Markus looked to the two men as they continued briskly walking towards the hospital.

"This is all it takes for the guards to lose control? A few ingrates brawling in the streets?" he muttered. Ahead, another pair stood, one holding firmly to another that was fighting to break free. Jim could just barely make out the words of one of the figures as they passed.

"Let me go, she's still in there!" they said, through strange, struggled words.

He turned his head as he watched the two and bumped firmly into Markus, who came to an abrupt stop and briefly turned to deliver a derisive scoff at his assistant before looking ahead. They had reached the far side of the Municipal

District. Its wide streets were lined with pharmacies, opticians, dentists and similar outlets. At the end, one of the largest buildings in the city, the Vaughn City Hospital was facing them.

A black substance snaked along the white surface of the building like vines bleeding oil. More of the same material seemed to be spreading along the floor and was beginning to climb the surfaces of the surrounding buildings. The chaotic noise of the city had faded to a distant murmur. Few remained in the streets this close to the hospital, the epicentre of the events that seemed to cause this outburst of mania. In the distance, closer to the hospital a number of individuals seemed to be standing, or slowly pottering around, seeming unfazed by the events. One of the scattered few that remained closer to the hospital turned, and a glint of light reflected on the black armour encasing their torso. Markus started walking down the street in a direct line towards the guard that stood there, swaying as they observed the hospital. Jim quickly followed behind, growing more uneasy with every step.

"You, guard!" Markus yelled as they approached, eyes furiously focused on the armoured figure ahead. "What is going on here? Why are none of you responding?"

Jim whimpered behind him as they passed strange individuals that now stopped moving, and watched, as he followed Markus to the end of the street. He found his voice suddenly betraying him, reluctant to come forth when he saw the faces observing them. He reached out a hand and weakly took a hold of Markus' shoulder, shaking and struggling to make words, any words, spill from his mouth. Markus marched on a few more steps, slowing as the guard grew close, eventually coming to a halt a few feet away, as the anger fogging his vision shrivelled. Now that he was close, Markus grew uneasy. The guard looked wrong, their stance was strange and... buckled? Streaks of black liquid that he hadn't noticed from a distance trailed along the surface of the dark security uniform.

"Markus, we need to leave..." came Jim's voice meekly from behind him. The security guard turned with inelegant, staggered steps. Markus struggled to comprehend the face that came into view. A large spike of colourful glass was jutting out heavily from their right eye. What skin remained had been sapped of any colour, turned to a greyish, desaturated charcoal grey. The right eye looked back at Markus, one point of bright white crossed with tendrils of dark veins. The skin and muscle retracted, exposing the eye in full. Black liquid streamed from beneath like tears, only to mix with a heavier flow that poured from the limp skeletal maw beneath.

Markus turned to run and collided directly with Jim, who fell hard on his front, Markus landing atop of him with an unpleasant, hard snap. He scuffed his hands roughly on the ground, the rest of his fall cushioned by Jim who groaned heavily. Markus rolled to the side, letting out his own groan of dismay, looking at his cut and bloodied palms.

"My nose!" said Jim, who pushed himself to hands and knees. A crimson waterfall poured from his face, his voice muffled. "I think you broke it!"

Jim's face was heavily scratched and bruised after colliding with the hard floor, and his nose twisted hard to one side. Blood poured heavily from his nostrils, and trickled from a cut on his forehead. Markus, laying on his back, looked around and saw multiple figures lining the street, all featuring an array of disgusting maladies similar to the security guard.

Black slime trailed their faces and bodies, flesh and bone and entire limbs missing, with those queer colourful crystals protruding randomly from their ravaged bodies.

He turned his head just in time to see the security guard lurching towards him, falling heavily to meet him on the ground. He rolled to the side, screaming, a sickly wet crack as the guard collided with the floor. Markus lay on his side, eyes wide as Jim screamed and fell in the other direction, the decayed creature laying between them. The creature raised its arms and began pushing its torso from the ground, leaving a thick, black pool stamped on the floor. The arms shifted and began to turn in Markus' direction. Without a thought, he kicked out his leg, pushing against the armoured ribs of the guard-thing, shoving it away.

The creature tumbled back and fell into Jim, who let out a terrified scream. Its arms flailed as it fell, elbows snapping, the arms bending backwards, wrapping around Jim. It pulled itself into a tight embrace, the back of its helmet colliding with his already broken nose. Markus lay for just a moment, watching as Jim's screams turned from fearful, to agonised. He struggled and screamed, but the twisted arms held him tight. The metal of the helmet began to fall away, thin black tendrils of liquid reaching out to caress his face. His screams grew louder as they pushed into his pale skin.

Markus clambered to his feet, and started to run. The other broken figures had drawn ever closer as they struggled on the ground. One reached for him and fell to the floor as he ducked to the side. More figures had appeared, wandering from alleys and doorways lining the street. Jim's screams followed Markus as he ran, echoing from the walls until with a strange peak, they stopped, and an eerie silence fell. Markus reached the end of the street, the city plaza now visible in the distance, and turned to look back. Tens more of the figures had appeared, most heading towards him. Some staggered heavily, some crawled along the floor, and some took long, confident strides that overtook the rest of the crowd. The black tendrils that had just been touching at the base of the buildings when they arrived were now passing the first or second row of windows.

"Oh fuck this," Markus muttered to himself, and then he turned, and he ran.

Chapter 16

Aki tried contacting Robin again and again during the final portion of their worried drive back to the city. Warnings and concerns were spread over multiple messages that remained in limbo, twirling symbols indicating their failure to send. Voice calls left unanswered, or simply unable to connect. Rob had been trying to contact management, the outpost, or anybody else who came to mind. The communication network was either overloaded, or down entirely. Either one hinted at disaster, and left them both especially uneasy. Such concerns were confirmed as the black substance spreading outward along the glass dome became visible long before they reached the city.

The pipe network had burst open along its entire track. The dark alien slime that slowly spread along the ground now consumed what remained of the pipes and their support columns. It seemed to have spread with additional haste closer to the outpost. Half of the structures in there were already either completely coated or destroyed by the corrosive ooze. Black tendrils continued to creep along the floor towards the remaining structures, vehicles and storage crates. A dense crowd gathered to one side, the varied colours of their suits dulled by layers of yellow dust. As the truck approached, a small few of the group separated and ran to meet them, Riley's white suit standing out amongst them.

"Thank god you two are alright, I was worried something happened out there!" said Riley, helping Rob climb down from the tall vehicle.

"It did," Rob said, shaking his head. "We saw this… stuff. Whatever it is, climbing out of the drill site. Aki noticed the pumps were on and shut 'em down. We'd hoped none of it had reached the city yet, but I see we weren't fast enough."

Riley looked to Aki, and glanced towards the viscous growth clinging to the city walls, spreading up from the pipe connection below.

"It's been, maybe twenty minutes? The stuff leaked out of the input valve and started climbing the glass. Then the pipes started to burst and more of the stuff spread over the outpost. It reached the surface elevators before we'd even thought to try getting everybody back inside," Riley said.

"Bollocks," said Rob, looking at the elevators connecting the surface to the city. It was lost amid a void of spreading dark. "What about the other elevators? You managed to contact anybody inside to get them set up?"

"Coms have been patchy. I talked to a few of the crew inside, and managed to talk to somebody up in command for a while. But the call cut out and I haven't had any luck since. We mostly just tried to figure out what was happening. It hadn't quite dawned on us that we were stuck out here yet. At first we just thought this was going to be a quick cleanup job, until, well, you see what the stuff is like," Riley said, gesturing to the crumbling outpost buildings.

"Yeah, I see…" said Rob.

A large man in a red suit stepped forwards towards the

trio. A construction worker named George, well known for his gambling habits, and his sore temper when they didn't serve him well. "The fuck is that shit Rob?" he asked, projecting the words in a harsh snap.

Rob frowned as he turned to look at him. "I don't know anything more than you George. I'm just as baffled as the rest o' you," he said, maintaining a calm tone.

"That's bullshit, Rob! You telling me you're sucking this shit up and you don't even know what it is?" George said, stepping forwards, shoulders raised and hands balled into fists.

Aki reached out a hand and placed it firmly on George's shoulder. "Calm down. You saw the same charts as the rest of us. If Rob knew anything, he wouldn't have let this happen. You know that," he said, as George turned his angry eyes towards him. "Whatever that is, none of us have ever seen it before. And we aren't going to find out while we're stuck out here with it."

A fraction of tension dissipated from George and he stopped pushing against Aki's hand, though his own remained tightly balled at his sides. Riley nodded thoughtfully for a moment and looked to Aki.

"If I can't get through to anybody on the coms soon, I could try heading in through the service tunnels. They're narrow, and we have a few hundred workers out here. So I don't think we could expect everybody to get back in the city that way. But if we sent a few through…"

"They could get some elevators working," Aki said, nodding his agreement. "You're right. If the coms are down completely, that could be the only way. We can send a few in, an engineer and a few crew to help out if they run into any issues. The others can start heading towards the next dock and keep trying on the coms." He turned to look at Rob. "You good with that?"

Rob nodded warily. "I'm not much good with any o' this, but I prefer we do somethin' other than sit on our arses."

"I can keep on with the coms if you don't mind heading in, Aki, I've already got a few trucks ready to move. We can finish up and set off in ten, fifteen minutes maybe," Riley said.

"I'm alright with that. I'll grab a few of the crew to go with me. If we get there first, I'll set up the elevators in Hydroponics. Could take us a while to get there. Doubt the trams are in much of a state right now, but we'll be as fast as we can," Aki said.

The group walked back towards the large congregation of crew that were chattering among themselves. Aki opened a local voice channel, allowing him to talk directly with all suits in range of his own, which connected automatically as he approached. He turned on the exterior speakers of his suit, to ensure even those in private channels would hear. The chatter died fast when he started to talk.

"I'm going to be heading in through the service tunnels under the city. We should be able to climb up through to the Industrial District. From there we can walk to Hydro, and set up the docks, so the rest of you can get inside. If a few of you are willing to join me, I'd appreciate the help," Aki called out.

A murmur rolled through the crowd as they turned to one another, looked towards the city and weighed their options amongst themselves. For a moment Aki thought nobody would step forward, until a short, broad figure pushed through the crowd and walked over to him. Joyce wordlessly nodded and stood alongside Aki, arms crossed. Her eyes wandered along those at the front of the crowd, meeting each one until they turned away from her piercing gaze. A beat passed, and then another, and then a skinny younger man cautiously stepped forwards and walked to join them.

"Good lad Chuck," Joyce said, patting him hard on the back when he stood beside her. A moment longer passed without another member stepping forward. Rob looked towards George and offered a pointed cough.

"And my bloody axe I guess," he said with a heavy sigh, taking a few steps towards Aki.

"I'll come too," said Rob, joining the four. "I want to get back quick as possible. Figure out what the bloody hell is going on."

"Are you sure you'll be alright with your leg?" Aki asked.

"Don't worry about that, if I slow you down too much, or we run into anything I can't get past, I'll turn back," Rob said, tapping his cane on the floor.

"Alright then, if you're all set, I can get to work moving the rest of the crew. I'll leave a truck here in case you have to turn back," Riley said. The larger crowd dispersed as the crew of five began walking towards the city. As they approached, Aki looked up towards the mass growing along the dome again.

The substance spread itself out along the underside of the city as well, in places eating away at the pipework but leaving large portions of the structure entirely unharmed. Something shiny and multicoloured seemed to be appearing haphazardly around the ground and the metal pipes, but none appeared on the glass dome.

"I don't get it," came Chuck's voice timidly from behind him. "It burns through some stuff, like it's acid or something. But, not all of it? Like the pipes. Why is it making holes in some places, but not others?"

He'd said exactly what Aki had been thinking as he

watched the substance spreading along the dome.

"I've been on this job near fifty years," Joyce said, her rough voice crackling through speakers in their suits. "I ain't seen anything like that before. That's not just burning through stuff, it's eating it. Whatever that shit is, I think it's alive." A silence fell as they continued to walk.

Chuck looked at the way the liquid spread along the outer walls of the city, long snaking tendrils reaching out as though probing, exploring, or… tasting? A shudder ran along his spine and he looked away just in time to avoid bumping into George's back. The group stood before a large metal doorway, with Aki already typing a code into the keypad beside it. Large hatches flipped free and a thick circular hand crank slid out from a recess in the door. Aki turned the wheel and thick locks shifted with a metallic groan, and the thick slab of iron swung open. A trail of misty air eagerly fell out of the tunnel and dissipated in the planet's atmosphere.

"Alright, let's keep our helmets on. I'm not sure what parts of the pipe have air right now," Aki said, looking back towards his small support crew.

The sun was still just below the horizon, tinting the sky with colour as the planet remained dimly lit by moonlight. The lights of the city glowed bright far above, and the outpost stood out as a drop of light in the dark. Small electric bulbs dotted the walls of the service tunnel every few feet, cold white light bouncing between tight, rust-coloured metal walls. Thick pipes ran along the ceiling, occasionally twisting down separate corridors or vanishing into the walls. Aki stepped in, somehow feeling more unnerved by the illuminated tunnels than the dark expanse outside. Joyce walked behind Aki, followed in turn by Chuck, George, and Rob, who closed the heavy door behind them.

146

The sound of the door echoed through the metal corridors that stretched far in all directions. When it faded, the ringing echoes of their footsteps took over. Occasionally new doors would block their path, which Aki would twist open and Rob would pull closed behind them, each sealing shut with an audible suck as the air tight seal formed. Small plaques pointed down occasional offshoots, connecting the different factories and storage basins that made up this part of the ship. High above them through countless layers of metal, the processing plants would be filled with workers. Or, they should be. Aki hoped they would have all been evacuated by now, having seen the substance spreading across the surface of the dome outside.

The dome of the ship was made of multiple layers of an extremely thick synthetic carbon structure that was not dissimilar to diamond. Whatever that stuff was, it would surely struggle to eat through the panels, if it even could. But, Aki wasn't sure about the beams that connected the glass. They were made of something much tougher than the pipe network, a mix of synthetic metals and polymers, but would it be enough? If the dome started to collapse, it would put everybody in the city at risk.

"What do you think is going on up there?" said Chuck over the speakers within his helmet. "Do you think they know what's happening?" The group had remained in a local voice call, but not much had been said since they entered the tunnels.

"They know," said Rob. "The coms are still up, but it's struggling. That means everybody's trying to use it at the same time. Takes a lot to slow the network down this bad."

"How do you know the network is still up?" Aki asked, almost stopping to turn and look at Rob before remembering the procession behind him.

"One of my messages got through to a friend in orbit. I typed it on the drive back and it's been trying since. Finally went through a few minutes ago," Rob said.

"Any replies?" Joyce asked.

"No, not yet. I'll let you know."

Aki opened the communication window on his helmet's visor and looked at the messages he'd typed earlier. A small swirling symbol marked one as still trying to send, but most had simply turned grey. Text beneath read 'This message has failed to send, try again?'

"I've been trying to get through to my sister…" Chuck started, when a panel appeared on Aki's display. A picture of Robin, along with a request to answer the call. Chuck's voice cut out as the local group call was muted and a new call opened up between Aki and Robin.

"Aki! Thank fuckin' god. I've been trying t' get you for an hour! Where are you?" came Robin's voice, concern and relief fighting for control in his tone.

"Robin! I'm down in the service tunnels, working my way back into the city. Are you okay? What's going on up there?" Aki replied. Hearing Robin's voice seemed to pump energy into his body. His steps became faster and felt lighter, like he had dropped a heavy weight.

"I'm alright, but some crazy shit's happening up 'ere. The refinery got flooded with, whatever that shit is. Aki, it eats through… Everythin'! Metal an' glass, and people! But the people, they get back up. I saw it get Harris, ma boss. Ate through 'im. No way he could have survived that. But he got back up and came after me. Tried to get that shit on me too," said Robin, speaking fast and sounding near out of breath.

"Wait, somebody attacked you?" Aki asked.

148

"No, it wasn't just a person. That oil stuff, when it gets on people it's like, it turns them into fuckin' zombies! And iIt wasn't just Harris, there are more of 'em. They've been poppin' up all over the city!"

Aki struggled to absorb everything Robin was saying. It sounded insane, but so did sentient goo that climbed out of holes and ate through metal. "Robin, listen. The elevators to the Industrial District have been cut off by the oil stuff. None of the crew can get back inside, that's why we're heading through the service tunnels. But there are still a lot of people outside. The next dock is over in hydro. Do you think it would be safe for you to get there? Or to find somebody who could? We need somebody inside the city to activate the lifts," Aki said. He heard Robin shuffling and a beat of silence before he responded.

"I think I can get there. How do I set up the elevators?"

"I can talk you through it, it's not hard," Aki replied, reaching another door and starting to turn the heavy wheel.

"Alright, I'm already on my way. I'm gonna dip outta the call for a bit, but I'll keep it connected, you do the same, okay?" Robin said, a clamour of voices faintly building behind his own.

"I will, keep me updated, yeah? We'll meet up once I'm in the city," Aki said. Robin's name turned grey, and Aki tapped out of the call and back into the local group, leaving Robin's call inactive in the corner of his visor.

He finished pushing the door open and took the opportunity to look at the four behind him. George and Chuck were talking over each other, the volume of their conversation striking Aki as the channel connected. "Hey! Listen up for a second," he shouted, pausing his progress and standing on the other side of the opened doorway.

"Thank god," Joyce said, as Chuck and George fell silent and looked towards Aki.

"I managed to talk to a friend who's up top. From the sounds of it, things are getting pretty bad in the city," Aki said, noticing he'd successfully captured everybody's attention. "He's going to head towards the dock and get it set up for the rest of the crew, so we don't need to worry about them any more. But I think we should pick up the pace a bit if we can. I'm not sure how much longer we want to be on this planet."

"Well shit, I've been ready to leave since we landed," Joyce said.

"Agreed," said Chuck, nodding emphatically.

"Think you can manage that, Rob?" Aki asked, leaning to look over the shoulders of the three between them.

"Don't worry about me lad, I'll manage fine," Rob said, wiggling the top of his cane in a gesture of affirmation. With a nod, Aki turned and started walking down the long stretch of corridor again. Joyce, Chuck and George followed. Rob stepped through, taking hold of the door. He paused at the sound of a high gasp, followed by a sharp expletive from George.

"Oh shit!"said Chuck, his voice growing high and cracking. Joyce and Aki looked back and saw a streak of dark liquid dribbling down Chuck's visor from the top of his helmet. George took steps back, looking up at the top of the tunnel, where a drip of the black liquid was forming on the pipe directly above Chuck. Chuck looked up towards the pipe and jumped back just in time to dodge the second drip. He grabbed his helmet, pulling hard and tearing it free. He threw the helmet to the floor where they saw the black liquid pierce through the exterior, and trickle into its now empty cavity.

"Hah!" Chuck said, a wide grin spreading despite his

panicked eyes. All colour had drained from his face and his hair clung flat to his head, drenched with sweat.

Then, in an instant, the drip became a momentary torrent. A sudden, heavy gush of the black liquid dropped from the pipe as a gaping hole tore into the metal. The liquid hit the metal floor of the tunnel and splashed outward, Joyce and George both jumping back to avoid it as Chuck fell backwards and began to scream. His entire front was covered in viscous black ooze, his legs laying in a pool that filled the ground beneath the hole. His head turned to look behind him, towards George, as his face seemed to shrink away beneath the layer of obscuring liquid. A metal whine joined Chuck's screams and Aki looked up to see the gap in the pipes beginning to widen and more of the horrible substance pouring its way into the tunnels.

"Run!" Aki yelled, grabbing Joyce and pushing her past him further into the tunnel. He stood just long enough to see George lift up Rob, carrying him awkwardly over one shoulder as he started running heavily back the direction they had come. Aki turned and followed Joyce as the sounds of screams and metal buckling echoed through the long tunnels. The hole continued to spread, and the liquid continued pouring in, as though chasing after both parties who fled the horrible scene. Aki could hear George swearing and panting as he ran, and Rob protesting as the pairs sprinted in separate directions. Joyce reached a door ahead and started turning its wheel, then swinging the door open and running through. Aki caught up and pulled it closed behind him, not bothering to spin the lock.

They outpaced the black substance, but could hear the echoes of pipes bursting as it continued to follow behind them. They passed another heavy door when the sounds of

George and Rob cut out, as the distance between them had grown too large to maintain the voice channel. Aki tried to keep track of the plaques on the walls as they ran, reading each one as best he could without slowing down, praying that they hadn't missed what he was looking for. They passed through another door, the sounds of the pipes faint but still following, when his eyes passed the plaque he had been watching for.

"Joyce! Left at the next intersection!" he yelled. Joyce wordlessly continued her run, strained heavy breaths carrying through the voice call. When the next intersection arrived, she turned left and Aki followed. This new passage didn't feature the same pipes overhead, but that didn't make Aki feel any safer. Joyce continued running, so he presumed she felt the same. At the end of the tunnel was another door, but this time leading to a wide room with a desk, some lockers and a few monitors mounted to the walls. Aki sealed the door tightly behind them and turned to see Joyce, bent and panting with her hands on her knees.

He fell back against the door, feeling his own exhaustion hitting him. His heart pounded in his chest, the oxygen in his suit feeling hot and moist as the filter struggled to keep up with his breathing and perspiration. He looked to a vent in the corner of the room, then pulled his helmet free, taking a deep breath of the cold air in the room, rubbing the sweat from his face. "Are you managing okay, Joyce?" he asked, pushing himself from the door and walking to her.

"I'm too old for this," she grunted, looking up to him.

Aki pointed to a hatch in the ceiling of the room. "There, that ladder will lead us back up to the surface," he said, placing the other hand on her shoulder. "You up for the climb?"

Joyce straightened and took a deep breath. "Yeah, I can manage that."

Aki took hold of the hatch and paused for a moment, thinking of Chuck. Thinking of his helmet laying on the floor as the black liquid ate through the surface. He fixed his helmet back in place, only fastening the bolts loosely. Then reached for the hatch.

Chapter 17

The Transport Hub heaved with activity. A mass of human bodies surged together, pushing against each other in an attempt to reach the elevator that could take them all back to the prospective safety of the Outer-Ring above. In the distance, the alien mass spreading across the glass dome of the city grew ever larger. The morning sun increasingly brightened the sky, which only served to make the dark mass all the more imposing as its shadow now blocked the natural light from reaching much of the city.

Markus, huffing and stumbling his way towards the crowd, hair and suit dishevelled, looked upon the writhing mass with dread. He needed to reach that elevator. The boarding platform on the far side was dotted with heavily armoured guards. Large barricades had been erected before the platform. The landing pad was empty, but above, the elevator could be seen descending down the thick cable that held the two halves of the ship together.

Markus skimmed his eyes over the scene. The stone pavilion in the centre of the hub was nearly filled, packed tight with what must have been thousands of citizens. More barricades had been constructed along either side of the crowd, creating two thin walkways that stretched the length of the hub. Guards were patrolling the space, watching the crowd as they brandished the tools needed to maintain a semblance of control. Each walkway featured a heavy locked gate along with guards who would surely allow their Mayor through.

Markus stumbled towards the pavilion. The crowd was dense and the noise was cacophonous. He crashed into it and began pushing his way through, shoving and squeezing between anyone that would part for him. He felt hot and clammy with the body heat from so many people packed tight radiating into him. An occasional shove threw him off balance, and a stray elbow hit him hard in the side of the head, dazing him, but he continued pushing through. The fenced area was only a fraction of the distance that those looking to the elevator platform faced, but even this much was hell. Even so, he persevered, pushing through and shouting at anybody that resisted. He could see the gate, glimpses flashing between the movements of the crowd. A small cluster of guards stood on the other side. He called to them, waving his arms above the crowd. His voice could only rise so high above the screams and shouts of everybody around him, but he continued to yell until a heavy hand fell on his shoulder and pulled him around. A large man in tattered clothing came close to his face and began shouting indecipherable words.

"What? I can't hear a thing you're saying you buffoon!" Markus said, pushing away from the man. He tried to continue forging through the crowd in the direction of the gate. But the man grabbed him again, and pulled him close.

"Tell them to let us on the fucking elevator!" the man yelled into Markus' ear. Markus shrivelled in the tight grasp of the man.

"W-what?" he said, growing increasingly wary of the brute, and now painfully aware of the situation he had put himself in as more eyes turned to look in his direction.

"They're not letting us in fast enough, we have fucking children for god's sake!" the man yelled, spittle flinging into Markus' face. More and more faces turned to look towards him, and soon a portion of the crowd turned inward. Hands swarming, scared and angry faces, crying and screaming, surrounding, and all making their demands of him. Begging for help, asking for protection, and making threats.

A heavy tug pulled him from the man's hands and he fell backwards into the crowd, more hands grabbing at his shirt and jacket, pulling and shoving him in every direction. Faces were flashing before his eyes, screaming at him, the words mingling together into incongruous nonsense.

"Please, I'll do what I can! I'm trying to help you all! But you must let me through!" he yelled, trying to hold his hands up, pleading. "I'll tell them to let you all on! I'm here to help you all! Just let me through!"

But his words couldn't penetrate the crowd. It seemed the faces only grew increasingly angry, venom filling the voices, the hands that reached for him rough and bearing ill intent. He found himself begging, pleading, promising whatever he could. A black mass smashed its way into the crowd, pushing through the grasping hands that yearned for his destruction, batons swinging and transparent plastic shields forcing the crowd away. A ring of guards surrounded Markus, beating and pushing back the ravenous hands and faces. They pulled him to his feet and dragged him, still dazed and lost, towards the gate. He fell through and collapsed to the floor, turning to look back as the crowd surged against the fence. The guards locked the gate behind them and screamed back into the crowd, spraying a mist of brown liquid into the faces pressed against the metal bars. The crowd fell back, dissipating, the gap soon filled with new people pushing towards the elevator platform.

Some of the brown spray drifted down towards Markus where he lay on the floor. The faintest remnants sprinkled across his wide eyes, and he let out a yelp.

"Ah, fucking perfect! You idiots pepper sprayed me!" he yelled at nobody in particular, rubbing at his face as his eyes and throat began to burn. He saw a hand padded in thick black gloves reaching towards him through blurry, tear-filled eyes. The guard pulled him roughly to his feet.

"Glad to see you, Mr. Mayor, sir. We were ordered to keep an eye out for you," the guard said, a stern face to match his voice.

The guard turned and began to walk away in long military strides. "If you follow me we can have you on the next shuttle, departing in just a few minutes. Keep up."

Markus ran to catch up with the guard, struggling to match his elevated pace. He continued rubbing at his burning eyes, tears streaming down his face. He looked at the symbol on the guard's back. A thick white ring, with a dark circle in the centre, a guard from the Outer-Ring of the ship.

"Captain Octavia sent you, I take it?" he asked, fruitlessly brushing at his shirt and jacket.

"Yes sir. We lost contact with almost all city guards within the first ninety minutes of the incident. The Captain issued an evacuation order and deployed a squadron to maintain order when the severity of the situation became apparent," the guard replied.

"Yes I'd say it's pretty bloody severe," Markus said,

glancing towards the crowd on the other side of the fence. The metal bars the guards had erected must have been made of something incredibly strong to hold against the pressure of so many pushing against it. Each bar was relatively thin, bolted roughly into the ground.

A chime sounded along with a metallic whirring from above. The elevator shuttle passed through the airlock. An automated voice barely registered amid the continued orchestra of chaos that only seemed to intensify at the shuttle's approach. The heavy whirring from motors that clung to the tether lessened as it settled on the platform. The large doors opened and a small group of armoured guards stepped out, joining the already sizable squadron that surrounded the platform.

"If you'd like to take a seat inside, we'll be loading quickly and departing in just a few minutes," the guard said, leading Markus to the doors of the elevator and gesturing for him to enter. Markus turned and looked towards the crowd. The guards were holding the gates and brandishing their weapons against the condensed mass of panicked civilians desperate to escape the city. In the distance he could still see countless people fleeing in different directions, in some misguided attempt to find safety within the city. Idiots.

As Markus boarded, automated metal arms lifted heavy crates onto the opposite side of the elevator, clamps pinning them into position. He took a seat by the door and pulled the harness securely over his shoulders. Once the storage compartment was filled, the guards opened the gate and people spilled through, tripping over one another as the pressure of the crowd behind forced them onward. The guards yelled, swinging their batons and spraying their stinging mist indiscriminately. The flood of battered and bruised ran up the platform and poured into the elevator, claiming their seats. Families carrying wailing children struggled to fasten their harnesses while being jostled by the flow of others searching for seats of their own. Eventually the guards forced the gates back shut, punishing those who pleaded not to be trapped again with more swings of their batons and sprays from their metal canisters. The seats within the elevator quickly filled, and the remaining people stood or crouched in the ample space between the seats, clinging to the harnesses of those around them.

Finally, a dozen guards entered the shuttle and the doors slid closed behind them. They spread along the entrance, taking hold of hand rails that lined the walls besides the door. A passenger that held onto the farthest handrail was shoved viciously by a guard who took their place, leaving them dazed and bleeding on the floor. The elevator shuddered, and the metallic whine of the motors signalled the start of their climb. Markus noted the guards activating the magnetic systems in their boots that would hold them firmly to the floor. The closest guard saw him watching and leaned towards him.

"The motors have been overclocked to get the thing moving faster. Get the civs up in less time. But it makes for a rough ride. Lucky you got a seat," she said with a toothy grin. She straightened again and held firmly to the small hand rail on the wall. Markus found himself gripping tightly to his harness as well.

Chapter 18

Aki and Joyce rested for a time when they reached the access room at the top of the ladder. The room was barely more than a closet with a locked door to keep anybody from accessing the tunnels beneath the ship without permission.

Usually the Industrial District would be flooded with noise. The sound of machines carrying through the thick surrounding walls, the chatter of workers on break or moving between factories. The buzz of forklifts and cargo shuttles. Now they sat in near silence. The fan in the corner of the room squeaked as it idly spun, and beyond the room, electric sparks flashed with occasional jolts of static snaps.

Joyce looked exhausted. Aki wasn't feeling much better. But he remembered what Robin had said, about part of the city being overrun, about the black goo filling the refineries. He was eager to leave.

"We should get a move on, are you feeling alright?" he asked, looking towards Joyce. She grunted in affirmation with a dismissive wave of her hand, pushing back to her feet. Things could be a bit weird out there," Aki said, taking hold of the latch on the inside of the door.

Joyce gave him a smile. "You're a good lad, Akachi.

We'll get it done," she said with a wry wink. Aki smiled back and pulled the door open. Steam poured in from the tight alleyway outside, metal walls just a few feet apart stretching either direction. Aki stepped out and walked cautiously down the alley towards the broader streets that connected. He tried to watch for the glint of liquid on the floor or walls, but the steam filling the alley obfuscated his view.

The alleyway led to the main street that wound across the Industrial District, the one through line that connected all factories and warehouses. Parts of the street had already succumbed to decay. Large metal walkways collapsed to the ground and pipelines burst, spewing hot steam or leaving pools of fuel spreading below. An electric cable swung loose, its end snapping loud and firing sparks when it touched the walls. The fuel pouring from a pipe was slow, but would inevitably reach the wire, igniting and engulfing the street in flame. One of the few roads in the city designed for vehicles, trucks and forklifts littered the scene.

Aki scanned the road, looking for the best way to pass through the gauntlet of debris. It was only then he noted the shimmering black liquid trickling from some of the walls. Hidden amongst the carnage, it had been hard to notice. Now he began to see it everywhere, leaking from vents and seeping from walls as it burrowed its way out of the factories. He imagined the walls inside were coated in crawling, shimmering black tendrils, exploring and consuming, ready to break free and spread into the street below.

Joyce nudged his shoulder, scattering the images from his mind. "I don't much trust the street, with that fuel line bust," she said, looking towards the swinging cable. "We can head the other way, see how that's looking. Or we can cut through that alley over there, should get us through a lot faster," she said, nodding towards a steam-filled alleyway across the street.

"I think we should avoid the alleys," Aki said, shaking his head. "We should stay away from walls. Look how many are starting to leak. I think we might have got lucky with that last one."

Joyce's eyes scanned the walls, noting the scattered trails of spreading ooze, its surface shimmering when it caught the light. "We better get moving then," she said, rolling her neck and turning to walk down the road, away from the ruptured fuel line. Aki followed and together they jogged down the long and winding road, twisting between abandoned vehicles and collapsed debris that blocked their path. Aki found himself watching the alleys and doors as they passed, observing the dark and obscured spaces for movement, but everything seemed still. As they ran he became aware of a distant rumble of voices, raised in a chaotic union. It was the sound of the entire population of the Inner-City pushing towards the elevator that would take them back to Outer-Ring in orbit. They could be heard from halfway across the city.

As they worked through the Industrial District, the buildings grew increasingly tarred in the viscous black fluid. Holes large and small dotted the walls, and huge, chromatic crystals grew in patches from the more decayed ruins.

A flash in the corner of his vision drew Aki's attention. Robin's icon blinked to life. "I'm hopping in another voice channel, just wave a hand if you need me," he said to Joyce, who offered a thumbs up as he flipped out of the local channel. "Robin! Are you doing alright?" he asked.

"All good! I'm at the elevators in Hydro. The crew are on their way up now. There were already a few people working on it by the time I got here, so, I've just been helping out best

I can. How you managing? You sound out o' breath," Robin said.

"I'm on my way out of the Industrial District. Not too far from the intersection to the city centre," Aki replied, his voice jostling slightly with each step.

"Wait, you're in Industrial? Aki you've gotta get out of there! I was there when this all started. I can't imagine how bad it's gotten!" Robin said, voice rising with concern.

"I know, it's okay. We're being careful, and fast. I haven't seen anything, but I'm looking out. It's not great here. But we don't have another choice. I'll be fine, I promise. Look, when we get out of here we're going to head towards Transport and try get back up to The Vaughn. You finish up there and we can try meet up on the way alright?" Aki said, trying to sound confident. Robin paused for a while before his response. He was uncomfortable leaving Aki to run through the dangers but was lost for any other suggestions he could make.

"Alright, yeah. Just, be careful, alright?" he said eventually.

"I need you to do me a favour. Look around the crew coming up, see if you can find a guy with a walking stick. His suit is white with a yellow stripe," Aki said, his voice hitching as he climbed a barricade blocking the road. Joyce watched him and turned to continue jogging just ahead.

"He's already here," Robin said. "Was with the last group that came up."

Aki let out a sigh of relief. "That's great, god I was worried he'd… Well, that he hadn't made it back. Can you grab him? Tell him me and Joyce are on our way."

"Yeah, I'll have to dip from the call. The crowd is pretty intense but I'll see if I can get to him. I'll let you know when we're passing the centre and see if we can meet up," Robin said. Ahead, Joyce tilted her head and glanced over her shoulder towards Aki, then raised her hand in a wave.

"That sounds great, I have to dip too. I'll see you soon Robin," he said, and the voice call turned grey again as they both swiped out of the menu.

"We have a problem," Joyce said as soon as he rejoined the local call. She slowed to a stop as Aki caught up with her and he immediately noted what she had seen.

The buildings around them were heavily marred with the black substance, odd crystals poking out from cracks and corners. Small pools of dark were forming at the base of some of the buildings. The roads were strangely clear, but another problem presented itself. Ahead, a large portion of the road had collapsed, creating a gulf a few feet across.

Aki approached cautiously, judging the distance. The gap wasn't huge. He may have even dared to jump it under other circumstances, but in his EVA suit and with Joyce, it seemed unlikely. He peered over the edge and saw a two storey drop. The sides of the road collapsed as the support beneath had been eaten away. And there, at the bottom, a writhing river of the hungering liquid. One of the thick pipes that connected the factories ran under the road here, and the substance had flooded the network. They must have crossed countless pipes just like it on their journey, and who knows quite how much of the stuff there was pooling down there in the vast storage chambers. Aki looked to Joyce, who had stood beside him. "Well shit, if that doesn't look like a bad time," she said, sounding almost amused.

"We're going to have to find some way across. I don't know if I trust any of the walkways though…" Aki said, looking at the thin metal paths mounted to the sides of buildings, many already falling away or disintegrating where the ooze trickled from the walls.

Joyce turned back and walked to a truck they had passed moments ago. It had been left parked askew in the middle of the road. "I've got it," she said, pulling a compartment open on the side of a truck.

"You've got to be kidding," Aki said, watching as Joyce pulled a compact ladder free from the compartment.

She looked back at him with a grey eyebrow cocked. "Well what the fuck else are we going to do?" she said, carrying the ladder back to the gulf in the road. Aki watched as she extended the ladder, looking up at it and across the gap, then letting it fall to land with a hollow clash comfortably covering the distance. "You first," she said, looking to Aki and wafting one hand over the ladder.

"What?" Aki said, looking at the flimsy looking makeshift bridge.

"You're lighter, it makes sense. Don't worry, these things are sturdy. I'll hold it in place back here as you're crossing," she said, dropping to one knee and placing a hand on the base of the ladder.

Aki approached and looked across the gap, and then down into it. The shifting pool writhed eagerly below. He looked to Joyce, who seemed calm and almost impatient as she watched him, but didn't say a word at his hesitation.

He took a deep breath and reached one foot forwards onto the side of the ladder, carefully transferring his weight. It did feel surprisingly sturdy. He had expected it to bend and sway under his weight. But still, the sides of the ladder were slim, and he could feel his feet hanging over the edges. He took another step, as careful and steady as he could manage. 'It's just walking in a straight line, this should be easy...' he thought, as he felt himself swaying, uncertain in his footsteps.

"Crawl, if you need to," said Joyce from behind him. As

165

soon as she said it, he regretted walking along the ladder like he had. He looked down and quickly regretted that too. Seeing the pit and what waited beneath him made his legs shudder and his guts spin. He looked away and reached his hands out, trying to breathe steady.

"It's alright lad, you've got it," came Joyce's voice again. There was a certainty in her tone like she was stating a fact rather than simple words of encouragement. Aki held his arms ahead and lowered slowly, squatting closer to the ladder until he could reach down and take hold of the sides firmly. Holding the sides of the ladder immediately made him feel more secure as he folded each leg out and rested his shins across the rungs of the ladder. The thin metal pressed uncomfortably through the soft portions of his suit and the metal plates caught as he shifted his legs. The distance hadn't looked like much when he had been standing at the edge, but now he was crawling across, it seemed much worse. He kept his head up, looking at the road across from him as it drew ever closer, studying what was on the other side. There was more of the sparkling ooze trailing along the walls, and crystals jutting haphazardly from any structure the material took hold of.

The road looked clear though, and not too much further ahead they would be at the crossroads that lead out of the Industrial District. He knew if he looked up, he would be able to see the cable that connected the two halves of The Vaughn, and the Outer-Ring hovering high in orbit, their path to safety away from this horrid place. He wanted to look, but focused on the road. He was close now. Two more shuffles with his hands sliding along the edges of the ladder, and there, the road in reach. His palms met the flat surface of the road gratefully. It felt solid under him, and he continued crawling

166

until he was entirely past the ladder. A huff, almost a laugh, escaped him, and he wanted to let his weight collapse onto the ground below. To lay and laugh, and cry, and breathe.

"Good job lad, you did good. Now come on, my turn," came Joyce's voice over the speakers in his helmet.

"Right," said Aki, turning to look back. It shocked him to see how close she was. The distance seemed to have stretched out as he'd crawled, convincing him the gap was so much bigger than it really was. But still, it wasn't small, and Joyce had to make her way over their makeshift bridge. He took hold of the ladder with both hands, planting his knees on the rungs at the end and pressing his weight down to keep it as steady as he could.

He looked to Joyce and nodded, and without hesitation she began to crawl across. Her movements were stiff and slow, but she kept her eyes fixed on the ridge where the ladder met the road. Aki watched her, feeling confident as the ladder seemed sturdy beneath him. He looked down through the gaps in the ladder and into the pit, and his grip somehow tightened even more when he saw a tendril reaching up from the black pool beneath. A long, thin strand of the substance was slowly lifting out from the centre, wavering slightly like a snake rising its head high above the ground. The liquid stretched out in tendrils as it spread along walls and floors, but to see it reaching out on its own, supporting itself, was surreal. He thought of videos he'd seen where ants use each other's bodies to build structures and reach great heights, or to form bridges over gaps. It was moving slowly, but it was already half way if not more towards the ladder. He looked up towards Joyce, her eyes remaining fixed on the road ahead of her, making her way, slowly, struggling to pull her legs across the metal rungs. It must have started when he was crossing

167

the gap. Had she looked into the pit and seen? She must have. Must have known what was happening beneath her. He watched, tense and uncertain, but he kept quiet. Impatience was bubbling in his blood, eager to see her move faster, but he knew that nothing he said would help. Instead, he willed her in his mind, and held the ladder firm.

Joyce breathed heavily, grunting occasionally as her sore legs pressed into the hard metal rungs of the ladder. Her body aching, sweat and breath starting to condense on the inside of her visor. But she was getting close. The other side of the road was almost in reach, Aki's hands on the ladder in sight. The tendril wavered, the tip coming to a thin point, its surface shimmering like dark glitter mixed in ink. Joyce was a few rungs past the middle now, away from the thing. But the tendril rose ever closer to the ladder as she struggled across.

Aki carefully shifted his weight, and moved to the side, ready for Joyce to crawl past. He kept his hands firmly on the ladder. Joyce reached out and placed one hand on the surface of the road, and the ladder shifted ever so slightly. Aki shot out one hand, grabbing Joyce's arm, and the tendril behind her touched the ladder, dark liquid starting to spread out along the surface of the metal and coated the middle rung. Aki pulled and Joyce crawled, and she soon slid onto the solid ground. Both of them collapsed to the floor panting heavily.

"My shins are going to be so bruised after this," Aki said.

"You think yours'll be bad? Once you get to my age you bruise like old fruit. My whole legs are gonna be purple," Joyce said, breathing heavily, but a smile clear in the tone of her gruff voice. Aki chuckled and pushed up to his elbows, looking down towards the ladder. The black ooze had spread along the rung, the tendril still connecting it to the pool below. Viscous black spread along the edges of the ladder. Aki pushed himself to his feet and reached a hand to help Joyce to her own. They both looked at the ladder and the substance that crept along it.

"It's coming for us," said Joyce. Aki had noticed the same thing. The fluid wasn't spreading evenly along the ladder. It was moving only towards them, out from the centre rung where the tendril connected. It hadn't even dissolved any of the thin metal of the ladder. Aki stepped closer to the ledge, touched the tip of his boot to the bottom rung, and pushed forwards until it tipped, and fell into the pit. As it fell, the structure of the tendril collapsed, falling back into balls of liquid that disappeared into the mass beneath. Joyce watched the ladder fall with him, and when it landed in the pool they turned from the pit.

Aki froze. Joyce took two steps before she stopped too. Dotted along the edges of the road before them, numerous figures had emerged from alleys and buildings. They were twisted, misshaped humanoid masses of torn flesh and black liquid, with iridescent crystals protruding from torn clothing and exposed bone. A gallery of defaced corpses continued to appear from the buildings around them, and stumbled or strutted in their direction.

"Don't let them touch you," Aki said under his breath, as though whispering would keep them safe.

"I figured the same," Joyce said.

"They don't look fast, we can get past them," Aki said, taking a long step to stand beside Joyce.

"Then we'd better get runnin'," she said, and set off. Joyce's sudden sprint shocked Aki, but it only took a moment for him to join her. The creatures were mostly lined along the sides of the street, close to the buildings they emerged from. So Joyce stayed centred in the road as she ran, only shifting to run around the vehicles and debris in their way. Her running was unstable, one of her legs clearly injured and causing her to falter with every other step. Aki quickly caught up but, reluctant to get too far ahead, slowed to match her speed.

The tar-creatures turned to watch them as they sped past, too slow to reach the centre of the road. Some of the creatures ahead turned. Instead of walking towards Aki and Joyce as they had been, they began to walk directly into the middle of the road. The creatures were planning ahead, trying to cut them off.

Aki and Joyce weaved a course through and over obstacles, avoiding the creatures. Some lunged and collapsed to the ground as they ran past, hitting the floor with a heavy, liquid thunk. One of the creatures lunged towards Aki and narrowly missed as he twisted and dodged out of the way, the creature falling to the floor.

Joyce let out a yell as she flung herself to the side, almost running directly into the prone creature. She landed hard and on her side, but rolled and started to push herself back up immediately. Aki helped her to her feet, watching the growing crowd that flooded the street behind them.

Joyce pushed him forwards, encouraging him to continue running as she followed behind. Ahead, a wall of tightly packed vehicles and storage crates formed an impromptu barricade. Aki aimed towards a thin gap between a van and a stack of boxes.

"Come on, this way!" he yelled, glancing back towards Joyce. Aki turned sideways and shuffled through the narrow gap easily, but Joyce grunted and swore as she crammed her broad build into the tight space. Aki looked around, surveying the street, but saw no more creatures on this side of the barricade. Joyce pushed, reaching halfway, when a tar-covered creature pressed itself into the gap behind her. Two eyes, dyed black and suspended in a half-destroyed face, pressed into the hole. A crystal grew up from where the tongue should be and jutted through the right eye socket, squeezing the eye out of shape.

The impact of its shoulders on the van caused the skewered head to fall forwards and, with a snap, it fell to the ground at the creature's feet. It pushed, its body crumpling inward, compacting within the narrow space. One arm lifted, its dripping, clawed fingers scratching along the front of the van, before they snatched at Joyce's hand.

Joyce let out a yell. Aki screamed her name, reached back into the gap and, gripping Joyce's other arm, pulled hard, yanking her free of the creature's grasp and out of the space entirely.

Joyce looked at her left hand, the thick glove of her suit now coated in a thin layer of the shimmering dark liquid. She used her free hand to clutch her left arm and yanked the suit downwards, letting her arm retreat back up into the sleeve as far as its tight fit would allow. She pulled a utility knife from her belt and started cutting at the soft section of her suit below the metallic elbow pad. The black ooze crept up the glove, and burned its way through the layers of polymer to reach inside. Her left hand curled into a fist, as small as she could make it within the sleeve of the suit, and then the sleeve dropped free, thumping to the floor. She jumped back, looking at the severed suit sleeve where it lay, a thin pool of black beginning to spread around it.

"Your hand," said Aki, trying to look at her clenched fist. She held her hand up for both of them to inspect, fingers splayed. A trickle of red ran down her forearm and stained two fingers; she had cut herself while slicing the sleeve free.

But there was no black ooze. They looked at each other, observing their faces through the visors of their helmets.

"I need a fuckin' drink," said Joyce, the faintest waver in her voice. Aki let out a joyous laugh and grabbed her shoulders, then enveloped her in a tight hug. "Alright, Jesus! I'm glad I ain't dead too. Now get off ya lanky pest!" she said, pushing him away with a smile on her face.

"Sorry, I was just… Really worried," Aki said, still smiling back at her.

"Yeah well, you're not alone there. I can't say I'm entirely comfortable just yet though," Joyce said, looking back towards the gap they had just squeezed through. The creature that grabbed her wasn't visible, but a tendril of the black substance had started trailing its way from underneath the truck.

"Those things… There were so many of them. Robin mentioned they're in other parts of the city too," Aki said, looking at the fortuitous barricade separating them from the horde forming beyond. He wondered how long it would be before they climbed over. Or, the goo simply ate its way through the barricade. He could see why Robin called the creatures zombies, they weren't dissimilar to the classic shambling monstrosities from so many films. But that wasn't what these were. A zombie had to bite you, and all it took to kill them was a hit to the head. A lot of these tar-creatures didn't even have heads left, and they didn't need to bite. All they had to do was touch you, to transfer even a little bit of that terrible oily substance to your skin, and then you were infected too. No, not infected. Consumed. These weren't reanimated. They were not the living dead.

They seemed to just be corpses, being used by whatever this substance was. Riding the empty husks like a parasite, puppeteering the remains of their meal. He thought of the tendril reaching to the ladder, thought of the way the ooze spread only towards them before he kicked the ladder into the pit. Whatever the substance was, it was sentient.

"We should get moving. Hopefully we can meet up with the others on the way to the elevator. And we need to find you something for that, it's bleeding pretty bad," Aki said, looking at the cut on Joyce's arm.

"It isn't so bad, we'll find something on the way," she said, as she started walking away from the barricade.

Aki looked back one more time. More tendrils had appeared, climbing along the sides of the structure, and out from beneath it. He turned and jogged a few paces to catch up with Joyce, the intersection out of the Industrial District wasn't far ahead of them. The Column signalling the centre of the city looked close now, and from there, there wasn't much further until they could escape the city entirely. Looking up, he could see the black substance had coated so much of the dome that it now acted as a shroud over the entire Industrial District. He was glad to be heading away from it, and wondered how much longer the dome could last.

Chapter 19

Markus stormed through the shuttle doors as soon as they opened, eager to escape its claustrophobic confines. The ride up into orbit had been horrific. The shuttle shook like it was angry at him, throwing him raggedly around despite his harness. The screams of the other passengers bouncing from the metal walls and the cries of the children left him with a headache and ringing ears. The guards seemed nothing but amused at his distressed and dishevelled state, and scoffed at his admonitions.

He paced the many long corridors of the ship's head, peering into every room as he passed, looking for Captain Octavia. Each room bustled with tense activity. Terminals whirred, observed by stern faces. Some rooms had large monitors showing footage of the crowds moving throughout the city. One showed a small group of rioters, opportunistic thieves, seemingly ambivalent to the immediate threat invading the city, mere streets away from them. Security teams filtered through cameras taking records, identifying as many of the looters as they could. One room offered a glimpse of the city from a distance. A drone was flying high above, watching the black mass that now covered near a third of the city. Markus paused here for a moment when he realised the substance was growing ever closer to the pillar that connected the two halves of the ship.

When he reached the navigation chamber at the heart of the command deck, he pushed through the door, skin tingling with irritation and his blood starting to boil with impatience. He skimmed the room, ready to yell out, demanding to know where Octavia was hiding, when he met eyes with Duri Gim, the Head Navigator and his co-conspirator. The rage in her eyes forced the wind from him like a punch to the gut. His intently authoritative stance crumbled and his voice failed to project from his open mouth. When he realised those demonic eyes were approaching, he reflexively started walking backwards, back out of the door and into the long corridor. He looked behind, thinking to run away, when Duri passed through the door frame and shoved him hard into the wall.

"You!" she hissed, her voice bubbling like lava. "Where the fuck have you been? This—whatever the fuck is happening to all those people down there—this is your fault!"

Markus realised his hands were held up, palms out like he was surrendering to a gun-wielding maniac. He lowered them and stood straight, trying to stretch every millimetre of height his spine could offer. "Where—" he croaked, stopping when he heard the squeal his voice had become.

He cleared his throat and, with as confident a tone as he could muster, continued.

"Where have I been? I've been down there! In the thick of it! Do you realise what horrors I was forced to fight my way through to get here?" he said, indignantly.

"Whatever you've been through, you deserve worse. I warned you. I told you this would go bad, and now there are people down in that city dying," Duri said, her lips drawn

175

back and flashing her teeth like a snarl as she talked.

Markus scowled and shoved her away from him. "You plotted the course, Duri. You played your role in this just as I did. We need to take control of the situation. Control the narrative, and make sure that—" Duri cut him off.

"Control? What the fuck do you think we've been doing up here this whole time?! We've been trying to understand whatever is going on down there. To stop—whatever is going on down there! Octavia's had everybody on the ship working to handle this mess! You think this is another situation you can worm your way out of? When we get out of here, people are going to learn what happened. This is going to fucking destroy you," she said, with a particular, venomous pleasure emphasising the final sentence.

Markus squeezed his fingers tight, the muscles in his shoulders twisting into aching knots. "Any consequences I face for this, you will be subjected to just the same. If you don't want to spend the rest of your pathetic life sealed in a prison cell, you'll be every bit as eager as I to find an equitable narrative," he said, stepping close to Duri.

Duri shook her head and leaned in, bringing her face close. "Markus, I am going to tell every court and reporter who is willing to listen, the absolute truth. With every shred of detail I have the capacity to recall. I will happily face the consequences, knowing that you will rot in hell for what happened today." She turned and started walking back to the navigation chamber, Markus seething with a rich hatred as he watched her. She placed her hand on the door and looked back as she pulled it open. "I presume you were looking for the Captain. She's in the lower floors looking through equipment. Trying to find a way to get us out of this mess."

The door slammed closed, leaving Markus alone in the

corridor, his face feeling hot, knuckles white. His shoulders burned under the tension coiling through his body. He turned and walked down the corridor, back towards the elevators that would carry him to the lower floors. His mind raced. Duri would have to be dealt with somehow. Maybe a trustworthy guard could be bribed. Or perhaps, there was a way to twist the blame entirely onto her... An error in navigation, bringing the ship to an uncharted system? He would have to talk to Octavia. Duri had become a liability, but he owned Octavia. She would follow his lead.

The lower levels of the ship were much less hectic than the offices and control rooms of the command deck above. Most of the crew were on the planet, and those who remained seemed scattered. Markus cornered one idling worker who pointed him towards the Captain.

Octavia stood beside an engineer, both reading text on a tablet when Markus entered the dim storage room. She glanced at the door when he entered, placed a hand on the engineer's shoulder, and asked for a moment of privacy.

"Right, I'll start making some of the arrangements. I'll be just outside when you're ready," the engineer said, nodding, before exiting the room.

"You look like shit Markus. I wasn't sure I'd be seeing you again," Octavia said, not bothering to turn and look at Markus directly.

"You almost didn't," replied Markus, huffing. "I would have been eviscerated by those creatures, or the barbaric fools down there with them, had I not had my wits about me. The city is lost to whatever is down there, Octavia. We need to leave, immediately."

"I'm well aware of the situation Markus. We can't simply leave. We need to recover as many civilians as possible, first of

177

all. And of course, there is the question of how we leave." She watched for a moment as his face contorted, but continued when she saw questions forming on his lips.

"Markus, these ships are designed to work as a unit. We may treat the city as a separate entity when it makes landfall, but make no mistake, The Vaughn is one ship. There is no way to completely detach the interior structure from the Outer-Ring, without destroying the tether. The tether, that at this very second, is acting as the only route to safety for everybody trapped on that planet." As she talked, Octavia rotated the tablet resting on the crate beside her, and pointed to a diagram of The Vaughn displayed on its screen.

"Then set a crew to dismantling the thing!" Markus said, leaning in to look at the diagram.

"We don't have the equipment to dismantle such a large portion of the ship, Markus. Not in any manner that wouldn't take days of manual labour. We'd be cutting through materials designed to withstand the harshest conditions known to man," Octavia said, coolly.

"Then what exactly are we to do? Just wait up here and hope the stuff is scared of heights?" Markus said, gesticulating in frustrated waves of balled fists. Octavia looked at Markus with a calculated calm, then looked around the room, studying the racks of heavy containers adorning each wall.

"This room contains many of the more… volatile materials we keep aboard. I considered the possibility of putting a bomb in the elevator and blowing up the tether from within. Set it to explode on the way down to the planet. But most of the explosive materials in here are not strong enough. They would damage the tether, but from what we can tell, are very unlikely to sever the connection entirely."

She stepped back and placed a hand on the container the

tablet had been resting on. "Most of the explosives we have are for breaking through relatively small amounts of material. This crate contains the explosives we use to blow up entire planets." Her hand tapped idly on the top of the container.

Markus studied the crate, growing nervous as he considered the objects around him. The container was made of a dense, dark metal, with an intricate locking mechanism on the top. A litany of symbols featuring explosions, skulls and exclamation marks were printed on the side.

"I have been discussing the logistics of the operation with engineer Carr out there," she continued, nodding towards the door. "We believe, with the correct payload, we will be able to effectively vaporise the city, and a portion of the tether."

Markus slowly nodded his head as he listened, beads of sweat forming on his forehead. Octavia paused, offering him time to think.

"Then let's do it," he said, not needing much time at all.

"Let's drop it. Right now."

Octavia's cool expression faltered slightly, the faintest glimpse of irritation shining through. "It's not as simple as that, Markus. You cannot fathom the intricacies we have been working through to make this plan work. We want to give all civilians as much time as possible to evacuate. If we release the payload too early, we may lose more lives than is necessary. If we leave it too long, some of the... substance, could cling to the tether high enough to avoid the blast. We have no backup plan if that were to happen. There's also the debris of the planet to consider. Cracking a planet necessitates the use of a photon-mesh barrier to contain the pieces. Such a barrier takes days and multiple teams of crew to assemble. Without that, the explosion would jettison debris in all directions. A fragmentation mine of rock and dirt with this ship hovering in orbit above." Octavia swiped on the tablet, causing the image of The Vaughn to zoom outward. The ship looked minute compared to the planet below.

"But, we wouldn't be blowing up the whole planet, just the city?" Markus asked, furrowed brow as he tried to follow Octavia.

"We can only reduce the impact of the explosion so much. And without the time to run detailed simulations, we can't be certain how much debris will head our way. As such, I've advised the navigation team to prepare for a jump on short notice. They will remain on standby until we are ready, and as soon as we can confirm the tether is severed, we will jump to a new system and assess any damage before continuing."

Markus stood, looking at the image displayed on the tablet, not saying a word. Octavia watched him for a moment to see how he would react. When he seemed to have no immediate response, she picked up the tablet and let his eye meet her own. "Do you have any questions, or am I free to continue? I still have work to do," she said, tucking the tablet under her arm.

"Yes, yes just get on with it," Markus said.

Octavia stepped past him and walked to the door, sliding it open and looking to the engineer waiting outside. "Start preparing the bomb. Have it set up and ready to deploy in the equipment bay. I want us to be prepared for any change of circumstance." She handed the tablet to the man. "I'll join you in the bay as soon as my other tasks are seen to," she said, and set off down the hallway. The engineer stood straight, presuming a near-militaristic formality was expected in Octavia's presence, until she turned the corner and vanished from sight.

The door to the storage room slipped closed, leaving

Markus isolated in the dimly lit space. He was struggling to comprehend how things had gone quite so awry. And how he would manage to explain not only the navigation mistakes, but allowing the crew to demolish half of the ship. He also found himself eager to leave. He thought of the creatures he saw at the hospital, of the black substance crawling across the dome of the city. He pictured the doors of the elevator opening, and rather than screaming civilians, a horde of dripping, decayed creatures storming forth and taking over The Vaughn.

He could find ways to blame the others. Duri would take the fall for the charts, and the bomb was entirely Octavia's plan. He would find a way to escape consequences. But none of that mattered if he didn't escape this wretched system alive. He felt a resolve swell within him, and he set off towards the equipment bay. He would keep an eye on Octavia. On the workers preparing this bomb, and make sure they did what was necessary to keep him safe.

Chapter 20

Robin peered through the smashed windows and open doors lining the streets out of Hydroponics and into the centre. When he'd first seen the scattered fragments of glass glinting on the floor, he'd worried the creatures had already arrived in the centre, but it quickly became apparent the buildings had just been looted amid the chaos.

People still ran between the buildings, carrying whatever goods they could find. Even so, he couldn't shake the sensation that one of those creatures would appear at any moment.

The Column was now visible, peering over the buildings just a few streets ahead. A group of nearly two hundred followed beside him. Everybody had found their way up from the surface, but many insisted on spreading out to other parts of the city, searching for loved ones or seeking shelter in their own homes. Robin tried to warn them, as had everybody else that had seen the creatures spreading through the city. Those that remained travelled together toward the Transport Hub on the opposite side of the city.

His legs were beginning to burn and he could feel sweat building beneath his shirt. Working in the refinery was a hard job, and one that kept him in shape, but he felt like he'd been running across the city for hours now with barely a break. He watched Rob keeping pace on his bad leg, cane tapping quickly, his own face dotted in beads of sweat, and chastised himself for complaining, even if only in his own head.

After their encounter with Harris in the refinery, Robin and Kurt worked their way back home, uncertain what else to do. A crowd followed them out from the Industrial District as the other buildings connected to the pipe network flooded with the corrosive substance. The tram stations quickly filled and started to fall apart under the pressure. A handful of guards tried to maintain some degree of order, but most of them vanished, responding to a call for help at the hospital. Those that remained quickly gave up on order and decided to just observe the chaos. Some even joined in. Robin and Kurt agreed to run home rather than try their luck with the trams. By the time they arrived, the Residential District seemed to bustle with a fervour unlike anything they had seen before. A calamitous sound echoed through the lofty buildings, mostly coming from the hospital as guards clashed with a fearful horde trying to escape the building.

When they pushed through the door into their hab, Kimi spun to look at them, dread sapping all colour from her face until she recognised her hab-mates. She had a large bag resting on the sofa, half-filled with her belongings.

"Holy shit, are you two okay?" Kimi said, voice cracking. Her hair was a mess, and her whole body seemed to tremble.

"We're okay, I think," Robin said, falling exhausted onto the sofa beside Kimi's bag. "We ran here from the refinery. Something real fucked up is going on."

Kurt fastened the locks on the door and stood beside the sofa. "What happened with you?" he said, looking towards

Kimi. "Do you know what's happening out there?"

Kimi stopped stuffing items in her bag and looked back towards Kurt, then Robin, mouth open as she searched for the right words. "I'm… not sure. It was just… crazy. At the hospital, it—" she paused for a moment, eyes searching for focus.

"I went shopping to pick up some things for a friend, you know Jamie? Well, I got the stuff and went over to the hospital. Everything was fine, I was just sitting in the waiting room, and then doctors all started rushing past and people started shouting. The nurses told us to stay put until they knew what was happening, so we did. Eventually a guard ran into the room and started screaming at us, telling us to get out." She looked between Robin and Kurt as she talked, a near-pleading look in her eyes, like she was scared they wouldn't believe her.

"It was awful. I grabbed my things and tried to ask about Jamie, but the guard just shoved me out of the room. I got really scared, so, I just ran to the stairs and followed everybody else down. An alarm started going off, and people were all shouting and pushing each other. And then, there was this horrible screaming. People started turning around and trying to push back up the stairs, but everybody at the top kept pushing down and we just got trapped there. I could see over the edge, at what was happening lower down. These people were there, at the bottom of the stairs, all covered in oil or something. They were just, pushing their way into the crowd and wiping oil all over everybody. I couldn't make it out properly, but the screams were so horrible. Eventually we started moving back up away from the stairs, but there were people getting knocked to the floor and nobody would stop to help them. I wanted to, but, I was being pushed by the people behind me and I was worried that if I tried to stop I'd just get stuck on the floor too." Her frantic movements seemed to settle here, as she dropped into a chair exhausted.

"I got out of the stairwell, and a doctor had opened a fire escape and was waving people through, so I got out. The street was just full of people running away from the hospital. I could hear more screams from inside, and more people covered in that, stuff, whatever it was, were in the lobby. I could see them through the windows as I ran past. Loads of guards were pushing into the building and pulling out batons and pepper spray. I just kept running until I was down towards the plaza, and then I saw the stuff spreading on the dome behind Industrial and, I just thought, 'fuck this, I'm leaving. I don't know what's happening, but I'm getting out of this fucking city.' So, I came home and…" She gestured to the bag in front of her and looked back to them both, a tinge of the wild in her eyes.

"We saw them too," said Kurt as soon as she was done talking.

Robin nodded his head when Kimi looked to him. A look of relief seemed to wash over her, though one steeped in dread. "In the refinery. Whatever that oil is, the tanks are flooded with it. It covered our boss. Killed him, I think. But then, he got up again and, well…" Robin shrugged.

"So, it isn't just the hospital? It's in other parts of the city too? I think I have the right plan then. I'm packing up and heading to the elevator," she said, standing from her chair and pushing a bottle of supplements into her bag.

"That… actually sounds like a good plan," said Kurt, looking down towards Robin. "You think we should join?"

Robin pulled his tablet from the pouch on his belt and looked at the chat window. The signal was still trying endlessly to connect with Aki and Adie, as it had been since they left the refinery. He watched the screen for a few moments before he shut it off again and pushed to his feet. "That seems like the smart thing to do," he said, with some apprehension.

Robin and Kurt went to their rooms and after a time emerged again, each carrying a pack of supplies and cherished possessions. Outside, the Residential District continued its descent into disorder, frantic people running along the streets to and from their homes. Fights broke out in narrow walkways where paths were blocked. Screams and shouts from nearby streets, those in the direction of the hospital. Robin noticed increasing numbers running from that direction as they descended the stairways to the street below. Kimi led the way, struggling with her large bag on the narrow stairs. She occasionally glanced back to check that Robin and Kurt were following.

All three found themselves watching the narrow walkways across the street. The screams sounded much closer than when Robin and Kurt had arrived. Reaching the street was a relief, giving them room to avoid those that ran in the opposite direction rather than squeezing tight as everybody tried to climb the stairs. Just a few steps down the street, Robin paused. A voice rang out from the alleyways behind, screaming for help. He turned to look and Kurt did the same. A man ran from the alley, voice shrill and piercing, eyes wide, scanning the street.

He held one arm out in front of him, black liquid coating it from the tips of his fingers to his elbow. Tendrils coiled their way up the rest of his arm. He stumbled and fell to his knees, letting out an agonised scream as the arm bent, snapping at the elbow. Kimi appeared, her face nearly filling

Robin's vision. "We need to fucking go!" she yelled, looking first at Robin, and then up to Kurt beside him.

Without waiting for a response she turned and ran down the street. The man writhed on the floor now. Kurt placed a hand on Robin's back and encouraged him to join as they ran after Kimi. The screams continued behind them, and beyond the wall of hab units at their side. The twisting narrow alleyways offered no glimpses of what chaos reigned in the streets beyond. The sounds dimmed, left behind as they progressed out of the Residential District. The circular streets surrounding The Column at the centre of the city were swarmed. Tightly huddled groups idled in the streets, while others scattered to all corners of the city. Many stood and gazed up at the mass growing along the dome, now covering most of the glass above the Industrial District, tendrils beginning to stretch towards the centre. Robin noted how empty that part of the city seemed compared to the other spaces he could see. In the time they had been gone, the Industrial District had grown eerily quiet. He noticed he was lagging behind, and jogged across the road to where Kimi observed the elevated tramway above them.

"I don't think we'll have any luck with trams. They'll be a mess right now," said Kurt, noting where Kimi was looking.

"We'll have to run to Transport then I guess. You two good, or you need a break?" said Kimi.

"I'm good," said Kurt.

"Yeah, I can keep—" started Robin, when a chime in his ear piece caught his attention. "Hang on…"

He pulled out his tablet and looked at the screen. A picture of Aki at its centre. One of the calls he'd left open had finally connected. He watched the icon spin, waiting for an answer on the other end of the line. Words repeated in his

187

head as the icon turned. "Come on, come on… Pick up Aki, come—" The spinning symbol vanished.

"Aki! Thank fucking god—"

After the call, Kimi and Kurt agreed to go ahead to the Transport Hub. Kurt had taken Robin's heavy bag, a promise to keep his items safe and return them once they were reunited on The Vaughn above. Robin had made his journey to Hydroponics, and now he and the mining crew were approaching The Column again, where he had last seen Kimi and Kurt. He hoped they had made it through the Transport Hub safely.

Where before the centre was filled with a chaotic energy, now it seemed dormant, eerily still. All noise was distant, though inescapable. Black tendrils explored some of the taller buildings in the distance, and a heavy plume of smoke billowed up from the Industrial District, trailing the inside of the dome similar to the inky substance on the other side of the glass. Winding streets and buildings blocked the view to most districts, but the wide, straight street leading from the centre to Residential offered a glimpse into its heart. Robin saw figures lining the street, moving slowly between the buildings and up throughout the intertwining walkways that released viscous drips like the buildings themselves were bleeding.

His attention was pulled away from the distant figures when a voice called his name. He turned and saw Aki had appeared on one of the roads. Aki ran towards the group, his helmet swinging in one hand and a broad smile on his face. Robin found himself grinning, and forgot the pain in his legs as he ran to meet his friend. They came together and Aki's arms flung around Robin, pulling him into a tight hug, lifting him from the ground as they both laughed in near-manic joy.

188

Joyce walked behind, waving one bloody hand at Rob who separated from the crowd and walked to join them.

"Alright! Get off me!" Robin said, still laughing. "That suit don't make for comfortable hugs."

Aki stepped back out of the hug, but kept his hands firmly on Robin's shoulders. "Sorry. It's really good to see you," Aki said, then looked over Robin's shoulder. "Rob! I'm glad you're alright."

Rob smiled, placing a hand on Aki's shoulder affectionately. His smile fell away as he turned to Joyce. "I'm glad to see you two. Could do with getting that looked at though," Rob said, nodding towards the still-bleeding cut on Joyce's arm.

"It's not so bad," Joyce said, dismissively glancing at her arm. "It's not deep. I care more about getting off this planet than dribbling on the floor a bit."

"She's right, you all need to stop standing about and get a bloody move on," came George's voice, deep and tinged with frustration from behind them.

Aki looked past Robin and saw a few familiar faces from the mining crew watching them as the rest continued their march towards the Transport Hub. Most of the mining crew had removed their suits from outside, back into the casual clothing they wore beneath. A small few in suits still stood out, the colour-coded metal panels looking out of place within the city. Aki realised how strange it was to still be wearing the bulky suit inside. George offered him a stern look, still wearing his own dark orange metal panelled suit, before opening a buttoned pouch on his belt and pulling out a roll of thick black tape. "Here, plug up your leak," he said, throwing the roll of tape to Joyce.

"You can get stitched up when we're safe. Now come on,

I didn't carry Rob through those pipes for half an hour so he can die now." With that, George turned and walked away. Joyce tugged the tape loose and wrapped three bands around her bleeding arm, tearing it free and hanging the roll over a spare hook on her own belt.

Robin looked back towards the Residential District. The figures were still too distant for him to make out any details, but he was certain they looked closer. "Yeah, let's get going," he said, looking to Aki, who nodded.

The streets around The Column in the centre of the city were littered with a mess of debris. Looters had left the ground covered in broken glass, scraps of paper, and plastic packaging. The large screens on the side of the skyscraper displayed still text, apologising for the disrupted services. They passed the city plaza, more garbage scattered on the grass. The stage on the far side had been heavily vandalised, the scaffolding that surrounded the stage toppled and the screens it supported were smashed on the brickwork below. A continuous roar of unrest emanated from the Transport Hub ahead. The sight of the crowd pushing and gyrating between the guarded fences still came as a shock. The scale of the evacuation was immense, with what looked like thousands still waiting for their turn to ride to the safety of the Outer-Ring above.

"This could take hours," said Aki, looking over the crowd.

"I can't believe there are still so many people here…" said Robin despairingly. In the distance the elevator shuttle rested in the middle of the platform, robotic arms lifting tram-sized containers into the cargo compartment before the guards pulled the gate open and a frantic stream of people ran forward to claim their place inside.

"Useless pricks," Rob said in a near growl. "Come on, I

can get us through." He began confidently striding towards the crowd.

The shuttle set off, shooting into the sky as Aki, Robin and Joyce followed behind, watching to see how Rob intended to break through the tightly packed crowd. Rob had seen the fenced-off walkways where guards idly walked back and forth observing the crowd. The farthest entrances poked out from the body of the crowd, a small cluster of guards gathered beside the barred metal doors. They seemed to perk up at the approaching group and the guard at the front placed his hand on the spray canister at his side.

"I'm management, they need me and my crew up in the ship," said Rob, holding out his identification as he approached.

The guards at the door leaned against the fence and looked down at the card in Rob's hand. "Pass it through," she said after a moment.

Rob stepped forward and pushed the card through the bars. "It took us a while to get here from the surface," Rob said as the guard peered at the card, then to Rob. She stepped away from the gate and pressed a finger to her earpiece, talking in hushed tones, before nodding to the other guards who stepped toward them, batons brandished. The guard unlatched the gate, and pulled it open. Rob started forwards as Aki, Robin and Joyce followed behind.

"Just you, only management," said the guard, holding out Rob's card with a pointed look towards Aki.

"I need them, they're my crew," said Rob, looking over his shoulder. The guards on either side of the gate seemed to lean in, squeezing the handles of their batons, eager to act on any shows of disobedience. The front guard observed the suits Aki and Joyce still wore.

191

"You, come here," she said, pointing her chin at Aki.

Aki looked to Robin at his side, then stepped forwards, through the gate. "You're some kind of management, right?"

"I'm one of the head engineers," Aki said, pointing to the identification tag on the chest of his suit. The guard leaned in and looked at the tag, nodded, and then pushed the gate door closed. "Hey, wait!" Aki said, reaching to grab the gate before another guard pushed him back.

"Hang on, I need these two!" said Aki angrily, stepping up to the guard who flipped the latch closed, locking the gate.

"I said only management. Those are the rules." The guard said, standing firm against Rob, her hand lowering back to the canister on her hip.

"Aki, it's fine! You two go ahead, Rob needs to get out of here. We'll catch up," Robin called through the gate. Aki looked back at him, and looked to the guards surrounding the gate. One of them met his eyes, looking almost pleased with the situation. He shook the baton, near taunting Aki to try something.

Rob reached for Aki's shoulder and pulled him close. "Come on lad, we'll do what we can to get everyone through faster. Someone's gotta sort this mess out," he said, clearly working hard to keep his voice level.

"We'll stick together, keep each other safe," said Joyce, placing an arm around Robin. Aki looked back at them with reluctance. Both he and Robin could see the fear in each other's expressions, but Robin looked brave in spite of it.

"I'll come back, once Rob is on the shuttle and I know what's going on, okay? Stay around here, I'll be back!" Aki said, turning to walk before Robin had any opportunity for argument.

Rob smiled at Robin, nodded to Joyce, then turned to

join Aki. Intense aches pulsed through his bad knee. Were it not for his cane, he was certain he wouldn't be able to walk at all. Sharp twinges of pain had started shooting through his bones every other step, but he had always been good at hiding discomfort. He knew it wasn't smart, but it was in his nature. He walked beside Aki, managing to keep up with his quickened pace. Aki looked to his side and saw Rob, one leg stiff, his shoulders tense as he pushed off his cane. He slowed his walk and looked out over the sea of faces packed into the space beyond the fence.

"We have to get them all out of here," Aki said.

Rob slowed his pace, gratefully, and looked across the crowd in turn. "Aye lad, we'll do what we can," he said.

Guards turned to watch as they approached the shuttle platform. Aki noted that most of them were from the Outer-Ring, as denoted by the circular symbol on their vests. The Outer-Ring guards had a reputation for being less personable than the Inner-City guards. More often than not, they acted as glorified security detail for the wealthy. They kept teens away from the Outer-Ring gardens, and were known to check the ident of anybody they considered out of place in nice neighbourhoods.

The Inner-City residents called them doughnuts, both for the symbol on their uniforms, and as a jab at the generalisation of all Outer-Ring guards being lazy. A guard sporting a golden badge sauntered to the edge of the platform when he noticed Rob and Aki climbing the stairs. "Welcome to the eye of the storm gentlemen. I take it you're here for the express ride out of this hellhole?" he said with an aura of amusement, thumb casually tucked into his belt.

"I'm here to make sure everybody gets outta this hellhole," said Rob, his voice calm, his fingers gripping tight at the head of his cane.

The badge on the guard's chest read 'Cpt. L. Fitch.' "Well there sir, I can assure you we're doing all we can. The shuttle is operating at optimal speed, and we're loading civilians as fast as we can," said Fitch in a professional tone, tinged with that same aloof amusement he seemed to carry with such ease.

Rob looked to the other side of the platform where a sizable stack of heavy metal crates waited, huge mechanical arms on tracks ready to transfer them into the shuttle.

"Looks t' me like you're not quite doing everything you could," said Rob, a tingle of cold drifting into his otherwise calm tone.

"That cargo's taking up half of the room in the shuttle. Seems t' me you could get these people outta' here in half the time. Maybe faster, if they can pack in extra tight."

Fitch pursed his lips momentarily, brow pulling together as he shifted his weight to the opposite leg. "Well, that sounds like an uncomfortable ride to me. We're following standard protocol for mass relocation, sir," he said, some of his humour departed.

Rob turned and pointed towards the colossal mass of dark stretching across the dome above. The pool now stretched across half of the dome, its tendrils out and searching along the glass panels. One of the tendrils stretched towards them, close to finding the tether that connected the two halves of the ship, and the airlock that the shuttle travelled through.

"We have no idea how long that stuff is gonna keep playing nice. I've seen it eat through parts of this ship like it was nothing, and I suspect it could'a got through the dome by now if it wanted. Do you want to be here when all that glass starts falling? Or that stuff starts raining down on us?"

Fitch looked up at the ceiling for a long moment, and

looked down to see Rob's eyes locked firmly on his own. Fitch twisted his mouth, as though chewing, and clicked his tongue.

"Well, I see your point. But I don't much feel like taking the blame for any hits to company profits. Besides, I haven't the foggiest idea how to shut that thing down," he said, gesturing to the arms waiting beside the containers.

"We've got that," said Rob, looking to Aki who returned a nod. "My boy Aki here can shut down the loading mechanism. And you can tell whoever you need that I gave the orders. They can shove their money up their ass for all I care."

An electric chime sounded and a metallic whirring signalled the arrival of the shuttle as it passed through the airlock above. Aki ran past Captain Fitch, who still looked very uncertain about the turn of events, and towards the loading mechanism on the other side of the platform. The robotic arms were already shifting into position, setting their thick iron-clamped hands onto the cargo containers. A boxy terminal beside the tracks beeped to life as he tapped the screen, displaying a list of automated commands looping in time with the arrival of the shuttle.

He tapped through menus and typed in codes as the shuttle settled on the platform, its doors sliding open to reveal a small few guards who stepped out onto the platform beyond. Rob watched from beside the door until Aki held up his hand, thumb extended.

"Right, you two," Rob said, pointing to the guards stood at the shuttle doors. "Come on, we wanna get this done quick." He strode into the shuttle and toward the wide cargo bay that took up half of the space within. Under Rob's instructions, the guards gathered the thick tethers that extended from the walls and floors, and tied them to the beams dividing the cargo compartment from the passenger section. A web of tethers began to form a makeshift handrail system. Rob stepped out of the container as the two guards worked, walking to Aki who stood looking puzzled at the terminal. "Should be able to board in a few minutes. I take it you're intending to wait on Robin?" Rob said.

"Yeah, I can't leave him. I wouldn't be able to head up anyway, I can't find a way to permanently disable the orders on this thing. I can only delay it one cycle at a time." Aki said, frowning towards the monitor.

Rob took a step closer. "The commands are coming down from the ship. Same signal's just gonna keep sending until we can turn it off up there," he said, fingers tapping on the head of his cane. "You want me to wait down here with you?" He turned and looked up at Aki.

"No, don't be stupid Rob. I'll be fine, and I can handle this myself easy enough. You get up there and make sure they're ready for us, alright?" Aki said, smiling back at his friend.

Rob nodded and reached out to pat Aki on the back. "You grab Robin and get up there as soon as you can, alright lad?" Rob said.

"I will, I'll see you soon Rob," Aki said, grabbing Rob's forearm and squeezing gently.

"I'll be waiting for you," Rob said with a stern look as he turned to walk away.

Fitch stood in the entrance to the shuttle, arms folded as he watched Rob approach. "Smart," he said, nodding towards the tangle of tethers inside the cargo bay. "But remember old man, if they try to call me on this, you take the blame."

Rob waved a dismissive hand in Fitch's face as he passed, finding a seat in the shuttle and falling back into the stiff cushions. He let out a heavy sigh and closed his eyes, feeling his knee throb, tingles running along his legs and shoulders.

"Just let people on the bloody elevator," he said, eyes still closed as he tried to imagine the aches and pains in his body seeping away through the seat.

Chapter 21

A small crew in grey EVA suits huddled around a container within the equipment bay, careful hands unscrewing bolts that held the container closed. Mayor Markus and Captain Octavia observed the engineers from the command room above, the monitors on the terminals before them displaying footage of the spreading mass of black liquid across the dome far below.

Markus sipped from a cardboard cup and scrunched his face. He held the cup at a distance and scanned the room. "Is it so hard to get a damn tea made correctly? Where are the facilities down here, the milk and sugar?"

"The break room is down the corridor and to the right," Octavia said, watching the activity in the room below. Her knee tapped up and down gently, a metal token twisting between her fingers.

Markus looked at her, watched the coin twisting, flashing as it caught the light. He found the habit incessantly irritating. He wished he could strap her feet to the floor and throw that blasted coin into space. "Why do you insist on doing that? Withdrawal symptoms?" he said, grumbling as he took another dissatisfied sip from his cup.

Octavia looked back to him for just a moment, eyes flicking across the room around them before turning back. "I do not have withdrawal symptoms, Markus. As you well know, I am not withdrawing from anything," she said, keeping her voice low. A small few engineers dotted the room, sat at terminals far enough away for them to go unheard.

"It has nothing to do with any other habits of mine. I've done it since I was a child. It aids my focus, when I need it," she said, holding up her token, the face worn near-flat, whatever symbol or text it used to display had diminished beyond recognition.

Markus watched in annoyance as the metal disk returned to motion. He sat in silence, watching as the engineers below adjusted some heavy piece of machinery. His uncertainty at their actions tickled the unease nested in his spine, but he resisted the urge to ask Octavia. He didn't want her to confuse the hierarchy of their relationship.

A soft whir sounded as the door opened and a man walked in, dressed in casual clothing. Markus perked up, sitting straight and waving a hand at the man. "You there! I need you to make a trip to the break room for me and—" he began, before Octavia stepped past him and cut in with a greeting.

"Robert! I'm glad to see you're safe," she said, clasping the man's hand in both of her own.

"Lightly beaten, but still in one piece," said Rob, shaking her hand.

"We have a team trying to contact you, but as I'm sure you've ascertained, the coms are severely limited."

"I was going to ask about that. I want to get back in touch with somebody on the surface," Rob said, sparing a momentary glance to the Mayor who remained in his seat.

"At first the system was overwhelmed, and shortly after, we started losing transceivers. That's not all, that substance has been eating its way through the underside of the city. Power outages, fuel leaks," Octavia shook her head lightly as she talked, then gestured broadly to the many consoles within the room.

"Terminals are still able to link directly, if that could help you contact those you need."

Rob nodded his head, thankful there was still a means of consistent contact. Then turned his eyes away from Octavia. "Mind telling me what's happening in my equipment bay?" He looked down through the large windows, his face grim as he saw the bomb being lifted from its crate, held cautiously in the padded claw of a robotic transport arm.

"Of course, please, sit with us. I'll explain everything," Octavia said, stepping back and gesturing to the chairs. "Markus, this is Robert Denton, I'm not sure if you have ever met. He's the head of our mining operation."

Markus quickly raised to his feet and presented a wide and civil smile. "Ah, Mr. Denton! Surely I should have met you long before now, to thank you, for your spectacular contributions to this fine city. I am Markus Bailey, as I'm sure you know," he said, reaching out a hand.

"Aye, I know who you are. I'd offer a curtsy but, bad knees," Rob said, waving his cane as he pushed past Markus. Rob took the seat at the central terminal, hooking his cane on the edge where it so often waited for him. He spun the chair and looked through the window into the equipment bay below.

"We're making plans to evacuate, when the remaining civilians are out of the city. As I'm sure you've noticed, we've settled on a solution for the obvious problems we're faced with," Octavia said, returning to her seat and turning to face Rob.

"Your solution being to drop a bloody nuke on half the ship," Rob said, voice calm but stern.

"We've reduced the payload as much as we safely can. I can tell you with certainty that we won't be hit, but the city will be destroyed," Octavia said, sounding confident in her reply.

"And killing everyone down there who ran anywhere but the elevator. You okay with that?" said Rob, offering a quick look to Markus before focusing his eyes on Octavia.

She took in a deep breath, and released it as a sharp sigh. "I see no alternative. We need to sever the tether connecting the city to the Outer-Ring." She leaned forwards in her chair and tapped on the monitor before Rob. "The substance is already at the base of the tether. And I suspect when it touches the tether, it will keep climbing until it reaches our safe haven here in orbit."

"We don't know that it can survive out of atmosphere," Rob said.

"Precisely. We don't know. Is that a risk we should take? Endangering the lives of everybody who fled to safety, for the sake of those who, we can presume, are soon to die regardless of the actions we take? We have no way to save those who chose to hide rather than run." She gestured to the screen. "From what I've seen on the cameras, and I assume you've seen in person. We can offer them a better death. Better the speed of the bomb, than to be consumed by that substance."

Octavia spoke with a calm and collected tone, but her eyes spoke to Rob more than her words. She had clearly considered this, and genuinely believed her choice to be the most humane. There was a pain in those eyes, to know that this was the better choice. Rob nodded, slowly, and solemnly. He looked back through the window to the floor below. The bomb, now mounted upon the robotic arm, was running smoothly along a metal track in the ceiling. The track led towards the open doorway on the side of the ship, the photon-mesh barrier fizzing around the metal as the arm stretched away from the hull into the open space beyond.

"So how's this gonna work then? When are you planning to drop it?" Rob asked, as the arm came to a stop and rested with the bomb dangling above the planet.

"Once the last shuttle arrives and the last group are on their way to safety. We're setting up temporary accommodation in the residential sections of the Outer-Ring. There's plenty of room. I'll be the one to release the bomb. I wouldn't expect that of anyone else. I can do it from here." Octavia swiped on the monitor before them, opening a menu for the robotic arm below. "Gravity will do all of the work from there. It will take a little over ten minutes to reach the surface, and detonates shortly after impact. Most of the city will be destroyed instantly, and a portion of the tether along with it. I can't say exactly how much of the tether will be caught in the blast, so it's important we don't give the substance an opportunity to climb too high before we act. If any of it is left attached to the ship, I'm not certain we have any way to remove it." Octavia swiped the menu closed and returned the monitor to the exterior view of the city.

Markus looked at the screen, at the tendrils that began creeping their way up the outer shell of the airlock connecting the dome of the city to the tether. "We'll certainly do our best to see as many brought to safety as possible," he said, mimicking Octavia's confident, authoritarian tone as best he could. "Of course, we do need to prioritise those who have already made their way to safety. How many more trips would you expect the shuttle will take?" He looked to Octavia, who returned a steely gaze.

"As many as it takes," Rob interjected. "The shuttle keeps running until everybody is safe."

Markus wilted under the waves of heat from Rob's eyes, pushing back into his seat and stammering for a moment. "I, well, yes! Of, of course. I was just enquiring as to the numbers. For preparations!" he said, a lump forming in his throat, an anger already building within him, an acidic bile rocking his stomach in waves. He maintained his smile until Rob looked away.

The older man took hold of his cane and pushed to his feet, excusing himself. Markus twisted his face into a collage of vitriol and disapproval, which he snapped towards Octavia, who received it with an infuriating lack of consequence. Markus pushed to his feet and stormed across the room, leaving in search of the break room.

Octavia watched, relaxing her shoulders and letting the tapping of her leg intensify ever so slightly. She could tell Markus would be a problem at the end of this. But, for now, getting her crew to safety was the priority. She looked to Rob, who stood at a terminal in an empty corner of the room, tapping at the screen with one hand as his fingers drummed on his cane with the other. She reached for the cardboard cup Markus had abandoned, still near full.

Rob tapped through the menus on the terminal, finding a connection with the landing pad below. Connecting his earpiece, he sent an alert to the terminal, requesting an audio link, waiting the few minutes it took for a chime to signal the connection made.

"Rob! Sorry, I've just got back, I was checking on Joyce

and Robin," came Aki's voice through the channel.

"No worries lad, I've not been waiting long. How are things looking down there?" Rob's tension eased slightly as he felt himself distanced from his interaction with the Mayor.

"Well, the crowd is moving a lot faster than it was. There's still a lot to get through, but we're getting there. A few more have joined at the back since we got here but, not many." The sounds of the crowd and the shuttle arriving filtered through the voice call as Aki talked.

"Good. Make sure they're packing in as many as they can. We want everybody up here soon as possible. Listen, I'm gonna make a few calls to the upper floors, get that cargo arm stopped properly. Soon as you're off the call, go find Robin and Joyce. I want you all on the next shuttle outta there, alright? Tell the guards it's orders from the top, from the Captain. Whatever it takes to get the lot of you through that gate and out of there as soon as possible."

Aki remained silent for a moment when Rob finished. The background noise surged as a new group were allowed into the shuttle behind him. "Yeah, yeah I got you Rob. I'll see you soon, okay?" he said, eventually.

Rob smiled to himself. "Good, I'll see you boys soon."

Chapter 22

A stream of civilians rushed past the guards and into the waiting shuttle. Aki idled by the terminal, watching the unbroken flow until a guard called out and the heavy metal gates slid closed once more. The crowd had calmed now that the shuttle was transporting them in far greater numbers, but every time the gates closed again there would be an increase in the cries from those who despaired to be denied access. The guards would yell back, brandish their batons, and occasionally unleash a spray of mist from their canisters until the clamour diminished again.

Once the flow subsided, Aki started his way across the platform. Four guards entered the shuttle, taking position either side of the doors as they started to shut. By the time Aki had descended the stairs to the fenced-off side path, the shuttle was lifting away from the platform. He looked up towards the ceiling of the dome. The sun rested on the horizon, the sky shifting to green and blue hues. And there, an oil slick scar was blocking the colours of the sky from view, like the night sky refusing to acquiesce to the day. Its tendrils probed at the tunnel that contained the elevator airlock, and the tether that connected the two halves of the ship. Aki imagined it finding its way into the airlock, dripping down onto the platform below. He lowered his gaze and increased his pace until he was running along the path.

Robin waved and called Aki's name as he approached. He and Joyce still waited at the very back of the crowd. A few more people had arrived after Aki, but most at the rear of the enormous huddle were still the mining crew he had arrived with. "How things lookin' up there, any news?" Robin asked, leaning against the fence's thick metal bars.

"Yeah, I just heard from Rob," Aki said, taking some deep breaths to recover from his run. "He's sorting out the signal, so I don't need to work on the terminal any more."

"That's good, no more running back an' forth! I was starting to feel bad for your twigs," Robin said, gesturing towards Aki's legs with a smile.

"Thankfully, yeah. I'd give one of them up for ten minutes in a comfy chair about now," Aki said, with a slight but earnest nod.

"Well I told you not to run back to us every time the shuttle set off!" Robin swatted at the bars in the direction of Aki's arm, causing a hollow metallic ping of sound. "So, what now?"

"Rob wants us on the next shuttle. Said I should tell the guards that Captain Moore gave the order." Aki looked towards the small group of guards patrolling the enclosed path's entrance.

"Does he need you for something?" Robin asked.

"I'm not sure. He's probably just being protective and wants us to skip the wait. I'm not too inclined to argue with him though, if I'm totally honest," Aki said, looking at the crowd. Part of him felt guilty for a reason he couldn't quite place. But then he thought of the liquid tendrils climbing

206

towards the airlock and wondered just how many more trips the shuttle could make before the substance made it impossible. He looked back towards Robin. He could feel guilty about saving himself, but he wouldn't regret taking any advantage they had to make sure his friends got to safety.

Robin gazed into the crowd himself, looking towards the shuttle platform on the far side. He wondered if he should decline and insist that Aki leave without him, but he knew Aki. There was no way he would leave alone.

"Alright, let's see what we can do," Robin said, looking back towards him.

"Grab Joyce, I'll go talk to the guards." Aki turned to jog along the remainder of the fenced-in path. The guards seemed to perk up as he approached. One paced back and forth directly in front of the gate, whilst three stood idly to one side chatting together, throwing occasional glances towards the crowd on the other side of the fence. "Hey! I've just got off a call with one of the managers, we need you to let some people through," Aki said as he slowed to a stop before the guards.

The guards looked to each other in silence for a beat. One turned back and took a step closer to Aki. "We haven't heard anything about it."

"The coms are still down, I was talking to them directly through the terminal up there," Aki said, gesturing back towards the shuttle platform. "He said the Captain approved it."

The guard's face seemed puzzled briefly in response. "Is somebody important still stuck down here?" The guard said, looking towards the crowd. He saw two figures approaching, Robin and Joyce jogging towards the gate. He looked at Robin's casual clothing, heavy backpack slung on one shoulder, and Joyce in her partially-destroyed orange EVA suit. The confusion remained, but shifted somewhat. The guard was clearly not impressed. "What, these two?" he said, looking back to Aki with an indignant glare.

"That's right," Aki said, calm despite his irritation.

The guard looked back to his colleagues, seemingly looking for suggestions that none would offer. He turned to Robin and Joyce who stood by the gate, watching him curiously. Eventually he turned back to Aki. "Look, I don't think we can just let anybody through. You're gonna need to show me a message from the top at least."

"I don't have a message, we were in a voice call. What difference does it make regardless, it's two people. Just let them through as well and we'll be out of here." Aki looked to Robin and Joyce, the metal bars between them partially obstructing his view.

"Look, buddy, if you can't prove that this is coming from the top, I can't risk it," said the guard, shaking his head.

"Risking what? Nothing bad is going to happen if you just let them through. Something bad could happen if I tell my boss that you refused," Aki said, the anger starting to roll out with his words. He looked at the badge on the guard's chest. "So I just tell him, Officer Hill stood in our way. Refused to help. Maybe he goes to your boss and submits a complaint. Or maybe he even goes directly to the Captain?"

The guard, Hill, grew tense as Aki talked. His shoulders grew taught and his chest began to puff outward. Aki noticed the two guards beside Hill resting their hands on their batons, the fourth guard paused in their pacing to watch the exchange.

"I don't much care for the tone you're taking there, buddy," Hill said, spitting the final word out.

Aki looked to the gate, to the latch that held it closed,

and back to Hill. Robin looked to Joyce with concern, and noticed her pulling something metal from her belt, holding it to her side, out of view from the guards. He looked back and saw Aki and the guard staring each other down. It was a strange way to see Aki, angry and confrontational. He started thinking through the items in his bag, trying to remember everything he'd packed.

"I don't have anything," he said to Joyce under his breath, careful not to draw the attention of the guard closest to them.

Joyce looked at him with a questioning look, but understood when he pointed his eyes towards her concealed hand. "Don't worry, just let me lead. It's not my first time," she grumbled in her coarse voice.

A scream cut through the air, puncturing the bubble of tension that had been expanding between them. The noise of the crowd that had seemed to diminish as Aki and Hill talked, suddenly flooded back. More screams quickly followed. Screams of fear, screams of surprise. But at the centre of them were screams of an intense and awful anguish. Ripples ran through the crowd, out from the corner farthest from the shuttle platform.

"What's happening?" one of the guards yelled, stepping closer to the fence and peering through the bars. The screams continued to swell, and the crowd fell into a chaotic churn as people pushed against each other, falling and condensing.

New figures appeared in the doorways and windows of the buildings beside the transport centre, creatures coated in shimmering black with twisted limbs and long, chromatic shards protruding from their bodies at random. Robin ran a few paces back, bringing the epicentre of the screams into view. There, at the edge of the crowd, where the screams began and from where they continued to spread. A tangle of bodies writhed on the ground, the glint of multicoloured glass and liquid black just visible amongst the fray.

"The things are here! One of them got into the crowd!" Robin yelled, looking back towards Joyce and Aki with wide eyes. The creature had emerged from the nearby building, silently approaching the crowd from behind. Few had noticed it, and fewer still called out to warn the people that would soon be tackled from behind, its arms held wide as it fell into the crowd.

The few directly touched by the creature started to scream as the sentient fluid spread over them and through them, a sudden anguish as their bodies burned and shrivelled. Skin, flesh, and bone disintegrating and twisting at the whims of an alien invader. The creature raised its arms, reaching to brush its clawed, dripping fingers along anybody it could reach, spreading its infection with the lightest graze. Each new person it touched began to scream in turn as their bodies became host to the spreading liquid. They fell, or tried to turn and move away from the creature, which almost seemed to be melting and spreading along the writhing few who still screamed beneath it.

Two of the guards immediately ran, heading down the fenced pathway towards the elevator platform. Hill watched, shocked, as his companions so quickly abandoned their station. He stammered, spilling syllables to the floor without forming any words. He turned to look at the last remaining guard. Something silent passed between them, and then they ran.

For a moment Aki simply watched the back of the guards, aghast as they made their way down the long path. Joyce's voice calling from behind snapped him back. He turned, ran to the gate, and unfastened the clasp that held the heavy metal

210

panel closed. "Come on, we have to go!" he yelled, catching Robin's attention.

Joyce stepped through the gate with a firm pat on Aki's shoulder, meeting his eyes for a moment before she started to run alongside the fence. Robin passed through and paused, watching as Aki pinned the gate open before joining him. Together, they ran. Joyce held out her arm, a heavy metal tool in her hand, clanging along the bars of the fence. Faces from the other side turned to see Joyce pass, followed by Aki and Robin. Some started running back towards the open gate, but most paid no attention to the sound and only continued to push forwards, against the constraints of the heavy metal bars.

Above, the shuttle was descending towards the city, still small in the distance. The crowd pushed in surges against the fence, but its thick alloy bars held against the combined strength of hundreds. The guards became frantic, screaming and lashing out at those closest to the gate. The black substance continued to spread outward from the far corner, multiplying itself at an exponential rate.

As more of the crowd became aware of what was happening, some started to turn and run away from the platform, out of the Transport Hub and back into the city. A rift began to form between those who continued to push forwards, and those ensnared by the creatures and their infectious tar. Hundreds vacated, launching themselves blindly back into the streets, away from the immediate danger. The flow of escapees thinned as the creatures and the substance that controlled them continued to spread, catching those attempting to flee until soon enough, a spartan wall of writhing, screaming bodies coated in the ever-expanding dark liquid formed a blockade between the two fences. Those who

211

remained in the Transport Hub found themselves locked into a bell-shaped enclosure, the fences on either side too strong to destroy. The guards refused to open the gate, and certain death, pulsating and consuming, was not far behind them.

As all of this occurred, Aki and Robin continued to run, breathing heavily, along the path towards the platform. Many of the guards gathered in the centre of the structure, talking in hushed tones and glancing up towards the approaching shuttle. By the time Aki, Robin and Joyce were climbing the stairs, the shuttle was passing through the airlock above.

"Hey!" Aki shouted, aiming his voice at a particular guard within the crowd. "You have to open the gates!"

Captain Fitch turned towards Aki with a look of pure exasperation. "Mr Isaacs, glad to see you're back safe," he said with a toothy faux grin.

"That stuff is spreading, Fitch. We need to open the gate. Get as many people on the shuttle as possible, and get that fence between us and those things," Aki said, pointing towards the panicked masses beyond the fence, the line of undulating black liquid and twisting bodies not far beyond.

"We will be letting them on the shuttle as soon as it's ready. But we'll let them in when I say," Fitch replied, the grin vanishing, his face turning stony and cold.

Aki faltered, looking to the crowd and back to Fitch, unable to figure out what was happening. Some of the guards were packing away their tools, folding them neatly into heavy bags and cases. "You're all getting ready to leave," Aki said.

A new, unpleasant smile tugged at the corners of Fitch's mouth. He turned and looked to the crowd below, back to his circle of guards, and finally tilted his head up to see the shuttle descending the final few feet to the platform.

"Well, I'd say we've earned our tickets for the ride,

wouldn't you? My crew here have been working tirelessly to get as many people out of the city as possible," Fitch said.

"You've almost got everybody! It'll only take two more trips to get everybody up. We just need to pack in as many as we can, and slow—" Aki's words were cut by a sharp wave of Fitch's hand, like he was cutting the air between them.

"Listen. Far as I can tell, this is going to be the last trip out of here before those lubed-up rot-jobs reach the platform. So I'd advise you to shut the fuck up and get in the shuttle too, unless you're planning to die today," Fitch said, the disconcerting smile lingering on the corners of his mouth.

"There's still a good distance between us and those things. We just need to slow them down enough for one more trip and everybody can get out of here. If the guards—" Aki said, before getting cut off again.

"The guards have had enough casualties already!" Fitch said, spitting the words out with a snarl now, all pretence of polite mannerism abandoned. "Maybe you haven't seen what those things are like, but I don't much rate our chances holding out against them. And it's only a matter of time before that shit up there eats through the dome and then we're all fucked!" He pointed a finger up towards the mass of black ooze coating the dome directly above them.

"You can stay and die if you want, but I'm not throwing my life away to look like a hero when it's so obvious there's no chance of surviving." Fitch lowered his tone as he said these final words, turning his back. The shuttle settled into the platform as he walked away, leaving Aki standing in the middle of the platform, uncertain of what actions to take. He turned, looking for Robin and Joyce. A thin stream of civilians started to appear, those who had noticed the gate Aki had left open. Robin and Joyce stood towards the back of the platform, having pried open a metal first aid cabinet fastened to the wall beside a defibrillator, fire axe, and assorted other health and safety trinkets. Robin held a thin plastic bag in his hand, looking at the small text on the back with focused eyes as Joyce ripped the tape from her arm that had acted as a makeshift bandage.

"Yeah, this is what we use first. Disinfect with that," Robin said, passing the pack to Joyce. "Then use… these bandages." He reached into the container and retrieved another sealed packet. "Oh, wait, there's a canister of coagulant! We should just use that," he said, reaching another hand into the box.

"It ain't that bad, Jesus. Just give me the bandages," Joyce said, wiping her cut with the disinfectant.

Robin put the can back in the first aid box and fumbled with the plastic wrapper. The bandages eventually came loose and he unfurled the end, reaching out to wrap them around Joyce's bleeding arm.

"I've got it, you go check on Akachi," Joyce said, grabbing the roll of bandages from Robin's hands.

"Oh, alright, I guess?" Robin said, reluctant but figuring Joyce wasn't a woman worth fighting with. He turned and saw Aki already approaching and jogged to meet him. "Everything good?" he said, glancing at the open shuttle doors, then back to Aki.

"Yeah, yeah everything good. We can take this next shuttle up." Aki smiled through tired eyes at Robin. "They're going to start loading it up soon, so we should grab seats. You head in and pick some out for us, I'll get Joyce." Aki watched as the guards started to enter the shuttle.

Fitch stood within a small huddle, pointing as he gave orders. Some of the guards seemed to be arguing with him, until a few split off and replaced those who were guarding the gate to the platform.

The crowd on the other side of the fence reached peak frenzy, though much smaller in number with barely a third remaining, many already lost to the mass of writhing creatures that had started to approach, and more lost to the city as they ran away in fright. Some worked to prop each other up, forming rough and uneven human pyramids in the hopes of climbing above the fence, but the jostling of the crowd as it pushed against the bars, and each other, made any attempts to climb too unstable.

Aki realised Robin was watching the crowd with him when he tore his eyes away, both wore deeply sorrowful expressions. Aki tried to smile, to show a confidence that was entirely lacking within him.

"I hope everybody makes it out okay," Robin said.

"So do I," said Aki, looking back to the crowd.

Robin turned and ran towards the shuttle's open doors, with Aki turning to jog towards Joyce, her arm now freshly bandaged. One hand contained a crumble of plastics, bloodied cloth and torn bandaging, which started to reach towards a pocket on her belt before she paused, looked up at the mass of dark liquid writhing on the glass dome above them, and threw it on the floor instead.

"Joyce, you ready to get on the shuttle?" Aki said as he arrived.

Joyce rubbed a hand along the bandage silently for a moment, checking its hold. When she raised her eyes to look at Aki she wore an odd expression. "Guards are leaving, aren't they," she said, a statement more than a question.

Aki scrunched his brow, confused. "Yeah. Yeah, they're leaving on this trip. They said it will be the last one before they reach it," he said, looking towards the row of creatures.

They had started their slow journey across the large stone pavilion, towards the tantalising mass of entrapped screaming flesh at the other end. Joyce gave a solitary nod.

"Look at that crowd. How many trips you think it would take to get them all up?" she asked.

"Just two. This and one more. I told that to the guards but, they don't really seem to care."

"I figured the same. And, those things, how long you think it'll take for 'em to reach us?" Joyce said, crossing her arms.

Aki fell silent for a few seconds as he watched. The black substance now coated the floor in a thick strip. Tendrils had started to appear, still small and thin, along the walls of the buildings that the creatures had emerged from, on the far side of the Transport Hub. Though the substance itself moved slowly, when it commandeered the bodies of those it killed, it seemed to move faster. The creatures' lurching steps were slower than a person, but not by enough. Lines of the black slime trailed behind them like slugs, those strange multicoloured deposits forming and growing like crystalline stalagmites.

"Not long enough," Aki said finally, after watching the creatures advance. "Even with the shuttle moving faster, I don't think it will get here in time without the guards slowing them down."

"I thought the same, 'cept, I never had much faith in the guards in the first place," said Joyce. She started to walk towards the centre of the platform, Aki following alongside her. "You an' Robin get out of here. With any luck, I'll be meeting you there soon enough." She scanned the crowd as she walked.

"What? Joyce, you can't stay," Aki said.

"Like hell I can't. I'm gonna to do what I can to slow those fuckers down and get on that second shuttle. I'm old, and I'm stubborn, and I'm not one to pass up an opportunity to make those guard goons look like fools. I mean it though, you get out of here. I know you've been worried sick about Robin since you lost Adie. You two can be safe. Just make sure they send that shuttle back down again, right?"

Joyce paused to look at Aki, a firm confidence set in her gaze. Then with a nod, she turned and started towards the fence. Aki watched for just a moment, before he ran towards the shuttle.

Guards carried their equipment inside, tucking it into compartments or stacking it along the walls. Some of the seats had been filled by those who came through the side gate, but distressingly few. Aki scanned the rows of seats looking for Robin. "Aki! Here," came Robin's voice from just beside him. Robin sat in one of the seats mounted to the wall of the shuttle, with two empty spaces between him and the door.

Aki fell into the seat beside him, landing awkwardly as the helmet fastened to his belt pushed into him; he'd forgotten it was there. He unhooked it and placed it on his lap, letting out a heavy breath and closing his eyes. The guards began finding seats for themselves.

"Where's Joyce?" said Robin, confusion tinged with concern in his tone.

Aki opened his eyes, but didn't look at Robin right away. "She's not coming," he said, looking at the metal ceiling of the shuttle.

"What? Where is she?" Robin said, the concern rising, leaning forwards in his seat.

Aki turned to look at his friend, meeting his eyes for just a moment. "The guards are leaving. They think this is the last safe shuttle out of the city, but Joyce wants to stay and help get one more. She said we should head up though," Aki said sorrowfully.

Robin looked back, a variety of expressions crossing his face as he comprehended the words and tried to settle his mind. The last few guards had entered the shuttle, a small few either side of the door. One whistled and waved a hand, signalling those who remained to open the gate. An intense clamour came as the terrified civilians outside began to push their way through the opening, steaming towards the shuttle.

"We have to help too." Robin looked at Aki, his face finally set in a look of fearful determination.

"Wait, Robin—" Aki said, but Robin was already moving towards the doors. "Robin!" he yelled, pushing himself from his seat and setting after him. A torrent hit him like a tsunami, panicked and frenzied people rushing in through the doors of the shuttle trying to claim their trip to safety. They very nearly knocked Aki to the floor, but he managed to hold himself upright. Robin had vanished beyond the door just before the inward flood began. Aki pushed forwards, against the tides, but struggled against the force. He focused on moving towards the wall, and once he could tuck himself into the metal he pulled along the handholds, pushed and bumped, but making progress. What should have only taken a few broad steps felt like scaling a mountain as panicked people streamed by him. A guard clung to the wall in front of him, and watched, baffled, as Aki inched his way towards the door.

"Let me out!" he yelled, fruitlessly, at those who worked against him. His left hand tucked his helmet tightly against him, as the right searched for more handholds to help pull across the last small few steps of his journey. As the hand searched, another palm met his own, the guard beside the door clasping and pulling to help him reach the exit, then pushing him from behind as he tried to twist around the tight corner of the door. Bodies crashed into him roughly as they passed in the opposite direction, almost forcing him back into the shuttle, until Robin's hands grabbed at the panels of his suit and pulled hard from the other side and together they fell outward, collapsing to the ground.

They scurried back and picked themselves up from the floor, looking back at the mad torrent beyond. "Are you alright? I'm sorry, I thought you would be right behind me!" Robin said, panting with a panicked, but relieved look in his eyes.

"I was," said Aki. "Then they pushed me back, and I couldn't get back out again. Thanks for helping."

They moved back, farther away from the shuttle as a crowd began to clump around the metal container. The inside had been filled and now the crowds pushed hard, trying to force those inside to compact tighter and tighter together. Some began clambering, trying to climb over the others, like rock stars at a concert, only to fall or get pulled back down. They screamed and yelled and only grew more frantic as the heavy metal doors started to slide shut, severing the tightly packed crowd like a surgeon's scalpel. The crowd bowed out slightly, those fearful of being crushed pushing hard away from the doors, then collapsed back in again as fists banged against the now sealed shuttle and calls for help went unanswered.

Robin scanned the platform, and spotted Joyce in a small gathering away from the chaos. "Aki, come on," he said, patting Aki on the arm and gesturing to the small group. Aki looked back to the crowd for a moment as the shuttle started to lift away, then joined Robin as he ran to meet Joyce.

The small group was made primarily of crew from the mining team, familiar faces Joyce had clearly pulled from the crowd, with a few guards mixed amongst them. "Joyce! We're staying to help!" shouted Robin as they arrived.

Joyce snapped around, looking truly shocked for the first time, though it was quickly replaced with anger. "What in the bloody hell do you two think you're doing!" she yelled, stomping away from her group. "I told you to get out of here you fuckin' idiot!" she said pointedly at Aki, lowering her voice but very much maintaining the angered tone.

Aki flinched back, worried for a moment that she was going to hit him with the way her fists balled at her side. "Aki said you were gonna stay, help the last few. I want to help too," said Robin. "Aki came too, though I didn't really give him much of a choice, now I think about it... Sorry Aki." He turned to look up at him. "You didn't have to come, you know."

Aki shrugged. "To be honest I think I would have stayed down here too if I wasn't worried about getting you up there. But, then you ran off anyway," he said.

Robin frowned. "Why you worryin' about me? I'm exceedingly competent y'know," he said with a smile.

"Well you better be, we'll need plenty of competence and plenty of luck to pull this off," Joyce said, turning back to her gathering.

Aki and Robin joined the loose circle and noticed a variety of tools laid out on the floor between them. All were basic handheld tools, wrenches, plasma cutters and knives. Joyce reached down and took up one of the cutters. It was a device shaped like a shortened cattle prod and a handle with two widely separated points in a U-shape at the end. The tool was typically used to trim metal bolts, or to help break down scaffolding or mining equipment that had rusted or frozen in a planet's atmosphere, standard issue for any of the mining crew heavily involved in the construction and deconstruction of equipment.

"So here's what we've been thinking," Joyce said, holding out the tool for Robin and Aki to observe. "We don't need to fight. We know there's no point trying to kill the things. All we need to do is slow 'em down, right? We could just lock up the gate, but me and Aki saw how quickly they can eat through metal. It'd only hold them back a few minutes. At best."

She took a few steps towards the fence, a few of the group parting to give her room for her demonstration. Aki noticed George was with them. The burly man was watching Joyce intently, arms crossed and clad in his metal padded EVA suit. Joyce looked up at the tall metal bars, stacked vertically beside one another to make the barrier.

"So, we cut it up, get all these bars loose, as we use them to shove the bastards back," she said, tapping on the bolts that connected the bars together with the tool in her hand.

"So… We're making spears?" Robin asked, glancing to Aki.

Joyce looked back at him and bobbed her head to the side slightly.

"I suppose. Won't be sharpening them or anything. We aren't stabbing, just shoving. We keep pushing them back, making sure they're moving as slow as we can keep them."

"How long? Until the shuttle gets back?" said a woman on one side of the circle. She wore casual clothing, but Aki thought he recognised her from the mining crew, though he didn't know her name.

221

"Less than twenty minutes if we're lucky," said one of the few remaining guards. His helmet had been removed and clipped to a carabiner on his belt, his nametag read G. Weaver. "They turned off the limiters a few hours ago, so it's moving pretty fast. It's already on the way up, so, less than twenty? Though, it depends on how long they take unloading it. And, that is assuming they decide to send it back down again at all."

Weaver said the last part with a decidedly mournful tone that dropped the group into an uneasy silence. Worried faces glanced between other members of their circle.

"Don't worry about that," said Aki. "Rob, that's the head of mining. He's up there. He wouldn't let them stop it when there's still a chance of getting people out. I can even talk with him through the terminal there, let him know what's going on." This pulled some of the grief from the faces of the group, though all still clearly had plenty of fear weighing heavily on their shoulders.

"That's right. I've known Rob for decades. If we were going to be trapped down here, he'd sooner die with us than be the one that left us here," said Joyce, nodding to Aki. "Twenty minutes is still a long time, and those things aren't waiting for us. Any o' you who know how to work a plasma cutter, start cutting up that fence. Pile up the bars just behind us."

She looked to one side of the crowd and pointed to Weaver who straightened his stance instinctively under her gaze. "You, guard. Why'd you lot stay? Draw the short straw?" she said, sounding harsh.

"No, ma'am. We all volunteered to stay behind," Weaver said, looking between the few fellow guards scattered in the group. "We argued with the others to stay and help get the

222

last shuttle here safely. There was no stopping them, but a few of us decided we'd stay anyway. We… we didn't want to leave people to die. Not without trying to save them," he said, looking back to Joyce.

She studied him with harsh eyes before nodding. "Suppose there had to be a few of you with a spine, even if you're rare. Alright then, Weaver, you go explain what's happening to that lot," she said, gesturing to the crowd gathered by the empty shuttle bay. "Get any that are willing to help, and make sure the rest know to stay out of the way. The rest of us, we're gonna to grab those iron bars or whatever else we can find, and start slowing those things down."

With that, she threw the tool in her hand to one of the workers across from her, and walked away from the circle with intent. The rest of the plasma cutters were quickly retrieved from the centre of the circle and five sets of hands started cutting at the fence. Two more started unfastening the heavy bolts at the bottom. One of the workers turned back from the fence as her hands continued working. "It will take us a while to get the first few down, look around for anything else you can use in the meantime," she said, looking to the few stragglers left standing uncertain of what to do.

Aki and Robin turned and observed the platform. Joyce was back at the wall of health and safety equipment, one arm full of items taken out of the medical kit, the other carrying the fire axe and what looked like a roll of rubber pipe.

Aki noted the stack of cargo crates on the far side of the platform. "We can check out those crates," Aki said, looking to Robin. "I don't know if there'll be anything useful in them, but it's worth checking." They both jogged to the crates as Joyce dropped her findings on the floor near the edge of the platform.

Weaver stood, straight backed, hands twisting as he talked to the group of civilians by the shuttle as Aki and Robin passed. The group had calmed considerably as they listened to Weaver, faces still fearful, but soothed by the opportunity to focus on something, and to hear people were trying to help.

Aki reached out for the latches on the first crate, straining to flip the sturdy metal lock open. Robin followed his lead, pulling at the second latch, and with two heavy clicks, the top of the crate lifted open. Aki leaned in and looked at the contents. "Nothing in here. Just scraps of ore," he said, turning to the next row of crates. "They'll be stacked in groups, so we just check the front of each row, see what we can find."

They worked down the row, finding little of use in each. "Could use the crates as barricades? They'd last a lot longer than the fence," Robin said, looking at the wide and sturdy metal containers.

"They're too heavy, I think. The crates alone are a lot of weight, and they're all full. If they were empty maybe a few people at a time could move them…" Aki looked over to the crowd, who still listened intently to the guard. A few separated themselves and waited behind him, those who had volunteered to help push back the creatures. "Hang on, keep checking the crates, I'll be back in a minute," Aki said to Robin, before running to the group. "Hey! Weaver right? I have a job for some people to fill. See those crates over there? I need people to empty them out. Most of them are full of junk, just metal ingots or lumps of unprocessed ore. If we get them emptied out, it'd take maybe four or five people to move the crates. Barricades don't last long against these things, but it's better than nothing."

"That's a good idea, I'll figure out the details. Thanks," Weaver said with a nod. Aki returned the nod, and ran back to the crates. Robin saw him approaching and dropped a dark silver lump of metal, walking back to one of the crates he had checked after Aki left.

"Here, this one could be useful," Robin said, reaching inside and pulling out a thin iron rod. "They're not as long as the fence posts, so they won't last long, or be as safe. But there are a lot of them, and they're better than nothing."

Aki took the iron rod. It was heavy, about four feet long and two inches thick. He held it at the end and mimed a pushing motion, struggling to hold the weight outright for more than a second.

"They'll work for now, good find!" he said, tucking the bar under his arm and reaching into the crate for more. Aki and Robin carried a few dozen of the bars between them, enough that the weight made their muscles burn and tingle at the strain. The bars made a heavy, reverberating series of clangs as they dropped to the floor. The pile Joyce had started with the axe and medical equipment had grown slightly, and now contained loose bricks and an assortment of plastic and thin metal bars that had been the handles of mops and brooms.

Joyce picked up one of the iron bars, feeling the weight in her hand and looking around her as others reached for their own. Some tentative, still afraid of what was to come, others almost eager. Beyond the fence, across the long stretch of stone paving, the creatures were fully set in their march towards the shuttle platform. Half of the pavilion was now thickly coated in the spreading, shimmering ooze, following the trails left behind by its puppeteered corpse vehicles.

Joyce was the first to step through the gate and begin walking towards the creatures, but was quickly joined by a small platoon of miners, civilians, and the few remaining guards. Aki and Robin walked side by side, sensing each other's tension. "This must be just like some of your old films," Aki said, glancing to Robin, who let out a soft chuckle.

"Yeah, I'd been thinking that," Robin replied, looking up to Aki. "You know something? I always thought fighting zombies'd be fun. I've literally fantasised about situations like this. But here we are, running towards a load of shambling, undead, infectious abominations. And I'm absolutely shittin' myself."

Aki smiled. "I mean, they're not really zombies though, right? They're just, goo. So it doesn't really count."

"They're close enough. They're goo zombies," Robin said.

"Gombies," said Aki.

"Goombies?" said Robin. Both of them were smiling now, somehow. Terrified, but happy to have each other in an insane situation.

The running began to slow as they came ever closer to the jagged line of marching creatures they faced, stopping with a few feet between them and the closest creature. For a few seconds, nobody dared to do anything. Just stood frozen, now faced with the terrible things. The closest of them still looked mostly human. No missing limbs, its head intact, but any defining features had vanished. Its face was entirely buried in thick, sparkling liquid, and shards of multicoloured crystal. Whatever clothes it may have once worn were gone, the black liquid squirting along the surface of its torso and burrowing beneath the skin. The creature took long, sturdy steps, carrying it faster than most of those behind it. It lurched closer with a wide sweeping step and shuddered to a halt for a moment before swinging the other leg forward in another deep lunge.

A man stepped forwards, quickly swinging his metal rod at the creature's bent knee. The knee buckled inward, causing the creature to spin and collapse to the ground. The pipe flung small globules of the black liquid sideways, but the weight of the substance pulled it quickly to the ground. The man stepped back and Aki saw it was George, his dark orange EVA suit and his towering size making the distinction obvious. The tip of his metal rod now featured a few inches of shimmering black liquid coating. He held the rod forward, watching as thin tendrils began to form, the liquid preparing to climb the rest of the way.

Joyce took a step and jabbed her hand forward, an inelegant attempt at fencing with her heavy metal staff. The tip of the metal contacted hard with the brow of a creature, snapping its head back and sending it falling to crack onto the floor with a thick slap of viscous liquid.

More stepped forward, increasingly emboldened, using their makeshift batons to push the creatures back. Each creature writhed, struggling for a moment, eventually finding its way awkwardly to its feet. The tall creature that George had hit adopted a strange waning limp as it walked, swaying with each step on its shattered leg. The liquid held their bodies together even when broken, but the damage slowed their inexorable approach.

Aki placed his bar on the head of a creature and pushed it back to collapse on the floor. Robin pushed on the sternum of another and sent it tumbling on top, entangling the two in a writhing indiscernible mess of twisted limbs, glistening black liquid and shimmering pointed shards.

"Keep an eye on the floor!" called Joyce, her voice projecting loud for all to hear. "We can push back the bodies, but the shit on the floor keeps coming! Step back!" Everybody looked down to see that the dark, shimmering substance was indeed continuing to spread along the floor. It moved much slower than the creatures were able to, but they had no way of slowing it or making it retreat. Collectively, the group took a step back and prepared for the creatures again.

"Keep an eye on your tools too," yelled George, gruff and displeased. The black substance coated nearly half of the rod he held, and continued to creep towards his hand. He stepped forward and jammed the bar into the mouth of a creature harshly, letting the bar go as it fell. "I'll bring more back," he said as he turned and started to run towards the fence.

The line continued their defence, pushing at each new creature that approached. A man on the far side of the line pushed forwards with a harsh jab, hitting a creature under the jaw and forcing its head up. With a wet snap, the head spun backwards and fell to the floor, the body left behind, rocking, but regaining its footing and continuing forwards.

The man stood, shocked in place for a moment. Another pulled him back, stepping in place and swinging their bar hard, hitting at the shoulder of the creature and sending it crumbling to the floor. The arc of the bar through the air sent clumps of the glistening liquid flinging up. A woman in casual clothing stepped forwards to push at one of the creatures, stepping directly into the path of the droplets, one small dark orb landing on her collarbone.

Instantly, she dropped her iron bar and began to scream. The line broke, separating as the surrounding defenders tried to distance themselves from the screams. All eyes turned to look at the woman and saw as she tried to wipe the substance away, spreading more of the viscous black to her hands where it shrivelled flesh and dripped to the floor, a few specks landing on her legs. The line retreated further, the fighting paused, horrified eyes watching as one of their own succumbed to the enemy. The liquid ate its way into the woman's torso, turning her screams to wheezes when it punctured her lungs and explored the cavity within.

More screaming began, from the other side of the row this time. A man had dropped his iron rod to the ground, nearly the entire thing was coated in black. The substance had made its way to his hand as he watched the woman screaming, taking advantage of his distraction. He turned, the screams dimming into a shocked, agonised silence.

Wide-eyed and mouth agape, looking to those around him for help as his bones and flesh shrivelled away. He staggered forwards, trying to form words, but those around him stepped back away. He stepped forwards again, trying to catch up with the people that retreated from him. Behind the row of defenders, metallic chimes rang out as George arrived with a large stash of metal fence posts under each arm, his face red and covered in sweat. He stepped towards the man and with a strong kick to the ribs, launched him into the row of creatures.

The man collided with them, sending one clattering to the ground beneath him. His screams returned with a new intensity, but faded quickly as the pool of dark shimmering ooze surrounding took over. George turned back and reached for one of the metal bars he had dropped to the floor.

"What are you waiting for? Get back to it!" he said, gruffly, as he turned to see most of the crowd watching him. George lifted the long bar seemingly with ease, took a few steps forward and launched it violently into the closest creature, which flung back a few feet before collapsing heavily to the ground.

Those closest discarded their small iron bars, throwing them into the row of creatures, and instead retrieved the fence posts. Despite their much greater size, the posts proved to be

229

lighter than expected. Lighter even than the dense iron bars they had previously used. They were hollow within, made from a very strong but light metal alloy. The new tools helped enormously at holding the creatures back.

The group grew in confidence. So long as the creatures were slowed, the ooze would only make slow progress as it crept along the ground. Quickly they fell into a routine. A pattern of motions, repeating to keep the creatures at bay. Pushing them back, watching the seeping tar as it crept along the floor and taking one long step back when it grew too close. The system was working. Now they just had to hope it bought them enough time, and that the elevator shuttle would return to save them.

Chapter 23

Rob sat, eyes fixed on the monitor before him. His fingers interlocked, his thumbs twisting anxiously as he watched the events unfolding below. A group in the Transport Hub were forming a line, seemingly preparing to fight the creatures that inched towards them. Many within the crowd were his friends, faces he'd worked with for decades, and now he was watching from hundreds of kilometres away, powerless to help. He had seethed with rage upon seeing so many of the guards abandoning the platform. Captain Octavia had done all she could to dampen his anger. Despite her calm demeanour, he sensed a touch of it within her as well. She had departed shortly after, intending to meet with the guards as they arrived.

The Mayor had been missing for some time, though Rob hadn't spared a thought for the man since he left. He only became aware of how long he'd been gone when he finally re-entered the control room, a spring in his step. Markus's head darted around the room as he walked, arriving beside Rob and peering through the window down to the equipment bay below. "I hear the last shuttle has arrived! Are we ready to set our plan into motion?" he said, eyes near-glistening as he observed the bomb hanging like ripe fruit from the robotic arm outside the ship.

Rob leaned back in his seat, pointing a stern glower at the Mayor who turned to look expectantly. "There's still one more trip to make. The last batch are waiting," he said, gesturing to the monitor.

The Mayor looked at the screen and watched for a few seconds. The camera feed showed a row of civilians standing against an army of the slime-coated creatures. It looked to him like a preposterous line dance was about to begin. He couldn't make out precisely what they were doing from the distance of the camera, but he could see that the creatures outnumbered the humans by a substantial number.

"You must be kidding, right? They're clearly a lost cause," Markus said, looking back to Rob, his eager demeanour vanishing in an instant. Rob sat silent, his fingers tightening around each other so much it hurt. His eyes didn't leave the Mayor's as he went on, "Look at them! Our very best guards have succumbed to these creatures, how do you think they expect to defeat these things? We're not even sure they can be killed?" Markus yelled, flailing an arm in the direction of the screen.

Rob extended one pointed finger from his knotted hands. "They don't need to kill them. Just need to slow 'em, until the shuttle gets back down," he said, tapping at his terminal twice and bringing the conflict closer to view on the monitor above.

"Ridiculous. You think they can, what? Just keep prodding them with sticks and that will slow them down long enough?" Markus said.

"I think they can do exactly that, aye. The shuttle will already be on its way back down, they don't have long to wait," Rob said, sounding supremely confident as he looked at the faces of his friends on the monitor.

"The shuttle won't be going back down," said Markus, voice cold and factual. He straightened himself as Rob's gaze turned from the monitor to meet his eyes again.

"What do you mean?" Rob asked.

"There will be no shuttle. I told the operators as much myself. We've given them more than enough time," Markus replied, tilting his shoulders back and his nose up as he talked.

Rob unclasped his hands and pushed to his feet, turning to face Markus directly. "There are good people down there. My friends are down there. We are not abandoning them!" he snarled through gritted teeth.

Markus's face started to flush red, affronted to be argued with once again. "Your friends do not take priority over the safety of everybody we already have aboard! We need to drop that bomb now and—"

"Nobody is dropping that thing until we have saved everybody we can!" Rob yelled, stepping closer to Markus.

"I am the Mayor of this ship and I decide when it's the right time!" Markus yelled, face burning hot.

"And I am the Captain," came Octavia's voice, projected firmly from the room's entrance. She had entered unnoticed and walked towards them, the door still sliding closed behind her. She glanced between the two men, face stern. "What, may I ask, is this altercation relating to?" she said, coming to a stop before them.

"The last few at the Transport Hub. He's trying to stop the shuttle going back for 'em," Rob said, glaring at Markus with firm and vicious anger.

"We don't have time to save everyone! It is imperative that we protect those already onboard and drop that bomb!"

Markus rushed out, as though trying to overwrite Rob's words.

"As the Mayor of the city, your counsel will be noted and considered. But you have no jurisdiction on matters such as this. I have the final say," Octavia said, holding her eyes on Markus for a moment before looking to Rob. "How are they doing? Can we be certain it's safe to extract the remaining survivors?"

Rob stepped back, placing a hand on the chair behind to support his weight; his knee was beginning to ache again. He gestured with the other hand to the monitor. "They're setting up defences. Holding those things back. They can make it. And if anything goes wrong, we'll see it from here, and you can make a call," he said, watching Octavia, trying to read her thoughts.

Octavia studied the monitor, watching how the civilians below worked together to keep the creatures at bay. Behind them, a group were constructing barricades. They seemed well organised, given the situation they were in. "We don't leave anyone behind unless absolutely necessary. I'll see to it the shuttle is returned," she said finally, turning to walk back out of the room.

Markus's hand shot out and grabbed her by the arm tightly. She turned and saw him leaning towards her with hateful eyes.

"Think about this, Octavia. Think about the choice you're making," he said, speaking with a hiss.

"I know precisely what I'm deciding, Markus. I suggest you prepare to explain what happened here. We'll be departing the system as soon as we have those people back on this ship," Octavia said, pulling her arm free, and walking briskly out of the room.

Chapter 24

Since George had arrived with the makeshift spears, the plan to delay the creatures had worked perfectly.

The tar-covered things had been kept at a considerable distance, and the viscous substance was condemned to crawling along the raw stone floor at its slow pace without the aid of its reanimated companions. Even so, they had lost a lot of ground. The black slime was slow, but inexorable in its progress. It crept ever-forwards, yearning to reach those who defied it. And some of the creatures had begun to act strangely.

Once the routine had proven successful, a few of the disfigured creatures had paused in their pursuits, standing back behind the line of lunging things like curious observers. They had yet to do anything to raise alarm, but their lack of action brought a sense of fresh unease to any who noted them. An unease that was validated, when they began to move again.

Split into two small groups, the creatures staggered parallel to the rows of clashing combatants. They aimed themselves directly at the fenced-in walkways that had previously kept the guards separate from the crowd.

"What are they doing?" yelled Aki, watching as the creatures pressed themselves against the metal bars. They pushed their bodies against the fence, their arms slipping through the gaps, and spread the black substance along each bar, where it started to eat its way through the thin metal.

"Oh piss. They're breaking through the fence!" Joyce yelled. She shoved the creature in front of her hard, then threw her metal bar forwards, discarding it into the black ooze. She stepped back and walked at a speedy pace along the row, singling out three individuals either side. Both groups dropped their spears and turned to run towards the platform behind them. Much of the fence close to the platform had now vanished, dismantled into a pile of loose metal bars stacked beside it. A row of large metal crates was forming a shallow wall, half complete, with a group struggling to carry another crate to add to the row.

The creatures continued their push forwards, those defending against them spreading thinner to make up for those that departed. More of the creatures stepped through the fresh holes burrowed into the fences, and began to stumble their way down the undefended pathways on the other side. The teams that Joyce had sent away ran to meet them, but not before the creatures had gained a few feet of progress.

The creatures were slowed again, but the black ooze began to seep inward, back through the fences towards the defensive row in the centre of the pavilion, forcing them to retreat and surrender those few feet of ground entirely. They used the short time to breathe, a rest of just a few moments, but one they welcomed despite the concern of losing a significant portion of ground.

Aki's metal bar was getting close to unusable. The black substance had not dissolved any of it, but it had crawled its way down the majority of its length, and would reach his hands soon. He looked back at the stash of weapons George had brought and noticed them dwindling. "We need somebody to bring us more of the fence posts!" he yelled, looking towards Joyce.

She looked to him, and then to the few posts remaining on the floor behind them. Even with the longer fence posts as their defensive tools, the oily substance would eventually eat through them. The bar she used had shrunken notably since she first picked it up, and half of what remained was painted in crawling ink. Everybody would need to replace theirs soon.

Joyce studied those on either side of her, each with their own spears in varying levels of disrepair. The substance ate at some, but not all, seemingly at random. It crept its way down each and every one, eager to reach the hands that held the other end of the bar. Aki's was one of the worst. "You go, Aki! Bring as many as you can manage, and ask somebody up there to start topping us up."

Aki nodded to her, placed the tip of his metal spear against the head of a creature and shoving hard, letting the bar fall away with it to land in the pool of creeping ooze below. As soon as the bar left his hands he turned towards the platform. The distance was much smaller now than when they had started. He hadn't noticed just how much ground they had lost. If it wasn't for their efforts slowing the creatures, the platform would surely be overrun by now. Not far into his run he reached the barricade of crates, now completed, and had to clamber over the wall on his way. Very little of the fence now remained, turned to a sizable pile of spears for them to use. More of the heavy metal crates had been stacked along the edge of the shuttle platform, leaving a gap at the top of the stairs with more crates to the side ready to block them too.

Aki ran up the stairs and saw a crate carried between a group of six moving towards the platform's edge. "Hey! Can you spare somebody to carry these pipes out for us to use?" he said, only realising how out of breath he was once the words had spilled weakly from his mouth. He leaned against a container and took a few deep breaths.

Five of the group seemed to look towards one member, expecting their answer rather than offering any of their own. "Yeah, we can manage that," said the sixth.

"Great! Oh, and those side paths," Aki said, pointing to the fenced in pathways. "Do you think you can block them off too? It should only take two or three crates."

"You guys good to start on that whilst I find somebody to carry those bars?" the sixth said, turning her head to each member of the group, who nodded in response. The group shuffled and redistributed the weight, now one member short, then continued to the edge of the platform as Aki ran to the pile of makeshift spears. He lifted as many as he could, quickly realising that, though they were lighter than the iron rods he and Robin had carried from the crates, they soon became a lot to handle. He lowered his expectations, dropping a few of the bars and started his way back to the defensive row, amazed at the number George had been able to carry on his own. When he reached the wall of crates again, he dropped the bars atop the blockade and climbed over. There was little distance between the wall of crates and the creatures now. Aki realised he had no idea how long they had been holding the creatures back.

A huge amount of ground had been covered, the ravenous ooze now claiming the majority of the Transport Hub. In the distance, the buildings of the connected streets were almost entirely black, covered in the dark tendrils. He looked up, much of his view blocked by the substance coating the exterior of the dome. But between patches of probing tendrils of liquid, still far in the distance, he could see the shuttle rocketing its way back down towards them.

"Just ten more minutes!" he yelled as he arrived back at the defensive wall. He handed a spear to Robin, and another to Joyce, then took up position to help hold the creatures back again.

"How do you know?" asked Robin, his face damp with sweat.

"The shuttle's on its way down," Aki said, watching as Robin and a few others around them looked up for just a moment.

"Feels like we've been at this a lot longer than ten minutes," said Robin.

"We have. They took their bloody time sending it back down again," said Joyce, a vendetta clear in her tone. They fell quickly into routine, pushing the creatures back, and retreating a step every time the black ooze drew close on the ground. Somebody began to bring them a constant supply of the fence bars. By the time they found themselves close to the wall of crates, Aki's bar was nearly ready to be discarded yet again, shrunk to half its original length.

"We have to hop the crates," Aki said, seeing some

239

further down the row already starting to do so.

"You first, you need a new spear. Mine's alright," Robin said, looking back at him. Robin's fence post had barely been affected despite picking it up at the same time as Aki. The substance was persistently unpredictable in a way that Aki found unnerving. He threw his spear, then turned and hopped over the barricade and picked up a new bar from the pile atop the crates. He looked up again as Robin started to climb over, and saw the shuttle much closer now. "It's almost here!" he yelled.

A cheer rang out along the row, those on the platform behind joining in as they all saw how close they were to victory. Aki turned and smiled to Robin who smiled in return. Joyce climbed the crates and landed beside Robin, turning and patting him hard on the back as she did. "You're doing good lads," she said, picking up a new spear of her own.

They turned back to the creatures, free to rest for a few moments until the things stumbled in range of their weapons again. Aki focused, his fingers tightening on the metal bar as confidence swelled in him.

Robin let out a yelp, dropping his spear. Aki turned and saw Robin, staring at his hand, black liquid coating his fingertips.

Robin snapped wide, shocked eyes to Aki. Joyce saw black trickling from the bar on the floor. A tendril reaching out from a hole that had formed in the base where Robin's hands had been. The outside of the bar was pristine, but the hollowed interior was filled with the stuff. Robin let out a scream as the liquid began to eat into his fingers.

Aki watched, not sure what to do. Robin fell to one

knee, clutching his wrist and watching as the colour was sapped from the flesh of his fingers. Aki started to look around, searching for anything he could do to help, but his mind became an overwhelmed, tangled mess. Robin's shocked eyes etched into his mind, and brought forth the memories of Adie, falling into the pit. Those impossible eyes that he surely couldn't have seen, but that felt so real and burned so fiercely within him.

The black reached the knuckles of Robin's hand, one finger dropping free entirely, and landing on the floor as an unidentifiable pile of dark mulch. A tendril started to reach down into the palm of his hand, each movement of the substance sending burning shots of pain through his arm and paralysing him.

Aki had vanished within himself. His awareness lost to a fog of fear and despair, the thought of losing both of his best friends, his family, enough to shred the core of him beyond repair. He was only dimly aware of what he was seeing, and barely registered when he heard his name. He heard Adie's voice, calling him again just as it had the previous night that now felt like years ago. The call came again, the voice shifting, and pulling him from his fugue as he turned his gaze to its source. Joyce was storming towards him.

"Aki, move!" she yelled. Aki stumbled back a few paces, looking back down to Robin who watched in despair as his hand shrivelled away. Joyce's hand shot into view, grabbing his forearm and slamming it firmly on the wall of crates. She took a step back, raised her arms, and swung down heavily, dropping the fire axe onto Robin's arm, just below the wrist.

The axe severed flesh and bone, then bounced hard as

it hit against the metal of the container below. Robin fell backwards, collapsing to the ground as though the force of the axe had pushed him away. Joyce threw the axe to the floor and grabbed him firmly by the jacket, yanking hard and dragging him along the floor and away from the crates.

"What the fuck…" Robin said, his voice lost in shock as he looked at where his hand should be, spurts of blood shooting from the end with each quickened beat of his heart. Joyce grabbed his arm again and retrieved a metal cylinder that had been jammed into a far-too-small pouch on her belt.

"This is gonna hurt," she said, using a thumb to flick the cap open. The can of coagulant spray burst a gush of white, dense foam over the stump at the end of Robin's arm.

"Fuck!" he yelled, as the foam began to burn and sting. "Oh fuck!" He tried to pull the arm away, but Joyce gripped his arm firmly and wouldn't let him leave.

"Aki, come here!" Joyce yelled, looking back to him. "It's alright lad, you're gonna to be good. Just give it a minute," she said, turning back to Robin, who had stopped struggling but grimaced at the pain.

Aki dropped to his knees next to him, grabbing at Robin's loose arm like he was worried he would float away. "Shit, Robin, I'm so sorry, I just froze up, I didn't know what to do," Aki said, eyes darting around Robin, looking for any dark patches on his clothes.

"You don't need to be sorry," Robin said through gritted teeth. "I wouldn't have known what to do either. Thankfully we have lumberjack Joyce over here," he said, smiling for a moment before a wince shocked it from his face.

"That'll do," Joyce said, wiping the white foam away with a cloth and holding it up to observe for a moment before finally releasing his arm. Robin looked at his wrist. A cloudy, semi-transparent gel coated the end of his arm where the foam had settled, the flesh around and beneath a bright red from the heat.

"Are you alright?" asked Aki, observing the wrist.

"Well, I'm in a lot o' pain. But on the plus side, I can slap a chainsaw on there and be just like Ash Williams now. Maybe poke an eye out, get a whole Ash-meets-Snake-Plissken-thing going on," Robin smirked at Aki, beads of sweat covering his face.

"Robin, I don't know who either of those people are," said Aki, smiling through his concern.

The creatures arrived at the crates, placing their hands atop the surface and pausing in their march as the black substance spread out from their hands along the metal.

"Aki, get him up the platform. He won't be able to walk steady for a bit," Joyce said, reaching to help pull Robin from the floor. Together they pulled Robin to his feet where he wavered dizzily.

"I do feel… real light headed," he said, blinking hard.

"You lost a fair bit of blood, and that kind of pain will throw you off," said Joyce, letting go as Aki gained a firm grip on Robin.

"You gonna be okay?" Aki asked, looking to Joyce

"I'll be okay when we're off this bloody planet. Luckily, that won't be long," she said, glancing up. The shuttle was right above them now, about to pass through the airlock and into the city.

"You two get up there and wait to get in, we'll slow 'em

down until the shuttle's open, just to be safe," Joyce said, picking up a fresh metal bar and turning from them, back towards the row of creatures that waited for the crates to dissolve.

Aki and Robin started walking together, climbing the stairs to the shuttle platform as the automated voice announcing the shuttle's arrival played through the speakers ahead. A small group waited at the top of the stairs, watching the events below. A larger crowd gathered, eager to enter the shuttle, occasionally looking back as though worried the creatures would sneak up on them at any moment. The final doors of the airlock above opened with a high pitched whine, and the shuttle started its final descent towards the platform. "That's a welcome sight," Robin said, his voice sounding optimistic in spite of his weary state.

"It certainly is. No doubt we have Rob to thank," Aki said, watching the large metal capsule descend the thick tether towards them.

Faces amongst the crowd began to look together with the spark of hope returned to their eyes. Thankful words were shared between friends that had arrived together, or those who had only met that day and forged a bond as they worked together to survive. A small ripple of laughs rolled through the crowd as one man let out a high pitched whoop of pure joy.

The shuttle arrived, settled in place, and its doors opened wide. The crowd rushed in, eager to feel the embrace of the safety its cold metal walls promised. Aki stepped into the doorway, carrying Robin with him, a wave of relief burrowing to his core at the sensation. Aki scanned the shuttle, relieved to see plenty of seating still available, and noticed Robin looking backwards.

Aki looked back through the doors, over the shuttle platform and towards the city. The Column, the thick tower at the centre of the city, bisected the scene cleanly in two. To the right of the tower the dome was entirely black, the buildings beneath encased in the liquid and beginning to fall apart. The other half of the city was not quite as decayed, tendrils plentiful, but still spreading.

The early morning sun and bright sky was still visible through the glass of the dome, though streaked with dark scars, like the claws of a great beast ensnaring its prey.

Columns of smoke rose from between the buildings with dark and shimmering vines climbing their walls. Those closest to the hospital were coated entirely, leaving only a streak of buildings near the centre of the city that had yet to be entirely claimed. It wouldn't be long before those were consumed too.

At the edge of the platform, figures started to emerge. Those who had worked with Robin and Aki to delay the creatures were now climbing the platform stairs to join them. The first few ran, though most struggled with a jog, exhausted after their battle of attrition with the creatures they left behind. George and Joyce were some of the last to appear, moving at an almost casual pace. Joyce was showing signs of wear for the first time since this ordeal had begun. The woman was strong, but clearly needed rest desperately. Aki watched them, endlessly grateful to Joyce for the role she played today.

A resounding, dry crack reverberated from the glass panels of the dome and filled the air around them. A heavy rumble rocked the ground, and a sudden shift beneath their feet made Aki's stomach lurch, like the entire planet had moved. Aki and Robin stumbled, bracing on the wall of the shuttle behind them. A few stumbled and fell on the platform, Joyce almost joining them until George caught her arm and helped her stay upright.

The ground stabilised, and a chorus of smaller cracks and pinging sounds rang out in the distance. Joyce and George turned, looking towards the city, just in time to see one of the large glass panes begin to fall away from the dome above the Industrial sector. A trail of viscous stringy black followed, clinging to the edges and dripping from the frame. A heavy whoosh of air like a distant tornado began to whistle across the city as the air in the city met the alien air outside.

"Run!" Aki yelled, as the glass panel collided with the buildings below, crushing the top two floors before sliding free. George and Joyce were already rushing towards the shuttle, and those who had fallen were scrambling to their feet and sprinting towards the doors. Behind, a second panel started to fall, the glass twisting and turning, one side painted in shimmering black. Another started to fall before the first had hit the ground.

Aki helped Robin to a seat as the roar of churning air was growing outside, along with the crash of gigantic glass panels crushing the buildings beneath them and slamming hard into the ground. He ran back to the door and grabbed the lever to start their escape, and watched as Joyce and George continued running, a growing rain of chaos in the distance as the city fell in upon itself.

His fingers tightened on the lever. He could feel the sensation of wind caressing his face, the helmet clipped to his belt started to rock as the air grew uneven and flowed past him. George tucked his arm under Joyce's own and launched forwards, flinging them both across the border of the shuttle and collapsing to the floor.

Aki pulled the lever down, stepping back and watching the city fall to pieces as the doors slid closed. In the last moment, just before the gap was sealed shut, he saw the slime coated creatures beginning to climb the steps of the platform across from them. A tall, bulky figure was at the front, its empty eye sockets pointed towards the doors, somehow menacing despite its lack of expression.

For the briefest of moments, a glimpse of shimmering red caught the light, and then the doors pressed together with a hiss.

Aki turned from the doors and ran to Joyce, helping her to her feet as George pushed himself from the floor. Both found seats and settled, exhausted, among the mass of nervous faces. The sounds of the motor above started, and the shuttle rocked and vibrated as it lifted from the ground. Aki walked back to Robin, eager to fall into the seat and wait for the ordeal to be over.

"Helmet," Robin said.

Aki stood, looking at him confused for a moment. Robin pointed at the helmet still hanging from the back of Aki's belt.

"Oh, yeah. Thanks," Aki said, unclipping the helmet before he sat down. He landed in the seat, thankful for the soft cushions even through his metal panelled EVA suit. He let his eyes close and leaned his head back against the chair, feeling the rocking of the shuttle shaking him gently as it lifted towards the airlock.

The voices within the shuttle fell away, a collective

held breath. Outside, the muted sounds of destruction continued to ring out as the dome collapsed and the city fell to pieces, and then the noises came to a sudden stop when the airlock sealed around them. A few moments, the hiss of pressurisation, and the metal churn of the airlock opening, and they were on their way again, finally out of the city. The turbulence of the shuttle built as it increased its speed.

"Hey Aki," came Robin's voice, close to a whisper from beside him.

"Yeah?" Aki asked, turning to look at his friend.

Robin leaned back in his chair, the wrist of his right hand tucked into his armpit like the missing hand was cold. Aki felt a pang of regret when he remembered what had happened to Robin.

"What do we do if that stuff got on the outside of the shuttle?" Robin said, looking to Aki with serious eyes. His voice was more curious than scared, but he talked low, trying to keep anybody else from hearing. Aki looked at him for a while, thinking.

"I'm not sure there's anything we can do," he said, eventually. "I think… we just have to wait and see. Our part in all of this is done."

Robin nodded and leaned his head back into his chair. The motor at the top of the shuttle whirred angrily as it ferried them up towards The Vaughn's Outer-Ring, the pull of gravity already growing weaker. The chatter of voices eased into the wide metal container as people grew more secure in their escape. A few faces spoke of the discomfort the heavy turbulence caused them, eyes knotted tightly shut and breathing deep, slow breaths.

Minutes passed, the gravity continuing to diminish

as the shuttle passed out of the planet's atmosphere. "Hey, Aki," Robin said again, the expression he held much softer now.

Aki turned his head, opening his mouth to reply, when a vicious shudder rocked the shuttle, throwing people hard into the sides of their seats. An unpleasant squeal pierced the air from the motor above them, and another heavy crash shook the shuttle and its terrified contents.

Screams and curses were shared amongst the passengers as the shaking seemed to settle, a few more small bumps and clangs from the metal walls before an uneasy stillness fell upon them all. Aki found his heart racing, breathing heavily. Robin's hand had appeared in his own, he wasn't sure if he had taken it or Robin had reached out for him first. They clung together for a moment, waiting in the silence for anything more to happen. The shuttle sat, silent, the whirring electrical buzz of the motor no longer present.

"Are we back on the ship?" came a lone voice called out from a seat on the far side of the shuttle.

"No. We should still have a little way to go," said Aki, looking towards the terminal beside the door.

"But, we've stopped moving."

Chapter 25

Rob sat, watching the monitor thoughtlessly. The screen had long turned dark, the feed cut as the city collapsed. He had been watching as the last few survivors rushed towards the shuttle, a number of his friends among them. The last thing he'd seen before the screen turned dark was the last few falling on their way to the doors.

He was fairly certain Joyce had been at the back. He told himself she would be fine, he'd seen Joyce go through plenty in the past. She always bounced back. She was too stubborn to let anything get in her way. That had always been what got them in so much bother, they were both simply too stubborn.

Enough of the under-city had dissolved that it could no longer sustain the weight of the buildings above, causing a large section of the city to collapse. The dome began falling shortly after, the heavy panels crushing whatever lay below. It was safe to assume that everyone hiding in the city was dead, or would be very soon. He dreaded to think quite how many it was. How many of his friends and colleagues must have been down there. Still, the shuttle had arrived, and he knew it was on its way. Aki, Robin, and Joyce, were on their way to safety. That was something. Now he simply sat in his chair, awaiting news of their safe arrival.

Mayor Markus had taken up a seat in the corner of the room, distancing himself from Rob, but reluctant to leave entirely. He tapped at his tablet incessantly, occasionally grunting and grumbling to himself as he worked. Octavia had eventually returned to the control room and, after confirming the shuttle was on its way, had settled by the large windows looking into the equipment bay. She retrieved her small metal token and proceeded to twist it between each finger methodically, occasionally tapping her ear and speaking a few brief words.

They had been in this state for some time when Octavia again reached to her ear, her demeanour shifting heavily. "What do you mean? What happened?" she said, her voice snappy and concerned.

Markus and Rob both looked towards her, ears perked to hear what was happening. Markus placed his tablet on the chair beside him and pushed up to cross the room.

"I see. Yes, let me know any further details. I'll get back to you," she said, tapping the earpiece and turning to Rob. "We have an issue. The shuttle has stalled, a few miles yet from the ship."

"What? What happened to it?" Rob asked.

"It seems the substance somehow ate through the tether. The sudden slack caused a heavy jolt, and has either decoupled or damaged the pulley system atop the shuttle," Octavia said.

"Oh for Christ's sake! How many delays are we intended to endure? Just tell them to hurry and pull the bloody thing in!" burst Markus, flailing his arms and pacing.

"It's not as simple as that," said Octavia, giving Markus a moment to regain his focus, and looking to Rob. "The cable

251

can't just be retracted on its own. And without knowing exactly what state the shuttle is in, we don't know how long it could take to repair. The majority inside the shuttle have no protective equipment, so we have no way of retrieving them externally from the shuttle."

Rob reached for his cane and drummed his fingers along the handle. "Bollocks. We'll need to get a crew together," he said, after a moment of consternation.

"I'll leave you to pick out some engineers, you will know who's best suited to the work," Octavia said.

"You have to be kidding. How long will this take, exactly?" Markus said, crossing his arms.

Rob looked back at him with a scowl. "It'll take as long as it bloody takes. It depends on what the issue is. Hopefully it'll be an easy fix. But if it's a busted motor, with the time to put a crew together, get them suited up and flying a couple o' miles to reach the shuttle, we're looking at a few hours at least."

"Hours!" Markus yelled. "We don't have fucking hours!"

"Markus! Rob has been the head of every operation that has taken place on this ship for the last thirty years. He does not take commands from you, not today," Octavia said, a rare burst of unbridled anger and irritation in her usually even tone.

Markus glared back, hands balling into fists and face flooding with burning red. Rob looked back at the man with disgust, then pushed himself to his feet, leaning on his cane.

"I'll start grabbin' the crew, and I'll make you a list of some preparations we'll be needin'," Rob said, before being roughly shoved from behind. Rob's cane slipped and his bad leg buckled under him as he fell forwards hard. Octavia's eyes widened and she shot forwards, reaching out to catch him, landing hard on one knee with Rob sprawled awkwardly in her arms. Markus stepped into the space before Rob's chair, swiping at the terminal, trying to remember the steps he had seen Octavia take earlier.

"Markus! What are you doing?" Octavia yelled, watching with terror as he loomed over the terminal.

Rob scrambled to raise back to his feet, lifting his weight from the Captain and spun around, lunging forwards to grab at the Mayor who tapped at the screen one final time. Markus stepped away from the screen, unintentionally avoiding Rob's grasping hands. Rob looked at the man with confusion, then to the monitor, and saw what he had done. "No…" he said in a whisper.

Octavia pulled to her feet and turned to look through the window. Through the hangar doorway, she saw a short burst of light as the metal arm separated its claws, and the bomb it held released a single, short burst of flames that fired it towards the city below.

Rob tapped at the screen frantically, looking through menus. "We have to stop it or slow it down," he said, glancing at Octavia.

"We can't. It has no propulsion system beyond what it needed to launch. Once it's on course, gravity does the work," she said, looking back at him. Rob turned and looked to Markus, who stood back, panting, sweat on his brow.

"It had to be done! We don't have time for all of this nonsense when all of our lives are at risk!" he said, the hint of panic in his voice.

Rob took two long, confident steps towards Markus, fingers bundled tight in fists that near-creaked with tension. He swung a hand, fast and hard, his knuckles connecting with Markus's round cheek.

Markus snapped to the side, spittle flinging from his loose

mouth as he spun to a heap on the floor. Rob's body followed the arc of the punch, nearly falling as well, before catching himself on a desk. Long nails of pain shot through his leg and up his spine, but through his anger he felt an immense pleasure to see the Mayor sprawled on the floor.

"Ah! A-assault!" Markus yelled, palm to his aching cheek as he turned to look back towards Markus. "This brute assaulted me! You all saw it! And I will see him punished as such!" he continued, turning to Octavia.

"I need some guards in the command deck," she said, placing a finger on her ear, looking down at the man on the floor with a neutral expression. Markus breathed heavily, looking between the two as Rob rubbed his knuckles, leaning against the desk. A few seconds later three guards rushed into the room, observing the scene and looking to Octavia.

"What can we do for you Captain?" said one of the guards, stepping forward.

"The Mayor is relieved of duty. I need you to detain him for the time being," Octavia said, calm and effortlessly authoritative. The guards looked to each other for the briefest moment, as Markus's face dropped.

"What the fuck do you think you're doing?" he yelled as two of the guards pulled him to his feet.

"Lock him in my office for now," Octavia said, throwing a key to the third guard. "I'll want to talk to him later."

The guards nodded, then marched Markus out of the room as he screamed commands at them. When the guards ignored him, he began to hurl threats to both Rob and Octavia, that only stopped when the door sealed closed behind him.

Chapter 26

Aki drifted to the cargo containment section of the shuttle, a web of thick tethers filling the space. He observed the tangle and, selecting one, unlatched it from the wall and began untangling it from the mass.

"Alright, here's the plan," he said, returning to the centre of the shuttle and passing one end of the tether to George, who fastened it tightly to the support in the centre "We're going to open the doors, just long enough for me to get pulled out. It's going to be scary. It's going to be loud. But George will close the doors again right away. It should take no more than a second. As soon as the doors are shut again, the life support systems will pump more oxygen and warm air into the shuttle. You'll all be perfectly safe." Aki looped the other end of the tether around his waist. "Once the doors are closed, I can climb up the exterior of the shuttle. If we're lucky, whatever is wrong with the motor is something I can fix," he said, clipping the buckle closed and checking to make sure the tether was tight. He had gathered any tools that seemed useful from the supplies stored in the shuttle, or those carried aboard by his fellow crew. George, looking satisfied with his knot, pushed himself towards the wall of controls carrying a tether of his own.

"What if it's something you can't fix?" came a timid voice from somewhere in the shuttle.

"If that's the case, then we just have to wait a bit longer for somebody on the ship to come help us. I'm just making sure we get back as soon as possible," Aki called out, wearing a smile for the benefit of whoever asked, and anybody else that was equally nervous. He looked to Robin and pushed towards him, the tether trailing behind.

"That's fine for us, but what about you?" Robin said as Aki arrived, bracing on the chair to stop his inertia. "If you can't fix it, you can't get back inside. And we have no idea how long it'll take anybody else to get here, do we? Why don't you just stay inside, wait for them to come get us?" he asked.

Aki looked over his shoulder, as though he could tell by sight if anybody would hear their conversation. "I get why you're worried, Robin, but... We don't know what's going on out there. If any of that stuff got on the outside of the shuttle, it could be eating through the walls right now. We might not have that long," Aki said, squeezing Robin's shoulder.

Robin held Aki's wrist for a moment, nodding his head reluctantly, before Aki let go and pushed towards the door. George stood by the terminal with a tether fastened firmly around his torso and looped through the handholds along the wall. He reached his large hand up to the manual door lever, the heavy metal switch inlaid beside the terminal. "Hang on," Aki said, drifting to join him. "It won't open undocked."

George moved and gave Aki access to the terminal, where he placed his hand on the scanner and opened the engineer's menu. A few taps on the screen and an admin override lit up the screen with an intense warning sign, illuminating his face in red light.

Aki pushed away from the terminal, coming to a stop before the large metal doors. He unclipped the helmet on his belt, looked to Robin with a smile, then pulled the helmet over his head and fastened it firmly. He floated for a moment, looking at the doors and imagining what was on the other side. He checked the tether at his waist again, then nodded to George.

"Everybody, deep breath in, just for a second!" George yelled, the red light of the monitor painting his arm as he reached across to take hold of the heavy switch. George sucked in a large gulp of air. Aki found himself taking a deep breath of his own, taking hold of the tether and holding tight. George's arm pulled down hard and the doors started to swing open. The air within the shuttle was sucked out into the vacuum of space with a terrible screeching roar, and Aki pulled along with it. The sound was enormous, like a tornado had entered the room, then dissipated as fast as it arrived as the silence of space took over. Aki found himself outside, surrounded by stars, uncertain if he had closed his eyes for a moment or if it had simply been so fast he hadn't seen it happen.

The tether tugged roughly, his hands immediately losing their grip, but the buckle at his waist held easily. The force sent him drifting backwards again, back towards the shuttle like a yo-yo, though much slower now. He twisted his body, looking back to the shuttle, where he saw that the doors were already closed firmly. The tether that held him was clipped tightly in the seam of the door. A part of him had been worried that the doors would simply cut the tether, but the material had stayed strong.

It quickly became apparent what had actually happened to the shuttle. The tether had been cut. The sudden loss of tension had rocked the metal capsule, bouncing it between the pipes and cables around it. The tether didn't need to be tight for the shuttle to ascend though, so that alone wasn't the problem. He still needed to reach the top before he would know if he could fix the motor. He scanned the exterior of the metal shuttle, looking for any signs of the shimmering black, and saw none. He took hold of the cable at his waist again and started pulling towards the doors, wondering if everybody inside was alright.

He hit against the door lightly and held the tether tight so he wouldn't drift away. He paused, turning to look out at the stars, and then down towards the planet below. The yellow sphere was close enough to fill his vision entirely, he could still make out the city, minute in the distance, but visible. The oddly pristine yellow expanse of the planet was now marred by a black gash, a growing pool of it surrounding the city, and a thick line running out along the pipe network to an even larger pool of expanding dark that must have once been the drill site.

A flash in the corner of Aki's vision pulled him away from the strange sight of the planet below. A notification in the corner of his visor screen of Robin entering the local voice call. He was surprised they could connect through the thick walls of the shuttle, but he eagerly joined the call. "Robin! I'm glad you're okay!" Aki said eagerly as soon as it connected.

"You're glad I'm okay? You're the one that just launched into space with a piece of rope around yer waist!" Robin replied incredulously. The connection wasn't perfect, their voices sounding uneven as the audio quality wavered, but it was still good to hear Robin's voice.

"How are things looking out there?" Robin asked.

"Okay, from what I can see. I still need to climb up the

shuttle, but no sign of the goo on the parts I've seen. I'm gonna start climbing up now," Aki replied, looking around for handholds on the metal walls before him. He reached out to a small groove to one side of the door he could just about grip with his thick suit gloves. It took very little exertion to pull along in the low gravity, he just had to make sure he moved in the right direction.

Looking up, he could see the underside of The Vaughn, the star's light catching on the metal underside of the ship. Lights blinked across its surface, almost serene after the chaos of the city below. "Joyce is here. Came an' took your seat once the doors were shut. Seems pretty glad you didn't get blasted into space," came Robin's voice after a moment.

"Yeah, tell her I'm all good," Aki said. "I'm just reaching the top of the shuttle, no sign of the goo up here either." He looked out along the top of the shuttle as he crested the edge. A tangle of pipes and cables traced along the surface, connecting the life support systems. In the centre, a large block surrounded a thick cable of twisted metal threads.

"I can't see anything wrong with the motor from here. It hasn't exploded or anything so a good start," Aki said as he started to climb towards the centre of the shuttle. He reached out, taking hold of a cable and jolted suddenly as something pulled at his waist. Looking back, he saw the tether tied to his belt pulled taut. "Shit," he muttered under his breath, reaching to the tether with one hand.

"What's wrong?" came Robin's voice with a peak of concern.

"The strap isn't long enough. I should have figured that out, I guess I wasn't thinking that far ahead," Aki said, looking back at the motor a few feet ahead.

"Oh, crap yeah, that's no good... Doesn't yer suit have

little jets on it? You mentioned using 'em before," Robin asked, sounding eager at the recollection.

"The suits we use to go out of the ship have them. This suit is for planets though, not space," Aki replied.

"Is there somethin' we can do? We can tie more straps to it, open the doors again," Robin said.

Aki contemplated for a few seconds, then reached to his waist and unclipped the strap. As soon as it floated loose he grabbed at the pipes before him with his spare hand, feeling a wave of vertigo twisting his gut.

"Aki?" Robin called, responding to the queasy sound that escaped Aki's lips involuntarily.

"I untied it. I'm gonna keep going," he said, after taking a deep breath, and letting his stomach settle.

"What? Aki you can't!" Robin said, voice rising in panic. "The fuckin' idiot untied the tether!"

Aki heard a muffled response from Joyce, but couldn't make out the words. "It's okay Robin, I'm being careful! Making sure I always have a good hold. And I don't have far to go," Aki said, reaching between the pipes like rungs on a ladder. His hands shook and he could feel sweat building on his palms. He focused on breathing, and hoped that Robin couldn't tell how frightened he was. "How's your arm doing?" he asked, hoping to keep his mind occupied.

"It's manageable. I can feel a kind of… stinging, I guess? Y'know when you touch something really hot, and your fingers tingle? I've got that. Which is weird, considering there are no fingers there to feel. It's a lot better than touching the goo though. That shit was way worse. How much farther have ya got to go?" Robin said.

"I'm there," replied Aki, reaching a hand forwards and taking hold of the square casing that surrounded the motor.

Carefully, he lifted himself from the surface of the shuttle, pressing the sides of his knees into pipes to stick in place. He leaned forwards and looked into the mechanism. The problem became immediately apparent. The cable had been jostled out of position, no longer fitted into the pulley mechanism that allowed the shuttle to travel.

"Well, the good news is the generator looks fine. The pulley looks fine too," Aki said.

"What's wrong with it then?" asked Robin, his voice distorted lightly though the voice call.

"The tether was knocked out of place. It should start working again, but I don't think it will be easy to get it back in." Aki muttered as he moved around the cable, observing it and pondering the issue. "Alright, I'm going to try something," he said, looking at the tools offered to him by passengers on the shuttle.

He found the tool he was looking for, a long, thin pry bar that would have been heavy in other circumstances. He peered down into the gap between the tether and the mechanisms around it, lowering the pry bar and hooking it on one corner of the metal casing. Tilting the bar behind the thick, braided metal tether, he tried pulling on the other end. The lever action that he hoped would see the tether pop back into place, instead just pushed him away. The lack of gravity and friction would be difficult to work around.

Aki repositioned himself, moving around the tether and putting both hands on the pry bar, pulling it towards him whilst bracing against the metal casing. The tether shifted, ever so slightly, but not enough. He tried again, pulling the bar with one hand whilst pushing on the sturdy metal casing with the other, feeling his muscles strain.

"How you managin' Aki?" came Robin's voice.

Aki let go of the bar with a grunt. He wanted to wipe the sweat that trickled past his eyes but couldn't with his helmet on. "I should have brought you or George. Somebody with actual muscles," he said between breaths.

"You have muscles. They're just... cute little baby muscles," said Robin.

"The babies are not up for this task. Let me try again," Aki said, looking at the pry bar sticking from the mechanism. He pressed and pulled at the bar from a few positions, uncertain of what to do. He leaned back, huffed in frustration, and then leaned forwards, placing the bar against his shoulder. He reached forwards and took hold of the metal casing across from him, found purchase for his feet, and started to push.

His feet pushed up from the pipes behind him and his arms pulled at the casing ahead. The bar pressed hard into the flesh between his neck and shoulder. He could feel the bar shifting, see the cable beginning to push forwards, and pushed harder. The bar dug painfully into his shoulder even through the thick padding of his suit. He pushed through the tender ache, feeling like his shoulder may snap, when something gave and he flung forwards, the pressure releasing from his shoulder. He began to flip, twisting in the low gravity. Reaching out, he managed to hook an arm beneath one of the pipes trailing the surface of the shuttle. His body hit against the metal, his arm and shoulder burning as he turned to look back at the tether.

"Aki! Are you alright? Did you do it?" came Robin's voice, raised in anticipation.

"Yeah, I think I did!" Aki said, surprised in himself.

"I can hear noises coming from the motor," Robin said, a light crackle of static dulling his excitement.

Aki righted himself against the wall of metal pipes and

cables, trying to align himself back towards the entrance of the shuttle. The tether he had used on his exit still floated just beyond the edge. He started to pull his way towards it.

"I'm going to try and tie myself back—" he started, but cut off when a heavy lurch of the shuttle hit him hard into the surface below. The lurching shuttle knocked the wind from him and knocked him away from the pipes. Dazed, it took him a moment to realise he was now drifting slowly away from the top of the shuttle, still towards the tether which now twisted strangely in reaction to the sudden movement.

He stretched out his hands, trying to grab the structure below, but his fingers were inches away and growing more distant with every moment.

"What was that? Aki you good?" asked Robin.

Aki looked to the motor in the centre of the shuttle, growing increasingly distant. A light blinked on the side of the metal casing. "I think it's restarting," Aki said, snapping his eyes back to the tether ahead. The blinking light turned solid, and the gears within the shuttle began to turn. The structure began moving. Aki floated closer to the edge, reaching his arms out ready to grasp at anything that came close enough.

The shuttle quickly approached, gaining speed, and in a blink it had collided with Aki, catching his legs and sending him spinning. He snatched wildly at the blur of the tether that whipped away, grunting with pain at the impact on his legs. The shuttle shot past, Aki flinging out, spinning chaotically until his back collided hard with one of the pipes that had previously rocked the shuttle.

"Aki! What's happening?" Robin called, the static in the connection growing quickly and his words increasingly distorted.

"Robin, I'm sorry," Aki said, opening his eyes just in time to see the voice connection turn grey, Robin's voice cut off before it could form another word.

The shuttle sped towards The Vaughn above, accelerating at an astonishing speed as Aki caught glimpses of it as he twisted through space. He had bounced away from the pipe, and away from the cable connecting the ship to the city below. He breathed heavily, tapping through the menus on his suit, looking for anything that could help. The dull yellow planet scrolled past his vision, the dark of space, and then the ship above, with the shuttle shrinking into the distance. The images repeated as he spun. It was hard to notice the changes when facing the planet, but the ship was visibly growing slightly larger with each rotation. He was floating away from the planet, the force of the shuttle pushing him further into the void of space.

He closed his eyes for a time, slowing his breaths, willing his heart to ease its pounding in his chest, and in time, it complied. The sound of the air pump in his suit, usually so faint as to be inaudible, now filled the gaps between the sounds of his breathing. He opened his eyes to see the ship, still far, but close enough to make out some of the details. The shuttle had vanished within and the airlock doors were closed around the thick cable. Robin had reached the ship, and at that thought, Aki smiled.

The ship drifted out of view, the star-spotted dark taking its place. He saw the rings of the planet, shimmering in the blue light of the star, and then the yellow planet itself. He observed the dark scar that crossed its surface, and noticed that a number of smaller dots of black had appeared all along the surface, like ink scattered from a toothbrush. More of the substance was burrowing its way to the surface, searching for more cities to ravage. Then the dark of space returned.

Clicking through the menus on his visor, Aki opened the oxygen gauge; a little over forty minutes left. He could purge it, if he decided that was too long. He thought about it, until the ship came into view again. He thought about his friends aboard, glad to know they were safe on The Vaughn, and glad that he had helped them get there. He wouldn't purge the oxygen. Not yet, at least. He wanted to see the ship leave, and know they were on their way home.

He closed the oxygen gauge and scrolled through his visor settings, adjusting the tint of the glass to its heaviest setting. The stars became dim, the planet below enshrouded in a night-like dark once again. He wasn't sure the visor's tint would protect him entirely from the flash of a ship jumping out of the system, not from this close distance. But of course, it didn't matter much. The flash of their escape would be a good final thing to see, and he wouldn't have to live in the dark for long. If he was blinded, he could always just remove his helmet entirely, or wait for oxygen to run out.

Another rotation, and another followed that.

It seemed like he had been floating for hours, though he knew it must only be a few minutes. The shuttle had been close to arriving when the cable broke, with barely over a minute left in the journey. How long had it been since he saw it vanish into the ship? He could check the oxygen gauge again, but he didn't want to dwell on the timer. He wasn't sure how long it took him to first check it anyway.

The dark tint of his visor made the metal underside of the ship blend with the dark of space, only differentiated by the colourful lights scattered along its surface like multicoloured stars. The dark glass masked any further details, and hid the shape approaching from the ship, until it was already close.

Aki started, shocked and momentarily afraid to see a strange shape encroaching. The thing rotated out of view as he reduced the tint of his visor. The bright white of the stars returning, the yellow of the planet below brightened by its sun once more.

He waited, anticipating, as he turned. He tilted his head, trying to see what was coming, and there, once the ship started to come into view, he saw it. Spidery legs hanging from a thick metal body, a cargo container hanging from its back, and a stalked eye protruding out, whirring back and forth as the drone approached him.

The drone slowed as it drew close, twisting to orient itself with him before inching forwards. Aki reached out, too stunned to understand what was happening. He took hold of the wide casing of the drone, away from the thrusters at its back. The jointed metal eye stalk turned back, studying him, before it turned back, and with a few quick jets from the thrusters, they rotated to face The Vaughn.

The thrusters fired, pushing them through space at increasing speed. The Vaughn began to grow quickly, the ship currently ring-shaped without the Inner-City to fill the wide central space. The eye stalk occasionally spun back, making sure Aki still held tight to its iron carapace. Aki realised just how quickly they were moving as they got closer to the ship, and the speed at which it grew became more discernible. He saw the opening of the equipment bay, growing fast, and as it grew, so did a figure in the wide doorway.

The drone began to release small jets toward the ship, slowing it slightly as they grew ever closer to the opening. The figure, dressed in a grey EVA suit, waved an arm eagerly at their approach. The voice channel in the corner of Aki's visor blinked to life as it reconnected to the ship's communication systems.

"Hurry up and get in here!" came Robin's voice, jubilant through a clear voice call. Aki laughed as the drone started to slow. "There's a bomb!" Robin yelled.

Aki had just enough time to scrunch his brow, puzzled at the statement, before a flash of bright light came from the planet below. The explosion atomised the city in an instant, along with a few miles of the tether connecting the two halves of the ship. The Vaughn shuddered, its bulk shifting heavily as the explosion tugged at the structures between them, before pushing them away again.

Inside the ship, Octavia clutched at her terminal within the command centre. A mutter of surprise ran through the room, hands clutching at desks and walls to avoid falling as ripples ran through the ship. Already, small rocks and shards of metal flew past the windows, flung through the planet's atmosphere by the explosion. Octavia offered little time to recover. "Duri, get us out of here. Before that debris gets any bigger," she said, voice commanding, projecting through the room.

Duri nodded to the Captain, then turned to her terminal and set to work. The engines rumbled to life, a hum building to a roar. Octavia tapped at her terminal and heavy shutters began to descend over the windows of the control room, the debris outside, increasing in size and quantity, being hidden from view.

Above, within Octavia's office, Markus stood by the window. The explosion knocked him to the floor, but he quickly climbed to his feet and watched the destruction below as best he could. He wanted to see the city destroyed. Wanted to know that they were free from that terrible slithering substance.

The drone wavered at the explosion, twisting as it sped through the open doorway of the equipment bay. Aki's hands slipped free and flung towards the floor. Robin reached to catch him and grunted at the exertion, the magnetically locked boots helping to hold him sturdy.

Aki righted himself, his boots locking to the floor, and looked through the visor of the grey suit to see Robin's face looking back. "What the hell is going on?" Aki asked.

"We need to get to the airlock, now!" said Robin, clutching Aki's wrist and turning towards the door. Aki followed, the two trying their best to move quickly, slowed by the magnetic locking systems in their boots. Aki looked up to the control room and saw Rob, watching through the window. Rob smiled, briefly, before turning and rushing away. A faint vibration began to build in the floor, and Aki realised what was happening. He pushed with what little extra energy he had to help them reach the airlock door.

Robin let go of Aki's wrist and reached out with his hand to pull the door open. He pushed on Aki's back with his forearm, following behind as they crossed the boundary. Passing into the gravity of the airlock, the two collapsed inward, falling to the floor in a pile atop one another. The airlock door began to close, as they both pushed their faces into the ground, eyes squeezed tightly closed. The room illuminated for a fraction of a second with a dazzling white light before the doors sealed fully behind them.

Markus stood by the window, watching as debris drifted past outside. He watched for any sign of the dark substance travelling on the rocks, paranoid that it would yet find its way onto what remained of The Vaughn.

He considered the power of the blast below, the total annihilation of the city, and surely that terrible destructive tar along with it. His mind had been racing since his incarceration in Octavia's office, pondering the possible outcomes of their plan and how he would handle the allegations levied against him, should they escape. But despite these worries he felt a sense of pride intermingled with nerves as he thought of his actions this day. Maybe he could present himself as the hero?

He placed a hand against the window and felt a tingle in his palm, the lightest vibration passing throughout the whole ship, though dampened by the plush carpeting of Octavia's office. Confused, he looked to his palm for a moment, studying the skin, then placed his hand on the glass again, feeling the vibration grow. The view beyond the window vanished, as The Vaughn was enveloped in a searing white light, and Markus fell to the floor screaming.

The light fell away, the ship growing dark in its absence. Markus crawled back, hitting his back and head against Octavia's hard wooden desk. He heard something fall on its surface, roll, and tumble to the floor. He heard the door open and footsteps approach.

"Are you alright, sir?" came the voice of a guard, one of those who had dragged him here.

Markus turned to look towards the voice, still shrouded in darkness. "I can't see!" Markus yelled. "What happened to the bloody lights? Why is it so dark!" The guard looked back toward their companion who watched from the open doorway. The room was well lit.

In the bottom floor of the ship, Aki and Robin laid on the floor, eyes still closed tight. The airlock door opened, and a chuckle rolled into the room with them. "You can get up lads, you're all good," said Rob.

Aki opened an eye and saw metal floor beneath him. He

looked up, seeing Rob smiling broadly. He looked to his side and saw Robin staring back, looking as shocked as Aki felt. Smiles began to grow on their faces, and then they laughed in unison. Aki pushed to his feet, unfastened his helmet and threw it to the floor. Stepping forwards, he embraced Rob in a tight hug.

"Was that you flying the drone?" Aki asked when the laughter subsided.

"Aye lad, sorry about the rough landin'," Rob said, patting Aki's back through the thick suit. Aki let go of Rob and stepped back, checking over his shoulder to see Robin pushing to his feet, one hand of his suit dangling loose and empty.

"What happened? I thought I was lost out there," Aki said.

"I ran here an' told Rob what happened," Robin said, pulling his helmet loose. "He told me to put on a suit and wait by the doors, so, I did. He did the rest."

"And what about that explosion? What the hell was that?" Aki asked, looking back to Rob.

"The bloody Mayor. We had to detach the city, and that was the only way. We didn't intend to do it so soon but… well, I'll tell you the specifics later. For now, I think we all need some rest," Rob said, leaning against the wall and looking weary.

A wave of exhaustion hit Aki, as though the mention of rest reminded his body how to feel. He leaned back against the wall and slid down to sit on the floor with a heavy huff.

Robin fell to sit beside him. "These suits are very uncomfortable…" he said, grunting as he landed.

"You get used to them," Aki said with a chuckle. He turned to look at Robin, both of them sweaty and drained from the events of the day. Robin looked back, a light smile tugging at the sides of his mouth. Aki studied his friend's face, looked into his eyes, and then tears started to well in his own. Robin's face flashed through shock to concern as tears started to trickle down Aki's cheeks.

"Hey! Hey now, come on, what's up?" Robin said, shifting on the floor to better face Aki, reaching a hand to his shoulder.

Aki smiled for a moment, trying to reassure Robin, but couldn't get the smile to stay. He shook his head. "I'm okay, I just…" he said, his voice abandoning him. He paused, taking a deep breath, looking away from Robin for a moment. Rob stood before them, looking back at him with understanding. Rob gave a light nod.

Aki looked back to Robin, the tears flowing easily now.

"I need to tell you about Adie."

Epilogue

Blinks of light flashed around a space port, twisting freely between the planets of Gliese 581. The remains of The Vaughn settled, empty, within one of the station's thousand docks, sealed away from the public eye. The station was an immense bulk of unsightly metal, filled with millions working and living on the station, with more passing through between stints in the outer reaches of the galaxy.

Aki sat at a beer-stained table, sipping a half empty glass and watching a monitor mounted to the wall. Nobody else in the crowded bar seemed interested. The noise of the crowd drowned out any sound the speakers could hope to make, but he could read the subtitles. On the screen, a woman stood behind a podium, an array of microphones before her, and camera flashes blinking rapidly. A bar along the bottom of the screen read 'Former Captain Octavia Moore'. She stood straight, her clothing pristine. But something about her face belied a weariness. Almost as though she had aged greatly in the few weeks they had been aboard the station. She continued talking.

"I have provided, in full detail, the actions taken by myself, and the former Mayor Markus Bailey for the tribunal.

I did all I could to save as many of our crew as possible in extraordinary circumstances. I know many of you have questions. I believe that when you are provided access to the transcript, any answers I am able to provide will be found within. For now, I will only say that I accept accountability for the role I played in this travesty. I accept that many believe I did not perform my duty to any acceptable standard. For that, I have surrendered my licence and credentials. I will never again act as crew aboard a spacefaring vessel of any kind. If the tribunal's decision is to punish me further, as I suspect they will, I will gladly face those consequences, whatever they be. I will not deny the justice you all deserve. To those who lost family. Friends. Loved ones. I can only tell you that… I am sorry. I will carry the weight of their loss with me."

With that, she stepped back from the podium, and the camera flashes increased as hands appeared, holding microphones, a calamitous chatter as journalists shouted their questions. The camera panned as she walked away, vanishing beyond a curtain. A man appeared on the stage, a generic grey suit as perfectly tailored as the dour expression he wore. A lapel pin featuring a smiling fish identified him as a representative of Tao-Visser Inc., the parent company of Paxton Universal.

"Aki!" Robin called from the crowd, pushing his way through the packed bar. He reached the table and dropped into the seat across from Aki, picking up a beer that had been waiting for him and taking a long, eager gulp. "Thanks. I need a drink after all that. I miss anythin' juicy?" he asked, looking up to the monitor on the wall.

"Nothing new. The Captain gave a testimony, but no results on the tribunal yet. And still no word on where the Mayor is or what's happening with him," Aki said as Robin looked back towards him.

"The prick better not get away with it…" Robin muttered, sipping from his drink again. Aki nodded and took a drink of his own.

"So, how'd your meeting go?" Robin asked, putting the glass down.

"Well, I think. They offered more than I expected, after hearing what others have been getting. I'm not sure if it's because I was at the dig site or because I was management. It was about seven hundred K, I have the exact number written down somewhere. Not enough to live a life of luxury, but enough to retire early if I find somewhere cheap enough. What'd they offer you?" Aki reached for his drink again, eyes curious towards Robin.

"Yeah, offered me closer to five hundred. But, they also offered a new hand, which I guess makes up for a good chunk o' that," Robin said, holding up his arm and waving the rounded stump at the end. A beat of silence fell, Aki twisting the glass on the table in front of him and watching the foam within rock back and forth.

"Do you think you'll take it?" he said, looking back to Robin.

Robin hummed affirmatively. "Think so. I know I should feel shitty about it, but that money'll make a big difference. And the hand they get me'll be leagues better than anything I could afford, even if I spent half of what they give me," Robin replied, sounding almost sheepish.

"I get that. Don't worry, I'm taking it too. With the Captain, and a few other people already talking about it… I don't think us agreeing to stay quiet will make much of a difference. But, that money will make a big difference for us," Aki said softly, but more confidently than Robin.

"You think Adie'd be disappointed?" Robin asked, a joking lilt to the question, though it was genuine.

"I think Adie would take the money, then talk anyway and get sued into oblivion," Aki replied with a smile.

Robin laughed. "That is absolutely what he'd do," Robin said, grinning wide at the thought.

"I also don't think he'd blame us for taking the easy option after all that," Aki said, raising his drink again.

"I hope so," Robin said contemplatively, looking thoughtful for a moment before raising his own glass. The two sat in silence, thinking of their lost friend for a time. Aki wished he'd bought a third beer, to leave in the space where Adie would have been, though he wasn't sure how melodramatic that may have appeared. He watched the edge of the table, imagining the third glass, and an empty chair that wasn't there.

"I heard back from my pop," Robin said, breaking the silence.

"Oh yeah? How are things working out?" Aki asked, the image slipping from his mind as he looked back to Robin.

"Sounds like it's all worked out. There's a few places 'round Canis I could settle in, places I can make this money last a good bit. They sound pretty excited about me being back, close to home. It'll be weird, livin' on a planet again," Robin said.

"I think it could be pretty good, after all these years on stations and ships. And being around your family again will be nice," Aki said, glad to hear Robin's plans were coming together. "How long until you head to Canis? You think?" he asked.

"Few days maybe, week or two? Haven't decided just yet. What about you, decided what you're doin' yet?" Robin said, the fingers of his hand rubbing the empty wrist in a thoughtless action that was quickly becoming habitual.

"I haven't really figured it out yet. I was thinking about moving back to Lacaille, around where my mum lived. But I don't really know anybody that lives there anymore, and I was never all that fond of the place really. Once mum died, I was pretty content to leave, so, it'd feel weird going back," Aki said, looking at an empty spot on the table.

Robin looked in his glass for a moment, then raised it to his mouth again, taking a long sip. "Ever considered Canis? I hear there's a few places going 'round there. Luyten's particularly nice this time o' year," he said, a lilting tone to his voice.

Aki smiled, looking to Robin who hid a cheeky grin behind his glass. "I can't say I'd ever considered Canis, no. Heard the people from there have a tendency to be a bit irritating. But, yeah. Maybe Canis would be nice," Aki replied.

"Y'know, if you're still interested, we could look for a place t'share. It'd make that dirty company money last a fair bit longer," Robin said, putting the glass down.

"I think I'd like that," Aki said, smiling at Robin, who began to smile back.

"It'd make Adie happy, wasn't it his idea?" Robin said, leaning back in his chair.

"I think I suggested it first, but then Adie was very emphatic about it," Aki said, trying to remember the conversation they had those long weeks ago.

"Y'know, if we're gonna share a house, I am going to make you watch a lot of old horror movies," Robin said with a roguish grin.

Aki feigned a cartoonish look of exasperation. "Haven't we had enough horror for one lifetime?" he asked.

"It's research! So we know what t'do if it ever 'appens again!" Robin said emphatically, leaning over the table.

"Isn't the whole point of moving to Canis knowing we won't be around if something like that does happen again? Besides, watching all those films didn't exactly help you much, did it? Captain five-fingers," Aki said, pointing to the missing hand.

"Well I've never seen a film that has the blob and zombies at the same time. Actually… well, Return o' the Living Dead has a goo zombie, but it wasn't that kind o' goo. But next time it might not be blob zombies. It could be like, space vampires. There's a film for that," Robin said, looking pleased with himself, twisting his stump hand in the air in a gesture Aki couldn't quite figure out.

"There's a space vampire film?" Aki asked, eyebrow arched.

"Multiple, I think," Said Robin, sounding all the more excited at the prospect.

"That sounds terrible."

"It's got a lot o' nudity in it," said Robin, tilting his head, like he was making a tantalising proposition.

Aki smiled, shaking his head and chuckling at his friend. "Alright. Once we find a place, we can watch whatever you want."

End

To: P. Visser

I am sorry to report that the planet designated AG-17-74 was barricaded by the UER before we had a chance to extract anything from the site. All formal requests with the UER to investigate have, unsurprisingly, been declined.

I think it is safe to assume that they will not be willing to cooperate with us, and I fail to see any means we could confidently procure a sample of the substance without resorting to more clandestine means.

I have assigned a team to study the ship logs we withheld from the UER. My hope is that we can identify debris that escaped the UER's notice. I've also instructed a few of our operatives within the UER to attempt transfer to any site with a connection to the AG-17-74 operations.

It may take a while but I'm confident that we'll have a sample in time.

I'll keep you updated.

D. Harlan

Afterword

For a long few years, I had a job that I grew to hate. Genuinely despise. I suspect a lot of people who read this will have had a similar experience, or maybe even be in one similar right now! It sucks. A lot!

It turns out I had some real wacky mental disorder stuff going on which didn't help any, but even without that, the experience of sacrificing your body as part of a machine you know holds no concern for the damage it does can be an arduous thing. Often, I made it through by listening to audiobooks. Things to keep my mind occupied and help the bad days pass that little bit easier. A lot of fantasy, comedy and sci-fi. A lot of Terry Pratchett.

But more than anything, horror. Preferably a bit pulpy. A little trashy. Fun monsters, a bit of gore and body horror to really get my synapses tingling. When I decided I was going to try writing a novel, it made sense to try the same. I have so many ideas for books I want to write, and I'd done plenty of writing before. But never anything quite this long. It made sense to write something where I know I'd be comfortable. Something fun, and pulpy. A little trashy, fun monsters, a bit of gore and body horror...

I hope you enjoyed it. I if any of you are out there having a tough time, this silly little book full of men who unapologetically love each other and monsters that unapologetically want to tear them apart, a couple of gruff badass ladies, and a spaceship shaped like a badly-drawn turtle, I hope it helped keep your synapses tingling.

This is my first book but I have so many ideas, and so much intent to keep writing. It won't always be horror, it won't always be sci-fi but I hope if you enjoyed this book you'll try out whatever I make next. And I hope you'll let me know, in an email, a review, or a very well-aimed paper aeroplane. Thankyou for giving this book, and me, a chance!

Ben

About the Author

B.C. Brown, colloquially referred to as a "Ben", is a creature of some notable ill-refute. It spends much of its time sleeping, playing video games and fawning over cats.

For many years it focused on illustration and animation, writing and self publishing a variety of comics as part of the UK's small press scene. None of them were very good. Well, maybe one was alright.

Eventually the complex whims of fate saw it turn away from the visual arts, and towards the written word. The result is the book you're holding right now! Hello future person!

Ben plans to write more things, and may well have done already.

On rare occasion it is known to write about itself in the third person.

See more and keep up to date at:
www.bcbrown.co.uk

Content Warnings:

- Amputation
  - Blood
  - Death
- Eye Trauma
  - Gore
- Mutilation
- Violence
- Human characters being "eaten"
- Dissolving whilst alive
- Agoraphobia / Fear of open spaces
  - Vertigo/Acrophobia

LITTLE
GREY
ALIEN